Deep Cries Out

By Allison Nance

Hidden Shelf Publishing House
P.O. Box 4168, McCall, ID 83638
www.hiddenshelfpublishinghouse.com

Editor: Kerstin Stokes

Cover design: Rachel Wickstrom and Megan Whitfield

Interior layout: Kerstin Stokes

Library of Congress
Publisher's Cataloging-in-Publication data

Names: Nance, Allison, author.

Title: Deep cries out / Allison Nance.

Description: McCall, ID: Hidden Shelf Publishing House, 2025.

Identifiers: LCCN: 2025905935 | ISBN: 978-1-955893-56-5 (paperback) | 978-1-955893-56-5 (Kindle)

Subjects: LCSH Family--Fiction. | Man-woman relationships--Fiction. | Galveston (Tex.)--Fiction. | Romance fiction. Christian fiction. | BISAC FICTION / Christian / Contemporary FICTION / Family Life / General | FICTION / Women FICTION / Christian / Romance / General

Classification: LCC PS3614. A63 D44 2025 | DDC 813.6--dc23

For Mommy and Peb, who taught me
to believe in the impossible.

*Deep calls to deep at the sound
of Your waterfalls;
All Your breakers and Your
waves have passed over me.*
- Psalm 42:7

January

I threw open the French doors and stepped onto the balcony. The sun's morning light beamed hard and bright, rendering every color more vivid than anywhere else in the world. To my right, our host's terraced citrus groves swept the mountain's swell up to its pinnacle and the cragged keyhole formation. Below me, the single lane road snaked toward Montepertuso and even farther down, Positano still slumbered under a weakening shroud of fog, clinging to wooded cliffs which staggered into azure ocean. My husband's footsteps padded softly behind me. His lips grazed my shoulder.

"Good morning." Caleb's eyes shone honey gold. I'd never tire of seeing them. "You sleep okay?"

"Not bad." I rubbed my swollen stomach. "But someone decided to have a dance party in the middle of the night."

"Anna Marie's already practicing for when she gets here." His bearded face split into a grin, the corners of his eyes crinkling in the way I found irresistible. "*Merengue.*"

"More like *bachata.*" I smiled, arching my back against the open doorway. The miraculous life inside me shifted and curled, mirroring a single wave far out in the sea.

"Aimee?" My husband's voice sank. "There's something you need to know."

I turned toward him; one paradise torn from my sight in exchange for another.

Caleb stood by the bed, suitcase open in front of him. Love spilled from his eyes. "You're not going to survive this."

A chill knifed through me. "What?"

"You're not going to survive this." He made the motion of folding clothes, but his hands were empty.

"What are you talking about?"

His hands continued to cut through the air. "You can't survive, my love. Not this way."

I fought to step toward him, but my feet dredged the wooden floor like anchors. I looked down. Waves crashed through the balcony doors, seafoam rushing around my legs.

"What's happening?" My voice tore through the air. "This can't be real."

"Don't let go, Aimee." Caleb's tone was calm as the water rose around our bed. "Take a deep breath. God's not going to let go of you. I have faith." The lid of his suitcase slammed down hard, sending a convulsion through my body.

I jerked awake.

Night crept from my window toward dawn. Over the last few years, I'd met Caleb in my dreams countless times, reliving half-true memories of the past. But never in a nightmare like this. My body begged for relief, unable to shake the terror. Pain seared my head, front to back. My chest and neck burned with heat. I stood, stripping off my shirt. My vision turned black with the rush of blood to my head, forcing me to sit again.

Take a deep breath.

I shuddered, sweat freezing on my skin. Drenched sheets stuck to my palms. My vision cleared, and my slippers appeared in my line of sight, white against the floor in the darkness. I slid my feet into them and stood once more. I almost tripped over the McQueen suit I'd shucked off the night before and left crumpled on the floor, but I didn't want to turn on the light. I didn't want to do anything. In the bathroom, I threw my sweaty shorts in the sink. Ran the hot water. My head pounded, matching the pace of my heart. A wave of nausea came suddenly and I wretched, coughing up nothing. Tears scorched my eyes. Naked, I stumbled to the closet, searching for a shirt and clean shorts.

There's a saying that New York City never sleeps, but it's not true. Somewhere in the hours just before dawn, the lights finally flicker off, and a deep hush falls across the buildings and the water. I know, because for weeks, I remained awake as the city slept. I'd tried to ignore the amorphous worry that grabbed at my throat every time I swallowed, keeping me up late into the night. But I'd said nothing about it to anyone, not even Clint.

I picked up my phone from my desk near the window overlooking East 84th. In the velvet darkness of the bedroom, the screen was blinding.

6:16

Clint Myers

> *I need to see a doctor today.*
> *Something's not right.*

His reply was immediate:

> *Already made you an appointment.*
> *I knew something was wrong in the*
> *boardroom last night.*
> *Picking you up at 7.*

Every nerve stood on edge, tingling.
The boardroom.
Yesterday, my lungs had emptied, robbed of breath. My vision

had blurred and the room itself seemed to come alive, spinning on its own. Suddenly heavy, my portfolio slipped from my hands onto the mahogany table. Half-formed words about blow-out preventers and offshore rigs died in my throat.

"Jesus." Every ounce of energy in my body imploded, crumbling into my shoes.

"Aimee?" Clint rose from the chair in front of me, the tenor of his voice tinged with alarm.

"I don't feel well." I started moving, unsure of where I was going. "I need some air. Please excuse me." The faces around the table twisted with concern as the conference room rocked under my hurrying feet.

Only a few hours before our pitch, I had felt strong and focused, jogging with Clint through the chilly streets of Manhattan. But my exit from the boardroom found me locked in the accessible stall of the marble-tiled restroom, sobbing breathlessly on the floor.

A panic attack of that magnitude was enough to induce any number of nightmares afterward. The last time I'd glanced at the bedside clock was around five in the morning. But with sleep came the deluge of mangled manifestations from a decade-old vacation in Italy... now distorted into a nightmare I might never be able to shake.

"Mama?"

Her voice from the other side of my bed lit through the darkness. My daughter sat up and rubbed her eyes, a mass of sleep-tangled hair making her look like a wild thing. "Can we get chocolate chip pancakes from the restaurant downstairs before I go to school this morning?" With a clink, she turned on the bedside lamp. I winced. Brown, soulful eyes that reminded me of her father searched mine, and the small, determined mouth curved into a smile, half-hopeful about the pancakes. She nestled into my arms as I collapsed beside her on the bed. I kissed her forehead.

"I think maybe we'll just have yogurt from our fridge. Okay, baby?"

She slumped against me. "Ugh, Mama," she protested.

"Shh, shh, shh…" Calming her was second nature, even though I could do nothing to tame the throb of anxiety beating like a caged bird in my chest. "I have a doctor's appointment this morning. Clint is coming to pick us up soon. You're not going to school today," I decided on the fly.

"Are you okay, Mama?" The slight tremble in her voice chipped away at her confidence.

"No, Anna. That's why I want to see the doctor. To feel better."

"Will the doctor help you sleep?"

A pang of guilt cut through my panic. She'd noticed? Of course she had; she noticed everything.

"I sure hope so, love."

Clint pulled up at 6:55 with pancakes from the cafe downstairs.

"I had them add chocolate chips for Anna," he murmured, concentrating on the stop-and-go rush hour traffic.

"Charmer."

He gave me a tight smile. "Not dying today, are you?"

His voice brushed the interior of the car loud enough for me to hear, but not Anna. I looked away from him at frost-bitten clouds, shrouding the sun.

He cocked an eyebrow. "That bad?" The Mercedes he had rented for our six-month stay in New York entered the highway with a roar. "Anna and I will wait for you in the car." Clint's hand moved off mine as we pulled up to the hospital.

Walking down the snow-banked sidewalk, my head couldn't keep up with my feet, as if there was some kind of disconnect between them. I made it to reception, filled in my information. Waited. The exam room tilted to the left. My head felt like lead.

The doctor walked in, wearing plum-colored scrubs and a white jacket.

"Good morning, Mrs. Rojas. Tell me about what you're experiencing." How could she be so calm?

"Um…" My thoughts were like fireflies loosed from a jar. "Brain fog. Insomnia. I'm in sales, but yesterday I had a panic attack when I started to give a presentation. It's hard to concentrate." I blinked my eyes hard against the fluorescence of her office. "Sensitivity to light. I can hardly look at my computer or my phone. Headaches."

She passed her eyes over me critically. "How about pain or muscle tension?"

"My neck is tense. All the time. My head feels heavy."

"Anything else?"

"Extreme fatigue, like I'm about to pass out right now. It's difficult to eat. When I swallow, it feels like I could choke." As I relayed the symptoms to her, the anxiety in my stomach knotted. The golden wedding band felt like silk on my finger as I twisted it. It seemed loose. "I think I've lost a lot of weight."

"Any family history of diabetes or cancer?"

"No."

"Sales can be a stressful profession. What field are you in?"

"Oil. I'm from Houston, but my team and I have been in Manhattan setting up a satellite office since August. We're going to be here a few more weeks to close a deal."

"I see. Any other recent stressors in your daily life?"

I was unprepared for the sobs originating deep inside, even before the words formed in my mind.

"I…" My breath deserted me. "My husband died from Covid several years ago. It's just me and my daughter now." I couldn't see through the tears, could barely get the words out. "It's been hard. But recently, it's been harder." My voice broke. "Now I feel this way and I don't know why." The knot unraveled inside while I sat, helpless, hugging myself on the exam table. Her palms were warm against my cool, pale skin as she took my hands in hers. I met her eyes and was surprised to see tears in them, mirroring mine.

"I understand. I've also lost a loved one from Covid."

I fought to give her a smile.

"I'll order your labs." She completed her brief physical examination. "But I'm going to prescribe a hefty dose of vitamin D to take weekly. The pharmacy downstairs can fill it for you. Let's schedule a virtual appointment tomorrow to go over your blood panel." She scribbled out a prescription. "Everything will be okay, Mrs. Rojas." Handing me the scrap of paper, my husband's words echoed in her mouth. "I have faith."

"So?" Clint's eyes roved over me, green and lantern-like against the dark interior of the sedan.

I threw the bag with the prescription onto the floorboard. "Lab results tomorrow. She gave me vitamin D."

"Vitamins?" He said it as if the word left a bad taste in his mouth. "How are you feeling now?"

"Miserable."

"Why didn't you tell me you haven't been sleeping well?"

"I thought I could handle it." I tried to focus on the lowering clouds, which held the promise of more snow.

He glanced over at me. "You certainly have in the past." His phone dinged and he swiftly reached across me, opened the glove box and caught it up in his hand. An idiosyncrasy, Clint couldn't stand anything in his pockets while driving. "Are you up to giving the boardroom another go so we can close this deal today?"

I caught my breath. It was starting again, somewhere in my head... energy draining, my arms tingling, losing sensation. A surge of heat raced up my neck. "No, Clint. Take us back to the hotel."

There was no room for negotiation, and he knew it. His hand flexed on the wheel.

A forceful breath escaped his lips. "This bid won't survive without you."

You're not going to survive this.

"What did you say?"

His eyes remained on the road. "You heard me, Aimee."

Shaken, I turned around to check on Anna. Ensconced in the corner of the backseat, headphones canceling out all noise, she was absorbed in a cartoon on Clint's iPad, dark hair cascading down her shoulders. The sight of her face cleared my head for an instant, anchoring me. Caleb would have been amazed—

"Clint Myers for Valiant." His words splintered my thoughts as he made the call. "Our team needs to reschedule."

I closed my eyes and thought about snow.

Nighttime held no rest for me. My mind constantly jerked my body awake, preventing me from desperately needed sleep.

After taking Anna to school the next morning, Clint holed up in my living room wearing a three-piece suit, smelling powerfully of espresso and something from the Saks fragrance counter. The smooth timbre of his voice easily put out fires from the boardroom meeting we'd had to postpone.

He always knew what to say.

We dealt in contracts worth tens of millions, and we'd left this one on the line—our biggest ever—because of me. Clint glanced at me occasionally, witnessing my struggle as I attempted to build the preliminary sales order we needed to submit to accounting. The numbers blurred in front of my eyes, not adding up. I handed him my laptop and took the virtual call with my doctor on my cell in the bedroom.

"Good news, Mrs. Rojas. As I suspected, your results from the bloodwork are normal, except for an exceptionally severe deficiency in your vitamin D levels."

Her diagnosis sounded ridiculous. "What does that mean?" The computer screen's brightness stabbed at my vision. "A vitamin deficiency is causing all of this? What's the bottom line here?"

"The neurological symptoms, exhaustion, insomnia. It's all an outworking of the vitamin D deficiency."

"I feel horrible." The tears were sudden and silent. "And I'm letting my co-worker down. And my daughter."

Even through the camera, I could see her eyes soften. "You're going to feel the effects of the deficiency for a while. Healing from this will take time, several months at the least. This deficiency has been and will continue to affect your entire body. You need to rest." She set her glasses down in front of her. "It seems you've been carrying a great amount of stress for a while, Mrs. Rojas. Now your body is letting you know in an ugly way to take time to slow down. If you don't, your symptoms could get uglier in the form of increased anxiety and even potential depressive episodes. I'm no psychiatrist, but your brain records these feelings on neural pathways. You need to give yourself some time and space to heal." She paused to ensure her words had driven home.

"You're saying there's no quick fix?" My voice trembled.

"Exactly, Mrs. Rojas. I suggest you leave New York early and go back to Houston. You already have the weekly vitamin D supplement. We'll start with that. I'm also prescribing a metabolic supplement and an antihistamine."

"Wait, I'm confused. An antihistamine?"

"I'm not in the habit of offering something very strong for sleep and anxiety, as raising your vitamin levels should clear everything up over the next few months. This antihistamine, hydroxyzine, is an older drug. It's not typically prescribed for insomnia, but it should help you with sleep and anxiety if you are still struggling. I'm also recommending natural aids like valerian or melatonin to help with sleep, as needed."

I had no choice but to trust her. "Okay. Thank you so much for everything."

She smiled. "Get well, Mrs. Rojas. And please feel free to call my office if you need anything else."

I sat in my chair for a few moments. My phone weighed heavy in my hand as I scrolled and made the first necessary call to Houston.

"Aimee?"

Hearing my boss's voice, I could almost smell the aromatic spice of the Cuban which resided in the top left drawer of his desk.

"Hoff."

"Clint called me last night."

"I figured he would."

Hoff's grunt failed to mask his concern. "You sound terrible."

"I feel terrible. I just got off a call with my doctor." A sharp pain quickly crossed the right side of my head, from front to back. "It's a vitamin deficiency. It's not serious yet, but sounds like it could be if I—"

"If you don't slow down."

My throat tightened. I never took his kindness toward me for granted. "How did you know?"

"My own diagnosis." The chair in his executive office overlooking downtown Houston squeaked as he swiveled.

My nails dug into the flesh on my thigh. "This is Valiant's biggest contract to date. I can't just—"

He cut me off. "Yes, you can. Take all the time you need, Aimee. You didn't do that the last time around, and I'll see to it that you do now." Staving off his emotion, he continued, "One Rojas has already been lost on my watch, and I'll be damned if

I lose another."

I let his clumsily crafted vow fly away with the whirling snow outside my window. "Thank you, Hoff."

"Get things squared with Clint. Although you're the head honcho, I've no doubt he can close this bid solo. But he'll need to know you're still in his corner to pinch hit."

"I will."

"Keep me in the loop, okay? And touch base with Nat to configure your network settings before you go dark. Talk later. Sharon, get me—" He hung up abruptly.

HR, I thought. Get him HR to approve my sick leave.

One more conversation.

"Hey, stranger." Nat leaned in close to the screen, straining to see me clearly. I knew Valiant's young IT guru preferred video chat to a call. My husband had taken Nathaniel Si, a fresh-faced kid from Caltech, under his wing when he first landed a job at Valiant. Caleb was an expert at mechanical engineering and even better at making others feel welcomed. He was everything good and kind, and I had tried my best to continue the friendship he'd built with Nat.

"Hi, Nat."

"Why are you squinting?" He unconsciously mimicked me.

"The light from the screen gives me a headache."

He whistled, then grinned. "If I had that condition, I'd be out of a job real quick. Hoff told me to give you parameters to access the network directly from anywhere. You're in the big leagues now. Well, not that you weren't. You're the best. But now, you know. You've leveled up."

"Great." My eyes drifted, reaching for the opposite ends of my head. "All it took was a panic attack and weeks of insomnia. I'll have my laptop with me. Just let me know what info you need."

"All you have to do is tell me a few details about your IP at your next place, and I'll make sure your firewall configurations are all set." He peered at me. "Is it contagious?"

"What? Vitamin D deficiency? No, Nat."

"Well, that's good."

Clint laughed in the living room, apparently smoothing things over with our customers. I gave Nat a half-hearted smile. "I've got to go."

"Okay, Aimee." Nat waved goodbye. "Take care."

Blood rushed to my head as I stood, slowing my steps.

Clint wasted no time. "What did the doctor say?"

"Vitamin deficiency, like she said yesterday."

"So, what does that mean for us? What's the bottom line?"

He talked like me. Thought like me. I managed a smile through the brain fog, unsurprised at our success as partners over the last seven years. "Sunshine, apparently. Rest. She said recovery could take months."

Clint's hand moved to his mouth. He had a beautiful smile, and it hadn't been directed at me in days. "Aimee, we can't do that."

"We can't. I can." My knees trembled. "I just got off the phone with Hoff. He's putting me on sick leave. I'm going back to Texas."

Panic. Talk about contagious. It leapt from my mouth to his face.

Clint's erudite and invitingly irreverent wit had served him well, enabling him to both humor and ease even the stoniest client's slightest hint of concern. It was his job to read people as well as I could, and his recent promotion to Director of International Market Activation was well deserved.

But he hadn't been able to read me.

He stared through my suite's window wall. Central Park slept under a blanket of snow, but I was certain he saw none of it.

"I'm sorry." Another bolt of pain shot through my head, front to back. "I'm so tired. I can barely form a coherent sentence. You know better than anyone I won't be able to finish this pitch with you."

"Yeah." His eyes cut to me. He took in the sweatpants that

rarely left my suitcase and the state of my hair. "How did you manage to keep this from me?"

I shrugged, my eyes involuntarily filling with tears. "I guess it's easy to hide something you refuse to see. I'll call back Houston today. Griffin and Brooklyn can take my place on the close. They could be here this evening and they're good about getting up to speed."

"You know they can't replace you." His optimism waned, a rarity for him. "This is the contract we've been waiting for. The client wanted you, Aimee. They specifically wanted us for this project, and they're pushing to have this deal closed by the end of the month." He passed a hand over his eyes. "I can keep everyone happy for a few weeks, but liaising with accounting to have the bid and sales order completed by our deadline is going to be a nightmare without you. Surely, you'll feel better in a month?"

A sob tore through my throat. "I have no idea, Clint. I've never felt like this before. I feel powerless, and there's nothing I can do but wait it out."

His profile cut sharp against the sunlight. "You're hysterical, Aimee. You're not thinking straight."

My body slackened and I sank to the couch. The warmth of my palms couldn't soothe the pulsing pain in my head, no matter how hard I pressed.

"Hey." The sofa sagged as Clint sat beside me. "Hey. Look at me." For just a moment, the businessman switched off and I saw the face of my friend. "I'm sorry. My musing isn't helping anything. What do you need?"

It was the one question we never asked a client. We were the experts. We told them what they needed. What they wanted. How we spoke and what we said created worlds in the minds of those listening, worlds where we knew every cleft and crevasse. Asking the question left us vulnerable. Clint never asked anyone what they needed.

Anxiety bled through my twitching mouth. "I haven't been home since Caleb's memorial service. I have to step back from all of this. The work, the hours. Getting Anna used to a new place, a new school, and new friends every six months just because of my career. It's too much. I have to get better, and to do that, I need time."

He stared hard at me. "You know—" Then he stopped, opting for a touch instead of words. His hand was cool on my face as he kissed my cheek, a liberty he'd asked Caleb for years ago and never overstepped. "You couldn't possibly be better for Anna than you already are."

Despite the intimate gesture, I saw the cogs spinning in his head, his mind already inside a boardroom somewhere in the financial district.

"Do what you need to do. Book your flight and pack up." He took a handkerchief from his pocket and handed it to me before gathering his things. "I called room service and told them to send your lunch at eleven-thirty. I'll pick Anna up when school is out."

"Thank you, Clint," I whispered. "I'm so sorry."

"Stop apologizing Aimee, and start getting well," he murmured, opening the door. "I can't do this without you." He turned on his heel and left.

The turbulence intensified during our descent, flinging us from side to side in the quickening dusk. The plane nosed its way through a late January snowstorm—rare for Texas—and I concentrated on my breath. Anna slept, her small frame curled in my arm which had gone numb an hour outside of LaGuardia. I glanced out the window, watching cloud cover snuff the sun's dying rays as we flew farther into darkness. Making it onto the plane in the first place was a miracle. Anxiety and exhaustion had threatened to overwhelm me entirely, and my body ached from sleeplessness. I opened my phone, scanning the messages from the last few days through narrowed eyes.

Momma
*I talked with Cecily and filled her
in on your situation, she closed on
her house yesterday and can leave
Louisiana tomorrow morning.
Thank God my sister can be
with you since I can't!*

*Thank you so much, Momma.
I'll text her asap.
I can't wait to see her.
I'm not sure of where to stay.
I need to put down roots somewhere, again.*

*I was thinking about that too.
Aims, try Professor Tunc.
You know he would help you
out in a heartbeat.
Daddy and I spoke with him on
campus several weeks before
we headed to the UK, and he just
bought an investment property in
Galveston. It would be good to be
close to Mary and Chris, too.
I think their house might even be
in the same neighborhood as David's
new property. Between the Coles and
Cecily, you'll have an army at your side.*

> *That's a good idea.*
> *I'll message David now about the house.*
> *Love you Momma!*

Are you sleeping any better?

> *Not really.*
> *Please pray.*

David Tunc

> *Hi David, I apologize for*
> *messaging you out of the blue.*
> *Unfortunately, I'm not feeling*
> *well, and my doctor has*
> *recommended some R&R.*
> *Mom told me you recently*
> *acquired a house in Galveston.*
> *Would it be possible for me to*
> *rent it for a six-month term?*
> *My aunt, daughter and*
> *I would be the tenants.*

Hello Miss Aimee!
Yes, the house is in the Sea Isle
neighborhood of Galveston and
is available now.
Please let me know the best
email address for you and I will
send you the terms and contract.
Your mother emailed me about
your illness, and I am praying
for your quick recovery.

> *Thank you so much David,*
> *I appreciate you.*

Allison Nance

Cecily Fontenot

Hey Cici, it was so good talking
with you on the phone earlier.
The house in Galveston should
be ready for us tomorrow afternoon.
Anna is ready to make some cookies with you.

Maria Rojas

Mija, your mother called
and told me everything.
Are you sure you and
Anna will be alright?
I know Los Angeles is far
away from your job, but we
have plenty of sunshine here!
Please let us know if you'd
like to come out.
It was a treasure getting
to see you girls over Christmas
before you headed back to
the East coast.

Thank you for the offer, mama.
I'm going to try to stay put for now.
I can't stand screens for very long,
but I'll have Anna FaceTime you
once we're settled tomorrow.

Perfect, mija.
Please tell Anna Marie that Abuelito
and Abuelita can't wait to talk to her!

I will. TQM.

Nathaniel Si

Nat, I'll be in Galveston.
Will tell you more when I know more.

Clint Myers
Files for most recent BOP specs?

Inbox.

Maren Williams

Hey bestie.
Want to come to the beach?
I'm having forced R&R and miss your face.

Did you just call me "bestie?"
Are you dying?
I'm calling you at lunch.

Cecily Fontenot
Closing on the house was smooth sailing!
I'm leaving Morgan City around
5am tomorrow and should be at ur
hotel by nine.
Love u Aimee, see u soon!

Great.
Love you too.

Have u talked to Mary yet?

Not yet.
I'll shoot her a message to let
her know we'll be on the island.

I will too, Shug.

A beep pierced the cabin and static scratched through the ceiling as the lights came on.

"Ladies and gentlemen, we're beginning our final descent into Houston, George Bush Intercontinental. It's a brisk twenty-two degrees. No precipitation currently. Winds are at ten miles an hour out of the northwest. We should have you at the gate by 6:25."

The drone of the pilot's voice brought me back to the present, and I opened my eyes, stroking Anna's hair as the wind continued to fight the wings. The wheels bumped, kissing tarmac. For the first time in two and a half years, my daughter and I were home—whatever that meant—and things would get better. I would get better. I had to.

Cecily threw her Jeep into park as we paused to pay the toll on the causeway at the San Luis Pass. Gazing through the window, I'd forgotten how serene Galveston Island could be. Even in the ashen haze of winter it was beautiful, a tongue of cinnamon sand stretching out into the gulf. In the summer, fishermen clad in waders would stand waist-deep in the bay, their families claiming swathes of the beach under colorful awnings and umbrellas. Life was slower where sea and sand met sky seamlessly on the West End. Some twenty miles away on the opposite side of the island, adorned with architecture dating from the nineteenth century, the city of Galveston hummed a festive tune, defying the mainland's hustle, and hurricanes from the gulf. Perched on the bridge of the two-lane coastal highway, we could see the first of the West End's beach houses, looking like pastel crayons dumped out onto the dunes by a child. The sky and surf between them reflected a dull, slate gray. I blinked hard against the glare of the sunlight dimmed and bouncing off the clouds, the sensations in my head mirroring the motion of the waves below us.

"How much farther, Cici?" I rolled my shoulders, desperate to relieve the tension in my neck. We had to be close to the house, but I didn't want to get out of the car, didn't know if I could.

She checked the screen. "Not too far, Shug. Maybe five or six more minutes."

Shug, short for sugar, her favorite endearment for me.

"Thank you for doing this."

"Of course, Aimee. The timing of everything worked just perfectly, and I'm so glad y'all are here, where I can take care of you. And happy that your friends are coming around you right now. Who is your friend who owns this house, again?"

It took enormous effort for me to concentrate on her words and reply. "David. David Tunc." I closed my eyes. "He works at the university with Mom and Dad, but he also invests in rental properties. He said the previous owner of the one we're staying at built two identical houses. Ours is the one on the right." Yawning, I struggled to stay focused. "The other one is still owned by the family who built them. David said our house has a work truck in the garage, in case we need an extra car. Not that I can drive in this condition."

"You recited all of that perfectly. Are you sure you're not sleeping enough?"

"Ha, ha, very sure."

"It's not affecting your memory."

"Yet."

"And Maren is coming soon?"

"In two weeks."

"Well, I'm excited." My aunt's eyes glimmered like aquamarine, a stunning contrast to her smart, silver pixie cut and the bougainvillea shade of lipstick she was sporting. I couldn't suppress the smile that rose on my face, triggered by her genuine happiness.

"Anna's excited too." I glanced at her behind me, asleep in the back seat. "And happy not to be alone with a mother prone to panic attacks."

"She won't remember any of this a few years from now."

"I hope so." My head swam. "You're honestly this thrilled to be a vagabond with me? Homeless and all?"

She gazed at the road ahead with unflinching optimism. "There's nothing else I'd rather do!"

I believed her.

Some of my earliest memories are of Cecily, my Uncle Sam, my cousin Darius, and their stately home near Morgan City's historic district. At four years old, I'd aptly nicknamed the beautiful Victorian "The Dollhouse." Both only children and living less than a mile apart, Darius and I were more like siblings than cousins. I was roughly five years older than him, but the age difference held no sway over how close we were. We spent many summer nights sleeping on Sam and Cecily's screened-in porch, talking ourselves senseless. Their property hadn't been very large, but I was certain the age of the house demanded upkeep, which would have been too much for Cecily. Especially now that she was older, and Sam had been gone for almost twenty years. And Darius…

I shook my head, clearing the fog of memory. "I'm sure you're ready for something new. I know you need a reprieve, too."

Cecily laughed ruefully. "That's the truth. With you and your parents claiming Houston as home base, I figured it was time to leave memories behind. Besides, all that Spanish moss can be so depressing." She smiled, her tone lightening a bit as she referred to the giant oaks which had studded the grounds of her home in Louisiana. "I heard from him a few days ago."

An unwanted wave of anxiety rose, tightening somewhere in my chest. "Darius?"

"Yes, I'll have to tell you everything when we get settled, and when you're strong enough to hear it." Giving herself a little shake, Cecily brightened—perhaps a bit too forcefully. "Helping you get well and taking care of Anna is just what I need right now. God's timing in all of this has been perfect, Shug. Just perfect."

Cecily turned off the island highway and onto a curbless street boasting ocean front houses and lined with palms.

"I think this is it, Aimee." Cecily pulled into a narrow driveway.

Two identical cottages greeted us, striking modern colonials, both mainsail white and trimmed with black shutters. The houses stood high on stilts which bore their hulking weight. Doubling as both patio and driveway, each house had a single garage that wrapped around its full footprint. At the far end of the properties, bitter panicum bowed, wind-whipped as it met the sand. Wooden stairs flanked the left side of the houses, climbing up to meet decking. A lone hammock was strung between two stilts underneath our house on the beach end of the carport. The twin of our cottage boasted what would undoubtedly become lush landscaping in the spring, with waxy green shrubs that could easily be gardenias. Dormant spears of canna lilies and birds of paradise guarded our neighbor's staircase. A large American flag hung over their driveway from a mount on one of the stilts, and a picnic table with an assortment of chairs huddled on the ocean side of their patio. The handlebars and front wheel of a small, pink bike peeked out from under the stairwell leading up to the deck.

Anna awoke in the backseat, rousing in the uncanny way that children do when a car ride ends. "Mama, are we there? Where's the beach?"

"Yes, love. We're here. But I don't know if we'll make it down to the beach today. It's awfully cold, and Mama needs to take it slow."

The door handle might as well have been a crowbar for all the effort it took me to open it. But once I did, the brine in the breeze hit me, momentarily taking my fatigue with it. Even though the ground seemed to shift with every step I took, I made my way to the trunk to help Cecily with something. Anything. Together, we carried up the first load of bags.

The weathered stairs ended at a narrow landing in front of French doors. Beyond this, the deck widened to the right, flaring out to a large space that overlooked a hundred feet of grass and dunes which yielded to the sea. David had furnished the deck with chairs, and a table that would seat six. The key was under the doormat, just as he said. I unlocked the French doors and stepped inside the house. The heat was on, shrouding the house in a homeyness and warmth I'd experienced many times at Professor Tunc's personal residence in town. The kitchen ran along the wall immediately to our right. The living space and dining area in front of us gleamed with crystal and brass baubles. Built-in bookshelves filled with novels and volumes of Turkish literature flanked the walls, lending themselves to the academic nature of the room. Stairs along the opposite wall led to a loft overlooking the ocean with a dresser and bed where Anna would sleep. Down the long hallway on the first floor beyond the kitchen were two bedrooms: a guest bathroom and bedroom to the left, and the primary suite to the right, facing the identical cottage next door. Cecily and I would stay in these rooms.

Cecily blustered in with the last load. "This is perfect, Aimee. I'm sure you'll recover nicely here."

I spied Anna, investigating the walk-in pantry with fervor. "Mama, David put my kind of chips in here!"

"Bless him," I said under my breath.

Anna darted up the loft stairs.

Cecily examined the contents of the fridge. "We'll have to pick up a few more things this afternoon to be fully stocked." She glanced at me, assessing the almost visible tension pulsing through my body. "Shug, why don't Anna and I do a grocery run? I noticed a corner store right before we turned into the neighborhood, on the other side of main road."

I had glimpsed the convenience store on the island's coastal highway too, built up some twenty feet above street level to evade potential storm surges during hurricane season.

"Sure." I surrendered my need for control into Cecily's capable hands. "I don't think I could handle being out right now."

"Anna girl, let's take a quick ride to the grocery store across the street while your mama rests." Cecily's eyes sparkled at me. "We'll get you some Topo Chico while we're out."

Her mention of my favorite beverage did nothing to lift my spirits. Irrationality washed up in my thoughts, a result of too many sleepless nights. "You'll be back soon, right?"

"Of course, Aimee. We'll be fine." Cecily slung her purse over her wrist.

"Coming, Cici," Anna chirped. She hugged me before following Cecily out the door, her serious brown eyes signaling business. "You cannot go to the beach without me, Mama."

After they left, I gazed out of the large picture window which perfectly framed our view of the gulf. Deck and land both seemed to undulate with the waves, some hundred yards away from where I stood in the house, although I knew it was all in my head. I glanced at my phone.

10:41

"They'll be back by eleven." I attempted to conjure up calm. Despite my exhaustion, I didn't want to lie down; couldn't make myself go into the darkness of my new bedroom with its shuttered windows. Even though I knew there was no tangible reason to be anxious, worry gnawed my thoughts.

I headed for the French doors. Outside, the chilly wind whistled, and I pulled the hood of my sweatshirt over my head. I sat in an Adirondack chair. Breathed in. Breathed out. The sky and sea formed a stormy union far out in the ocean, appearing limitless, eternally tied together by an invisible string on the horizon. Peace existed out there on the waves, hovering over the deep. I wanted to love it, wanted to believe I could walk on the sand with Anna someday soon, but the weight of my body melded to the chair.

10:48

Four pelicans soared across the dunes in front of me, single file and flying east, oil-slick black against the winter death-hue of the sea grass. As I followed their path, a movement on the twin cottage's deck caught my eye. The girl was close to Anna's age. Seated at a table on her deck potting pansies, she wore a heavy coat and a light expression. The flowers popped yellow and bright against the monochrome landscape my view offered. Completely absorbed in her work, the child took no notice of me. She patted the dirt down and placed the pot in the center of the table. She looked up, considered the darkening clouds, and deciding that they would suffice to water her plants, twisted the bag of potting soil in her hands and picked up the plastic container the flowers had arrived in. She crossed the deck and walked through her living room windows which—unlike the large window in our house—had been converted into doors. She called to someone inside, closing the doors behind her.

I tried to chase away the thought but couldn't: she was safe and carefree in her home, while I was imprisoned by my body's unexpected riot, alone on the deck.

11:06

Rivulets of rain streamed down the windows and my head beat dully. Cecily and Anna weren't back yet. I reminded myself they were just down the road. I could unpack, and they'd be back soon. The hallway tilted to the left and I found myself in the primary suite, opening the shutters and flicking the switch on the wall. I needed light. Staying too long in the dark was how I'd gotten myself into this mess in the first place. I hefted my suitcase onto the bed.

Thanks to my nomadic lifestyle over the past few years, there wasn't much to unpack. My suits stayed in the garment bag, hung up in the closet. Toiletries went into the bathroom. I lined the menagerie of medication my doctor had prescribed along the desk, nestled in the bay window of my bedroom. I studied the bottles one by one. 50,000IU of vitamin D. A powerful multivitamin supplement. Melatonin. Some kind of natural sleeping aid cocktail. None of them had worked. Some worsened my tension. If anything, I dreaded the night more. Insomnia held me hostage in a twilight state, half-awake and half-asleep. I arranged the bottle of hydroxyzine at the end of the row. I hadn't tried it yet. The doctor was sure it would slow my mind, force me into sleep. As someone known both personally and professionally as always being in control, the prospect of being at the mercy of a drug terrified me.

I shook off the thought and continued to unpack. Sweatshirts, sweatpants, T-shirts, socks and underwear. I hadn't brought a swimsuit. Then the realization hit me: I didn't even own a swimsuit. I'd been working too hard. I took out my tennis shoes and a pair of flip flops, the only two kinds of shoes really needed on the island. I left several pairs of heels in the suitcase and zipped it up, shoving it into the closet.

I touched my phone.

11:20

Cecily Fontenot

Are y'all on the way back yet?

I sat on the sofa in the living room, tension stringing all my muscles together in a knot. I closed my eyes and tried to pray, but I could only speak his name. "Jesus, Jesus, Jesus."

Two things were true: I was safe in this house, and I was unmoored, adrift in some unfamiliar and menacing darkness. I heard the beep of Cecily's Jeep outside. They were back.

Anna blew in with the rain and ran past me with a shouted greeting, hurtling up the stairs to the loft to check out the toys and books David had stocked it with. Cecily set her grocery bags down on the counter.

"Next time y'all do errands," my voice shook, "please try not to take so long."

Cecily came over to me. Holding me, she began to pray.

I tucked Anna into her new bed in the loft upstairs. How many "new beds" she had slept in during the past few years? We said our prayers together.

In my bedroom, I flipped through the worn pages of my Bible to Psalm 139.

> *If I ascend to heaven, you are there.*
> *If I make my bed in the deep, behold, you are there.*
> *If I take the wings of the dawn, if I dwell in the*
> *remotest part of the sea,*
> *Even there your hand will lead me.*

"Don't let me go." The prayer struggled through my lips.

As I closed the shutters, a sound caught my attention. "Oye Cómo Va" in all its glory echoed through the neighborhood, drifting between festive patio lights that twinkled on the deck across the street.

I waited, listening. The twelve-string guitar intro to "Wanted Dead or Alive" caressed the windowpanes.

Tomorrow morning, I would ask Cecily to pick up a box fan from Walmart.

February

My memories of February are smudged, mere impressions of moments hastily pressed like a paint knife laden with color to a canvas. One day blurred into another, and my sleep didn't improve. Cecily enrolled Anna at the local elementary school while I sat on the couch, frozen with irrational fear, and doubting I could ever recover from what I'd unknowingly put my body through. The only respite arrived each day at dusk, when I would pull out my Bible and read through Psalms after tucking Anna in bed. I began leaving the pages open on my duvet so I could re-read the beautiful words, first thing in the morning. The weather warmed slightly, and despite my anxiety, Cecily and Anna often went outside for hours on the weekends, combing the beach for shells. Anna brought back her most treasured discoveries, showing them to me proudly; their perfectly formed lines and curves radiating the brilliance and beauty of heaven.

Anna left a shell near my plate during dinner one evening. "Will you come to the beach with me soon, Mama?"

The words had to wait until I swallowed my bite. "Soon, love."

"Mama, why are you eating so slowly?"

It had taken me almost an hour to eat the small plate of food Cecily prepared for me. "Because I'm tired, love." It had been six weeks since I'd slept more than two hours a night. The insomnia and anxiety had only seemed to worsen, and although my headaches had lessened in intensity, they were a baneful constant, never fully dissipating. The boardroom in Manhattan seemed like a lifetime ago.

"Can I sleep with you tonight, Mama?"

My phone dinged with a text.

"Sure, baby."

"Can you come with Cecily to drop me off at school in the morning, too?" Her hand slipped into mine. "I miss you."

I smiled at her. "Yes, love."

Clint Myers
Settling in?

Yes.
Still not sleeping well.

Please take whatever they gave you.

I will.

I reassigned Griffin and Brooklyn.
Handling the bid myself.
I'll let you know when I need you
to sign off on sales orders.

How long?
I'm on sick leave until March 13.

A few more weeks.

OK
Let me know.

Will do.

I read the instructions on the label of the small plastic bottle.
Take one tablet every six hours as needed for anxiety.
I checked the time.

6:11

I thumbed the security tab down and the cap fell off. Tiny pills spilled into my hand, white and hexagonal with a star that looked like an asterisk on one side. I left one in my palm and returned the rest to the bottle, twisting the cap shut. I walked into Cecily's room.

"I'm taking a new medicine tonight. The doctor said it would help with sleep."

"Oh, I hope it works." Cecily tapped her reading glasses on the cracked leather cover of her Bible. "I'm so sorry none of the natural remedies worked for you. I know you've been apprehensive about taking anything very strong."

"I hope it works too." I flipped the tablet over in my hand, star side down. "It only took me six weeks to admit I can't fall sleep on my own." I popped the pill in my mouth and took a drink, raw nerves making it difficult to swallow. "Anna wants me to ride with y'all to school in the morning. What time should we leave?"

"It's only seven minutes away. We're usually out the door no later than 7:30 so she's there in time for class to start at 8."

I didn't know any of these details. "You've done so much for us, Cici. Thank you." The hardwood groaned under my feet as I turned to go, then a thought stopped me. "Have you seen Mary yet?"

The aquamarine softened at the mention of Cecily's dearest friend. "Not yet, Shug. I told her you weren't quite ready for company. She and Chris understand completely. Let's see how the medicine does tonight, okay?"

"Okay," I conceded. "Night. Love you."

"Love you too, Shug."

Back in my room I turned down the sheets, sliding in quietly next to Anna who was already slumbering.

I closed my eyes. "Here goes nothing."

The hydroxyzine worked. I slept for four hours straight after taking one more dose at midnight as directed by the miniscule print on the bottle. When I woke up the next morning, I took another pill. We dropped Anna off at school on time, but my mind told me we were driving through mud, minutes moving at a glacial speed on Cecily's dash clock. The medicine was definitely taking effect now.

"We need to stop by the store, Aimee." Cecily's words wound through to my ears.

"We can go now," I said with some difficulty. I blinked, my eyelids heavy as lead, houses flickering by us like a stop-motion film. We drove up the ramp to the corner store. As I gripped the door handle, misgivings flew like meteorites. This was my first time out of the house in sixteen days.

"Cecily." Tension rose through the mud, stifling. "I don't think I can do this." It was absurd. Of course I could do it. Nothing would hurt me. But the sensation of helplessness wormed its way deep in my chest.

Cecily turned the key and took it out of the ignition. "I only need to get five things."

I exhaled, realizing I'd been holding my breath. "Just five things?"

"Five things. Want to hold the grocery bag?"

"Um…"

"Here." Cecily pushed a bag with Geaux Tigers! written in gold script into my lap.

Dingy from decades of exposure to the coastal climate, the storefront swallowed us with a rush as the doors slid closed behind us. Inside was spotlessly clean and organized. Guilt followed me into the store as I realized Anna must have come here with Cecily many times. I had taken my daughter all over the world, but now she was comfortable and confident in a new place without me. Cecily stopped at the produce stand just inside the door, then moved quickly into an aisle on the left. The store was bright with a high row of windows and fluorescent lighting which illuminated the freezer chests and doors lining the back of the shop. The light glared and a familiar pain refocused, centering behind my eyes. An older, deeply tanned man with horn-rimmed glasses and an affable face leaned against the counter.

He looked up from his paper. "Hi there, are you Cecily's niece?"

"Yes. Aimee Rojas." My stomach churned as if I'd been called on by my second-grade teacher.

"Nice to finally meet you. I'm Amos Guerrero. Cecily told me you were here to get well. The West End is the best place for it." Pride shone from his eyes. "Plenty of sunshine."

I turned, searching for Cecily, but somehow—in a store the size of my suite in Manhattan—she'd completely disappeared.

"This your first time on the island, Mrs. Rojas?" Amos asked.

I turned my head back toward him and blinked hard. "Aimee, please. And yes, several times as a child to visit friends, and then also when my daughter was young."

Cecily plonked an overflowing basket on the counter next to me. Definitely more than five things.

"Good morning, Miss Cecily." A jar of strawberry jelly beeped as Amos scanned it.

"Morning, Amos! Did you meet Aimee?" She handed him the

shopping bag I clutched in my hands.

"Yes, I did. We'll get her taken care of, won't we?" A grin slid up the side of his weathered face.

Anxiety twined around me like a cord.

"It was nice meeting you, Amos." I gave my best attempt at a smile and bolted to the door, literally leaving Cecily holding the bag. I melted into the Jeep's interior, warm from the sun. I closed my eyes. I had done it. I'd been in the store and survived.

Cecily hopped in the driver's seat.

"It was more than five things, Cici."

"Phoo, Shug. It didn't hurt you anymore though, did it?" She smiled wickedly as I shut my eyes against the sun. We turned down the ramp out of the parking lot.

"Looks like our neighbor took a day off from work," she commented, pulling up under the house.

My eyes yawned open, keenly aware of the effort it took. Swift as a slingshot, the anxiety released me, flinging me into an inconceivable drowsiness.

"I'm just gonna head upstairs. I'm in no condition to meet anyone else today."

The aquamarine pierced right through me. "You should at least say hi to him and introduce yourself, Aimee. Anna's played with his daughter several times already and they're sweet little friends."

The ground lurched as I stepped out of the Jeep, holding one of the grocery bags.

"Good morning, Mr. King!" Cecily knew everyone.

He called a greeting back to her as I rounded the hood of the car. "… yeah, I just dropped off Christina. I'm taking a personal day to do some work around the house."

A baseball cap and dark sunglasses obscured his eyes and hair. Not remarkably tall and with a slighter build, a quiet confidence emanated from the way he held himself. He was holding out his hand to me and I shook it, my head delaying everything.

"Aimee Rojas. Pleased."

"Jeremy King. Nice to meet you." The terse set of his mouth and the way he held his keys said otherwise. I didn't blame him. I swayed slightly, still grasping his hand.

"Please forgive Aimee," Cecily laughed. "She's a little doped up right now." The awkwardness of our prolonged handshake finally set in, and I took my hand back. "She started a new medication last night and it's catching up with her this morning."

"Sorry to hear that." The grit in his soft, monotone voice scraped over me like sandpaper.

"Cecily says your daughter and mine are having fun together. I know Anna enjoys that." I wondered if the words sounded as slow to him as they felt coming out of my mouth. Turning to Cecily, I announced, "I'm gonna head upstairs and stick this in the fridge." My eyes couldn't focus on my neighbor. "Nice to meet you, Mr. King."

He gave a curt nod. "You too, Mrs. Rojas."

Relief flooded across my shoulders. No more strangers, no more introductions. The cool burst of the open refrigerator cleared my thoughts.

Cecily breezed in. "Isn't he nice?"

"Seemed a bit dour to me."

She chuckled. "He teaches eighth grade algebra at the middle school. I'd be dour, too. He's always been very kind to me and Anna, though."

"That's good," I affirmed mindlessly. I pulled my wits together. "What's his daughter's name again?"

"Christina."

I remembered the yellow flowers on the porch our first afternoon in Galveston.

"She and Anna have played a couple of times, mostly at our carport. Are you going to close the refrigerator?"

I pulled my head out of the fridge. "I bet Christina's mom has it all together."

Cecily raised her eyebrows. "I've never seen anyone over there but Jeremy and Christina."

"Oh." Mud. I was sinking in it.

I pulled my phone out of my pocket. The screen blazed. Vaguely concerned, I typed in a search, then scrolled.

Recommended dosage for Hydroxyzine:
Adults with no underlying conditions should tolerate a maximum of 100 mg every 24 hours. In some cases, 50mg may be taken every six hours for anxiety, especially prior to surgery or major medical operations.

"I've just had three doses of fifty milligrams in the last twelve hours," I wailed. The sludge thickened.

"What are you talking about, Shug?"

"This doctor is trying to mess me up." I slithered back into the kitchen, intent on drinking as much water as humanly possible. "I have to pass this stuff. I've taken too much."

"An overdose?"

Cecily's eyes, large with concern, halted me. "No, Cici, just too much for me. Enough to make me useless for the rest of the day."

"If you're sure."

I slumped onto a barstool. "I'm sure."

"Maren will be here tonight." Cecily changed the subject. "If anyone can snap you out of this funk you're in, she's the one."

"Love, how does anyone survive down here, living more than ten miles from an international airport?" Like dark chocolate, Maren's voice warmed my mood and left me feeling just as satisfied. After having survived three hours of deadlocked traffic on I-45 with an Uber driver whose playlist exclusively consisted of Yoko Ono, Maren lolled on the sofa beside me, glowing in the heat from the fireplace. Her homemade rooibos Chai swirled in our cups as we stayed awake long after I tucked Anna in bed. My head cleared from its state of drugged stupor at last, and my best friend had me smiling.

"It's a way of life. We measure distance in time, not miles."

"Well thank God for Nashville." She grinned at me over the rim of her cup.

Maren was currently based in Tennessee, although her career as a global Marketing and Conference Manager took her to all ends of the earth. She'd dropped everything after our call to be with me for a long weekend, but her selflessness was the least surprising thing about her.

Randomly assigned as roommates our freshman year of college, Maren and I both showed up at our dorm scared witless and wearing Mingo Fishtrap t-shirts. Discovering we had much more than a favorite band in common, we became fast friends. Over the years, Maren stood beside me.

She was by my side at a crowded house party where Caleb Rojas introduced himself and asked me to dance.

"What are you waiting for, dummy?" she hissed as I stood frozen, gaping at Caleb's laughing face. She hooted with joy as Caleb took my hand and drew me close. Then, she'd stood with me as I took Caleb's hand again, this time for life. She paced our hallway with Anna after she was born, crooning lullabies as Caleb and I stole precious sleep, one hour at a time. She was one of the very few who stood with me as Pastor Hamada wept, struggling to whisper the benediction at Caleb's coffinless funeral. And now, while I struggle to stand on my own, she's right there beside me, reminding me of who I am.

"Where are you, Aimee?" Maren cocked her head, an exquisitely sculpted brow perfectly reflecting the angle of her smile.

"A million miles away."

"You can say that again. Speaking of which, why didn't you pick out a house in the Heights? Wouldn't it feel more like home?"

"I'm not sure what would feel like home." Memory settled with the dregs of my tea. "With Cecily just selling her place in Louisiana and my parents on sabbatical in Cornwall, I figured we might as well go to the beach." I held my palm open to her. "Thank you so much for coming."

She took my hand. "Of course. Fill me in."

I told her about the sleepless weeks in Manhattan, my panic attack in the boardroom, the diagnosis from the doctor, the residual anxiety and gutting fatigue.

"You're not working now, are you?"

"No, I squared it away with Hoff. I'm officially on sick leave, and Valiant is temporarily without a Sales Director. I had six weeks of vacation time accrued since I've never taken off for an illness."

"Or the death of a loved one," she said gently.

"No." I let the sting of the months of work after Caleb's death pulse in the shadows on the floor. I pressed on. "Clint seems to be getting along alright without me, although he was uncharacteristically defeatist about the bid when everything came to a head in New York. I told him I'd check in at the end of this month, but six weeks takes me through mid-March."

Maren rolled her eyes at the mention of Clint's name. I smiled and couldn't help but remember the first and only time she had met him, at my and Caleb's house in the Heights for a Fourth of July barbecue.

My eyes struggled to focus on her smirk. "Still holding a grudge?"

"I don't know why I didn't believe you all those years ago. I never should have taken Caleb's bet to get Clint's number by the end of the night."

"Can't say we didn't warn you."

"The man is like Saturn," Maren waxed eloquent. "Gorgeous and magnetic but encircled by rings of rocky, frigid debris destined to pummel you once you're within a certain proximity. I could never get him to warm up to me."

"You're terribly clever. It really is too bad he only lavishes attention on whoever can close a sale." I stuffed a pillow behind my back. "And his car. If anyone could make a devastatingly good-looking couple, it would be you and Clint. He needs someone."

"You're wasting your time." Maren sipped her tea. "You are the only thing that could melt him."

"I'm a guarantee for his bottom line."

"Hmm…"

"Believe me. I'm just a good listener, and people appreciate being heard. Clint's the charmer. Honestly, he could run the entire show by himself." A log popped and hissed in the hearth. "And I'm sure he is right now. The last few weeks he's laid low, but I'm waiting for the other shoe to drop. He did seem genuinely concerned the last time we were together. He was actually a little dramatic by his standard, told me that he couldn't do 'it' without me."

Her cup stopped, half-way to her mouth. "'It' being the bid you're working on?"

"Yeah. I mean we had a killer rhythm going. We brought more clients to Valiant in the last five years than they've seen in two decades."

"And he's still single?"

"Married to the job, quite literally."

"He's been very devoted to you over the last few years."

"He doesn't have anyone else to be devoted to. His mom died when he was young, and his dad was kind of a hot shot in the oil and gas industry. They moved to England, and he grew up there. Stunning academic and professional credentials. Zero social life. Like you said, he distances personal relationships."

"But you're well within the debris field." Maren inspected me like a beetle on a pin. "He's never expressed anything beyond a working relationship to you?"

"We're friends." I hesitated, remembering his hand on mine in the car and the fleeting kiss before he left my hotel. "It's complicated."

"What?" Her cup rattled in the saucer.

"It's not what you're thinking. Ever since Caleb died, he's relentlessly helped me take care of Anna. He's been there for me. For both of us. He can finish my sentences and we're very close but not in a romantic way."

The look Maren gave me said she wasn't buying any of it.

"How else can I explain it? The chemistry we have is fine-tuned for the sake of our work."

"You're certain he's aware of the distinction?"

"If anyone is, it's him. Clint can read anybody like an open book. He knows exactly what people want to hear and how to speak to them. More importantly, he knows what they need to hear. Success informs his every decision." I straightened, rolling my shoulders. "That's why I hired him. We've been so busy anyway, especially this past year. We've hardly talked about anything personal. It's this newest bid with the Philippines that's got him on edge. I know he wants to keep them happy."

"Well, don't take any of his lip." She shot me a look. "In any form or fashion."

I shook my head. "I don't want it, trust me. I have no interest in him whatsoever, and honestly, I don't believe he does either. He had too much respect for Caleb."

Maren eyed me. "You sure?"

"Positive. For Clint, love is love and sex is sex, and ne'er the twain shall meet."

"That's taking things a bit far."

"Agreed. The saddest thing is, I'm quoting him." We exchanged glances.

"To be a fly on the wall during that conversation."

"I'll gladly take Clint's love over the alternative any day." I admitted. "And as far as that entire department is concerned, I can barely say hello to the guy who owns the grocery across the highway."

Maren perked up. "Is he nice?"

"Very. I'm also pretty sure he's seventy. Besides, I'm not looking for anything right now."

"You don't have to be, love. You know it doesn't always happen like that." Her dark eyes softened. "What's in your heart? Spill it, sister."

I gave a little laugh then was quiet for a few moments. The tears were instant, unasked for and unwanted. "I knew you'd have me crying before the end of the night. I don't know what to say. No one deserves me like this. I think Anna is okay, but I know she's lonely sometimes. She's been playing with the little girl next door, and I think they've become good friends. I think? I've been here for almost a month, and I don't even know anything about my neighbors. Except that the ones across the street have an exceptionally loud stereo and excellent taste in music."

"Oh dear." She weighed everything I'd poured out. "What do you mean no one deserves you like this? That's a lie straight from hell, and you know it. Friends carry each other's burdens, and you need to let us help you carry this one. Me, Cecily, the Coles. We're all here to help."

"I know, but this feels so heavy and dark. You know what's strange, though? I feel like I've finally gotten myself back after years of grieving, but at the same time it's like I've also lost everything that made me, me. Like the way I am now is irreversible. I'm not cool and collected anymore. I can't think straight, and I can barely take care of myself, let alone Anna. I know I'm getting better, and the feelings are nothing, but it's paralyzing."

"It's not nothing, Aimee. You're right."

"I am?"

"You aren't the same woman anymore, sister." Maren took my hand again. "You're becoming something more. The lack of sleep intensifies everything, I'm sure," she sighed. "And makes everything less black and white, more gray. You're taking that antihistamine though, to help you sleep?"

"Yes, I started it last night, but I think I should only take one before bed. The prescription only has eight pills and I've already taken three, so I'll give it a try for the next few days."

"It's worth a shot."

"I might toss and turn. You really don't mind sleeping with me?"

"Of course not. We'll sing along with Vanilla Ice or whoever the neighbors have playing tonight. Next time I come I'll even bring matching pjs for us." She gathered both our cups. "But first, we pray."

I gazed out the window. On the other side of the glass, the morning had eased into a beautiful day.

Maren shut her laptop. "Let's go shopping."

"What?" My head jigged like a bobble-head doll.

Maren waved her glasses in her hand. "Anna's at school and you've been sitting in that chair all morning. It's almost lunchtime and you haven't left this house since I got here two days ago. After rummaging through your closet yesterday, I know for a fact you have nothing to wear that actually fits. Let's get out and buy you some new clothes!"

My anxiety ratcheted up. "You were in my closet?"

Maren in my closet was akin to the same explosive reaction of baking soda and vinegar. In college, Maren combatted stress with shopping. The problem was, she never shopped for herself, only others. Sophomore finals brought me the dress I wore when I met Caleb. Her promotion somehow earned me the Westwood suit I wore for my final interview with Valiant.

I didn't say anything. I only stared back at her, longing to sink into the couch and disappear.

Maren flung her hand toward the window. "Look at that! The sun is shining. The beach is beach-ing. If you don't get out, you're only going to make things worse for yourself. It'll be harder and harder for you to rejoin the rest of humanity. If we get out now even when you feel miserable, the next time it will be easier."

I rubbed my eyes. "I really hate it when you're right."

"I know! So, get dressed. We're going to the Strand."

I tried to imagine myself in the heart of Galveston's historic district. "The Strand? That's on the other side of the island."

"It's a nice day for a drive," she countered, unmoved. "And besides, you wouldn't catch me dead in Walmart."

I tried to deter her. "I'm just going to wear what I have on."

Maren eyed my sweats, wrinkling her nose. "When was the last time you washed those?"

"I don't know," I mumbled. I had been surviving in stretchy pants and camisoles for the past six weeks, alternating between what was hanging on my bed frame, and what I had the energy to drag out of the dryer.

"Well, at least it's the middle of the morning during a school day, so you'll minimize anyone having to see…" she waved her hand in my general direction, "…that."

Cecily tossed the Jeep keys to Maren with such glee that I imagined they'd coordinated this particular outing. Humming, Maren navigated the island and pulled up to a boutique near the bustling cruise terminal.

A proud turquoise sign touting *Aqua Crystal* hung over our heads into the street. "Maren, it sounds like a diet soda."

"The worst named shops always have the best hidden gems."

Stepping from the Jeep, I became light-headed. For an instant

I thought it would float away, untethered from my body. "This was a bad idea."

"Of course it's not. Come on." Maren linked her arm in mine as if we were going on a grand adventure.

Like Amos's store, the fluorescent lighting blinded me. My mind rejected it, small and incapable of processing everything my eyes were taking in.

"Over here." Maren steered me toward a rack of clothing. I crossed my arms. She eyed me up and down. "You've lost what, thirty pounds?"

"Over forty."

"Love, we'll get you set up. No more elastic waistbands."

She had grabbed a basket on the way in and began filling it. I saw her toss in a pair of cut-offs, several blouses that were quite a few steps above my oversized t-shirts, and some black and white flannel button-ups. "This way!" She said cheerfully.

My head split from overstimulation. "How much longer?"

"We've only been here for ten minutes. Go wander around and pick something out."

Her proposition paralyzed me. Maren left my side, and I headed in a daze toward shelves of shoes against the wall. I tried to concentrate, focusing on each individual pair but I couldn't. A pair of espadrille wedges caught my attention, and I held them in my hands. I didn't need them; these were shoes for someone who could actually function in public.

Maren popped up behind me. "Adorable!" she praised. "We're getting them."

A shop girl seemingly materialized out of nowhere, plucking Maren's full basket from her arm and offering her another one to fill. A strappy black linen dress with a full skirt flew into the newly proffered basket, followed by something slinky that looked like it would only fit my leg.

"You're daft if you think I need those out here."

"You have literally nothing like this that fits you." She tossed them both into the basket. "And they'll go with the wedges you picked out."

"I have literally no occasion to wear anything like that."

"Don't be peevish. Who knows when Clint will swoop down here and whisk you away to another boardroom."

"That's not exactly executive attire you've picked out so far."

"Be prepared for anything, love. And besides it's a local shop, not Nieman's. We have to take what we can get."

My stomach churned. "Are you done?"

"Not in the slightest. Toiletries."

"They have toiletries here?" I glanced around, wondering if the shop was really some kind of multi-dimensional clown car. "Do I smell that bad?"

"No, but you could use some pampering. Face masks and Epsom salts."

I closed my eyes slowly, consciously trying to relax. "Please marry a nice man, have four children and shop for them instead."

She shot me a look. "You know as well as I do that all the men I encounter regularly are on a tedious spectrum of self-involvement. They either see me as a nice diversion from the wife and kids they aren't telling me about, or obnoxiously in touch with their feelings.

"Surely there must be a happy medium?" I watched a bottle of rose vetiver body spray fly into the basket.

"God willing, I'll fall madly in love with some endearing beefcake who completely lacks any kind of self-awareness whatsoever."

"I'll start praying for him now."

"I'll forever be in your debt." Mascara and lip gloss went into the basket next. She gave me a playful look. "Your bank account can handle this, I'm sure."

I noticed the pattern on the third night.

Two hours after taking hydroxyzine, drowsiness would overtake me, and I'd sleep for at least four hours. Even in small increments, the sleep from the drug made me feel human again. But there was also an ugly side to the pattern. It ushered in a lingering mental fog and depression that laid heavy on me all day, only clearing at dusk.

Just before the next dose.

I coveted the few hours when my mind was clear and pain free, when I could hold Anna and almost feel normal again. Mary and Chris' visit tonight would coincide with the evening hours of clarity, when I would feel most like myself.

Anna tackled her homework at the kitchen table, getting it done before the weekend. I hugged her shoulders.

She looked at me and smiled. "Do you think I can play with Christina after I'm done, Mama?"

"Christina?" I drew a blank.

"My friend, next door. Mr. Jeremy's daughter."

"Oh." I glanced out the window. The thought of her going anywhere riled me. "It's almost dark outside, baby. Mary and Chris will be here soon, and I'm sure they're excited to see you. It's been a few years, and you've grown up so much since the last time they saw you."

"But Mama, Mr. Jeremy said I can come over whenever I want."

"I'm sure he did, but I bet Christina's also got some homework to do, and I don't have any way to ask Mr. King if it's okay for you to come over." Nor do I know anything about Mr. Jeremy King, I thought to myself. "I want you to be here for Mary and Chris."

Her eye roll could have set off a Richter scale. "Ughh, fine. I'll stay." She gave me a quizzical look. "Mama, who exactly are Mary and Chris?"

Mary, Cecily and my mother had grown up together as girls

back in Louisiana. With only five years spanning the difference in their ages, their bond was as strong as a pride of lionesses. Not long after I was born, my parents began seminary. Mary babysat me every summer while she went through college herself, graduated, and began her career as a kindergarten teacher. Chris and Mary met and married young and—like all newlyweds who need the extra cash—Mary had continued to be my nanny.

Childless herself, she fell somewhere between older sister and second mother, and I couldn't remember a time in my life without her in it. When I was six, the Coles moved to Galveston for Chris' job in shipping, and Mary started teaching at a local elementary school. After they built a house in Sea Isle, they only came back to Morgan City for Thanksgiving and Christmas. But distance couldn't prevent us from picking up exactly where we left off, our families playing dominoes and ragging on each other until the early hours of the morning. With marriage and work, the last time I'd seen them was at Caleb's memorial service.

"Mama?"

My thoughts snapped back to Anna's question. "They're as close to family as you can get, sweet girl."

"Aimee." Mary's eyes brimmed with tears as I met her at the French doors.

I let myself sob openly in her arms. After a few moments she took my face in her hands and studied me. "I'm so glad you're here. So glad we can help take care of you."

Anna fidgeted beside me.

Mary knelt and met her at eye level. "And you! You're so big, Anna. You look just like your momma when she was your age. Do you remember me?"

Anna gave Mary a shy smile. "Not really."

"That's okay." The warmth of Mary's smile could melt a glacier. "I remember you. And we're all going to have a really great spring together."

"Where's Chris?" I asked.

"Right here, darlin'!" His huge frame filled the entirety of the doorway. "I was just giving a quick shout to your neighbors next door." He grabbed me up into a giant bear hug. "Where'd you go, Aimee? I thought New York City was full of fancy restaurants with sandwiches you needed at least four other people to help you eat?"

His eyes danced with joy, and I laughed uncontrollably, for the first time in a long time. "It is, but it helps a lot if you're actually able to eat."

"Well." His voice was gruff. "We'll make sure nothing like that happens again, right baby?" He directed his last question to Mary.

"Of course, honey." Mary took my hand.

"I thought I'd make some hot chocolate tonight." Cecily carried a copper tray laden with steaming mugs. Her hot chocolate was legendary. Rich and creamy, and guaranteed to keep me awake, medication or no.

"I'll stick with tea, Cici."

"Whatever you'd like, Shug."

"Now tell us everything, Aimee." Mary took a cup from the tray. "From the beginning."

Hearing the words I was saying and speaking about the fear I suffered from to Mary and Chris made it easier to understand, even if I couldn't quite reconcile the events of the last few weeks. Maren joined us, sipping cocoa near the blaze in the fireplace.

I spied Anna, curled up in one of the oversized chairs. "Anna girl, why don't I get you ready for bed?"

She rubbed her eyes. "I'm not sleepy, Mama."

Chris chuckled. "We don't believe that for a second, little miss."

Anna giggled and stuck her tongue out at Chris, and readily accepted a passing hug from Mary.

I stood with Anna in the bathroom as she brushed her teeth, catching a glimpse of myself in the mirror. My clothes hung on me, cheeks sunken deep under the bones of my face.

Anna spit and wiped her mouth. "Mama, can Christina come to our house and play sometime? I mean, her house is fun, and Mr. Jeremy is really nice and has a like a million boats and everything, but…"

"Boats?"

"… but I think it would be fun to invite someone to my house for once." Her eyes shifted to the side, then fixed on me.

I smiled. "You're a hard one to deny, Anna Marie."

"So that's a yes?"

"Yes. We'll ask Cecily when's a good day."

"Thank you, Mama!" She hugged me and waved goodnight to the group in the living room as we walked up the stairs to the loft. She slid into her bed, and I sat on the edge beside her, smoothing the heavy quilt.

"What are you grateful for, lovebug?"

"You. Cici. Christina. The beach. And that you're getting better." Her hand found mine. "You are getting better, aren't you?"

"Yes baby." I smiled, not feeling an ounce of truth in my words, even though I knew it was true. "It will just take time for me to be back at a hundred percent."

"What percent are you now?"

"Mmmm… sixty-five percent."

"Well, that's no good."

"I love your optimism, child."

"Huh?"

I managed a laugh. "Come on, let's say our prayers. It's your turn tonight."

I turned Anna's box fan on high and came back downstairs.

Chris pulled his chair close to Cecily's and lowered his voice. "How's Darius these days?"

Cecily cast a glance at me as I nestled between Maren and Mary on the sofa.

"It's alright. I can handle it." Couldn't I?

Chris, my uncle Sam, and Darius were so close when we were kids. But that was then, and so much had changed…

There had been a phase in my early childhood where I had vehemently requested my parents to produce a sibling for me. For months after my fourth birthday, I took the apparent denial of my request personally. I remember none of this.

It would be a decade before I would learn that my conception had been a miracle for my mother, and another decade until I'd learn that I shared the same difficulty in carrying a child. What I do remember is the year I turned five, Darius was born.

At Cici and Sam's, I was given a pillow and a tiny person who wrinkled and cooed on my lap. His corn-colored hair felt like the down of a chick, and he was pink and perfect and mine. Now, he belonged to *them*. Or more accurately, *it*. The cumulative effect of the prescriptions, meth, opioids, cocaine, addiction, lies, hallucinations, numbness, overdoses, shame, arrogance, denial, bodiless enablers that dictated his every action. Every time he used, a part of him vanished. Over time, I expected to find myself staring at the voided consciousness of a living corpse. But it wasn't like that. He was still Darius, even underneath the star-bound eyes and slurred *I'm sorry's*. Maybe I subconsciously hoped his mind would be utterly vacant, so completely alien to the boy I grew up with, that I could abandon the love I had for him like a condemned house. But it didn't work like that at all.

Darius had been and always would be mine, just as he'd been since the first day I held him.

Frustration creased Cecily's face, suddenly aging her. "Where to begin? Well, I guess I could tell you about the most recent incident. I think you know some of what the past few years have held for Darius, right Mary?"

Mary nodded. "I think one of the last things was that his driver's license had been suspended?"

"Okay, then it's been a while since I've talked with you about him. His license was suspended about nine months ago, when he was working the night shift at Jack in the Box. Last summer, one of his co-workers who worked the morning shift noticed that Darius' car was still in the parking lot when he arrived at work. He saw Darius passed out in the driver's seat and couldn't wake him up by knocking on the window, so he called 911. The police and paramedics showed up and broke into the car but still couldn't wake him, so they took him to the ER. When he finally woke up, the police arrested Darius and cited him with a DUI since the keys were in the ignition when the EMTs got him out." Cecily pursed her lips. "But being arrested didn't stop him from driving. He was pulled over a few weeks after that and arrested again for driving with a suspended license."

Pain shot across my head like a streak of lightning. I had been in Tokyo at the time for a business summit when Cecily texted me the news. The lights from Roppongi had illuminated my suite as I found his mug shot online, showing me a face that belonged to a shadow of the boy I grew up with.

"Someone you know?" Clint had asked, over my shoulder.

"I'm not sure anymore," I replied.

Cecily continued. "One of his... acquaintances made bail for Darius both times. His trial was set for six weeks ago, but Darius never showed. So now he's in contempt of court and there's a warrant out for his arrest in Louisiana."

"No," Mary murmured. I caught Mary's expression and could

tell she was trying to reconcile Cecily's narrative with the silly, conscientious boy who always sought her out when they visited over holidays to read books and play jacks.

None of Cecily's news surprised me, but I caught myself twisting my wedding band around and around my finger.

"Where is he now?" Chris shifted in his chair, agitated.

Cecily paused. "He's actually in Houston, staying with Lord-only-knows-who in Montrose. Do you remember Tyler?" She glanced at us.

Tyler had been Darius' best friend in Morgan City. A sweet, skinny kid who hadn't crossed my mind in years. He and Darius lived two streets apart and played soccer together all through high school.

"Tyler Thompson?" asked Chris.

"Yes." Cecily let out her breath slowly. "He's also in Houston, receiving treatment for stomach cancer at MD Anderson, but he's been in palliative care for almost a month. His doctors have said there's nothing more they can do except to manage the pain."

My thoughts were crystal clear now, entirely free of the hydroxyzine, and I was fairly certain where this particular facet of Cecily's narrative was headed.

"I've kept in touch with Tyler and his wife, Kayla, throughout the whole thing. Tyler practically lived at our house when the boys were younger. He's like a son to me." Cecily bent her head and rubbed her hands. Her knuckles had grown large with age and the beginnings of arthritis. "Kayla called me a few days before I left Morgan City and said Darius came to see them in the house they're renting. She said of course he was beside himself when he saw Tyler, couldn't keep from crying."

"Darius has always been tender-hearted," Mary encouraged.

"Well." Cecily's eyes darted to her best friend. "Kayla called to tell me Darius spent the night with them on their couch and left before breakfast the next day. When she went to give Tyler his morning dose of pain meds, the entire bottle was empty."

My hand froze, stopping my ring from turning.

"Not gone, but empty?" Maren's eyes were wide.

Cecily's voice dropped to a near whisper. "The home health nurse brings Tyler's medication when she comes at the beginning of the week. She'd just brought a fresh prescription for him a couple of days before Darius' visit. Darius stole a week's worth of medication from them. From his best friend."

From a dying man, I thought. My own physical state seemed minuscule compared to what Tyler was facing, and what Darius was battling. Or maybe he wasn't fighting it anymore…

Cecily shook her head. "Tyler and Kayla know that Darius has had this problem with pain killers for the past fifteen years, and Kayla said he looked terrible. I don't know why she didn't think to hide the medication."

I spoke up. "Even when you know what's happening, sometimes it's still hard to face the reality of it."

Maren exchanged glances with me.

"I should go see Tyler and Kayla soon," Cecily said. "If only to apologize for what Darius has done."

"Have you heard from him directly?" Chris' chair creaked as he leaned forward.

Cecily shrugged. "He knows I sold the house. More importantly he knows why I sold the house. Morgan City has nothing left for me anymore. I called him a few days after we got settled here and told him I was enjoying an extended stay with Aimee and Anna while they're in Galveston. He doesn't know I spoke with Kayla." Cecily looked at me. "And he doesn't know you're sick."

I passed a hand over my eyes. "It's probably better that way."

Mary stirred beside me on the sofa. "Well, there may not be much we can do action-wise." A determined glint entered Mary's eyes. "But we can pray and share your needs with others who can be praying for you, Aimee, and Darius. Aimee, you know the Hamadas, don't you?"

Jason and Lilly Hamada. Our friends and pastors of the church Caleb and I had belonged to in the Heights. "I do. Jason conducted Caleb's memorial service. Didn't they move down here a while ago?"

Mary's eyes sparkled. "Yes, to pastor the church Chris and I have attended since we moved down here. West End Bible Fellowship. We have prayer nights once a month where we eat dinner and pray for each other. It's always laid-back." Her hand came up to rest on my arm. "If you're feeling well enough to host, I'd love to ask Jason if it would be okay for our next gathering at the end of the month to meet here. To pray for you all."

"That sounds really good, Mary." I looked at Cecily. "Is that alright with you, Cici?"

Hope returned to Cecily's face. "I think that's just what we need, Shug."

I slept for about five hours that night and the next. The morning before she was supposed to leave, Maren and I chatted about her upcoming trip to France as we shared her post-jog breakfast of berries and cream. She would be in Paris for almost two months, and we were already hatching a plan for her to come back to the island sometime in May.

Our conversation lulled and my friend gazed through the window. "Aimee, have you seen your next-door neighbor?"

"Yeah." He'd worn dark sunglasses and fidgeted with his keys. "I met him…" I wracked my brain, trying to recall when. "…earlier this week. Why?"

Maren popped a blueberry in her mouth, still concentrating on the outdoors. "No reason."

Monday morning brought rain, indicative of the impending cold front on its way to blast the coast later in the evening. Overcast and gray, the sky reminded me of the last time I had taken care of Anna on my own in New York. And for the next twenty-four hours, on my own I would be.

After conferring with me, Cecily and I agreed she should make the trek into Houston to see Tyler and Kayla.

"They didn't need to invite me to stay the night." Cecily zipped up her overnight bag. "But Kayla seemed happy to have some extra help for the evening hours."

Maren's Uber pulled up just after breakfast.

She hugged me hard. "You can do this, love. Don't be afraid."

"May is a long time from now." My breath crystallized in the frigid air.

"Enough time for you to get well. It'll fly, Aimee, and I can't wait to see how much better you'll be when I come back."

Watching her car pull away, I considered the day ahead.

Cecily would pick Anna up from school, then head to the Medical Center after dropping Anna off with me. With Cecily going away for the night, it was my task to check out the work truck situation so I could take Anna to school the next day.

The wind whipped my hair, and I glimpsed the slate-gray surf surging at high tide beyond the dunes. I turned the key in the rusted lock. The hinges of the garage doors groaned as I swung them apart. From the shadows of the garage, the grill of a turquoise Chevy C10 grinned at me. I opened the driver's door and hopped in.

The keys glinted on the bench seat, and the tank was full, praise God.

I ran my hand over the wheel. "It's you and me tomorrow, pal."

I stood in front of the bay window in my bedroom, listening.

Apparently, it was the greatest hits of Jimmy Buffet for this evening's listening pleasure from the residential concert hall across the street.

I closed the shutters. "Jesus, help me sleep tonight."

My hydroxyzine was gone, and—I hoped—the insomnia too. I turned my fan on high and flipped the pages in my Bible to Psalm 34.

> *Many are the afflictions of the righteous,*
> *But the Lord delivers him out of them all.*

"Amen." I said and flicked off the light.

My alarm went off at 7:15, but it didn't matter.

I had never gone to sleep. My body revolted without the hydroxyzine, keeping me abnormally alert and awake.

My fingers typed in a search, and I read:

> *Stopping hydroxyzine suddenly without tapering the dosage will often cause a rebound effect in the patient, heightening anxiety and insomnia.*

A nameless weight pushed me down into the bed, and my head reeled worse than before. Anxiety swelled in my throat at the thought of driving Anna to school.

Take a deep breath.

I sat up. Sweatshirt hanging on the bed frame, up and over my camisole. Pajama shorts stayed on. The room leaned to the left. I grabbed the water glass on my nightstand and drank.

Small sips.
Swallowing was hard.
"I can't do this."
Many are the afflictions…
I walked slowly down the hall to the living room. Anna was already awake, reading a book.
"Baby, get your clothes on. We gotta go soon."
"Okay, Mama." Her footsteps thumped like heartbeats, pounding up the stairs.
The floor lurched whenever I took a step.
There was no solid ground.

7:32

We needed to be on the road in 10 minutes.
I had to make her lunch. Lunch. Lunch.
I stood in front of the open pantry. How could I make her lunch?
I could barely put clothes on myself.
Bread. Strawberry jelly. Peanut butter. A knife.
I opened the silverware drawer.
No knives.
I forgot to run the dishwasher.
My eyes fell on the acacia knife block on the counter, fully stocked.
You won't be able to survive this.
The harrowing prompt entered my mind faster than thought, leaving as unexpectedly as it had come.
"No knives." I shut the pantry door.
I opened the fridge. A Lunchables.
"Thank you, Jesus."
An apple juice. Water bottle. All in the lunchbox.
"Anna? Remember to brush your hair."
"I am, Mama."

The cold air creeping under the French doors chilled my feet. Everything was the color of stone. The grass, the boardwalk, the sea. There was no hope hovering over the water, only fear.

… of the righteous…

"Anna!"

7:40

Breakfast. She needed to eat.

I wanted to throw up. I coughed, walking back into the kitchen.

She was tying her shoes.

I grabbed a banana from the fruit bowl. "Baby, you need to eat this in the truck."

"I don't want a banana, Mama."

"Anna, you have to." The coughing originated from somewhere deep, wracking my body.

Anna's eyes grew wide. "Mama, are you okay?"

"No baby, but everything's going to be fine."

Keys.

Wallet.

"Let's go to school."

The wind hit my face as I slammed the door behind us, the cold shocking me awake.

I fumbled with the lock.

Dropped the keys.

Rain had saturated the deck.

Picked them up.

The blood rush as I stood blinded me, forcing me to lean against the wall.

Anna hurried down the stairs.

… but the Lord delivers him…

I followed her.

Unlocked the garage.

Opened the passenger door. "You're in the front today, big girl. Tell me a story."

"Mama, I don't want to tell a story." I didn't miss the sob which caught the last of her words.

Key in the ignition, column shift up.

"Baby, don't cry." I flipped on the radio. "Let's sing." I checked the rearview mirror, glimpsing dark circles under my eyes from many weeks of sleeplessness.

I had no business driving.

7:45

"Seven minutes."

"What, Mama?"

"Seven minutes to your school." The adrenaline wasn't rushing, but trickling down my spine, my neck threatening to snap from the tension knotting at the back of my head.

Sea on the right, bay on the left.

We drove east.

I breathed in. Was it enough?

I blinked. Then blinked again.

Anna wasn't eating her banana. She was staring at me, scared.

I tried to smile. "We're almost there, love." Weren't we almost there? The day we dropped off Anna and went to Amos' seemed like a month ago.

I breathed in. Beach houses blew by us in a blur.

… out of them all.

It was enough. There was the school and the carpool line.

We were last. The doors seemed miles away. I coughed again, thirsting for water.

"Mama?" Anna started to cry.

"We're here." I caressed her cheek, tears smearing on my fingers.

Foot off the brake, ease forward, foot on the brake. Foot off the brake, ease forward.

"It's going to be okay, baby." Hadn't I heard those words before?

One teacher waved us on.

Another teacher waved us on.

And another.

Mary Cole waved us on.

Mary.

Concern flooded her face as she saw me in the driver's seat.

Jeremy King anchored the end of the line and opened the passenger door. "Good morning, Anna." His voice sounded upbeat, but his expression remained impassive.

"Have a good day, baby," I called.

She didn't look back.

Mary shouted something to Jeremy King.

Fear surged in my chest. What if I passed out? I knew I wasn't going to pass out, I never had.

Seven minutes back.

Why wasn't he closing the door?

"Sure thing," Jeremy called to Mary. "Tell Mike I'll be back in twenty." He looked across the seat at me with eyes Bob Ross would have called Prussian blue.

"Happy little trees," I mumbled under my breath.

"You don't look well, Mrs. Rojas. Let me drive you home. Scoot over here." He slammed the passenger door shut.

I obeyed wordlessly, unbuckling the ancient seatbelt and sliding across the bench seat.

The banana laid there, uneaten. I picked it up and cradled it in my lap.

My legs were falling asleep, cold.

Where were my shorts? They were bunched up high on my thighs and I wasn't wearing a bra. I shuddered and rubbed my legs.

Jeremy King was in the driver's seat.

"Buckle up, Mrs. Rojas." He turned on the heater. Burnt dust and salt.

Fatigue and guilt sprang out of nowhere. Anna was gone. She was going to be gone all day, and I had abandoned her. The tears coursed down my face, hot.

Column shift down, he gunned the engine and turned out of the driveway toward the road.

I breathed in.

Seven minutes.

I breathed out.

Sea on the left, bay on the right.

"I'm not usually at the elementary school." His voice sounded far away.

I blinked, the road tilted to the left.

"But since the middle school and elementary school are so close together, I still get assigned carpool duty occasionally."

The tears rolled, unceasing. My favorite song came on the radio.

"I don't have duty this afternoon. Christina gets off about ten minutes after Anna does. I can bring her home with us, if that's okay?"

His question brought me back.

I nodded. "Thank you," I managed to say. "I didn't sleep last night. My doctor said recovery could take a while."

"I'm sorry."

"Vitamin D deficiency." He didn't want to know this. Why was I explaining myself?

"I have a buddy who went through that. It's a tough time."

"It is." I breathed in. Exhaled quickly, the sudden realization unnerving me. "Wait, how will you get back to work?"

"Bike. Doesn't take long."

Dress shoes. Slacks. A shirt the color of his eyes and a dark tie.

"I'm sorry."

"Don't worry about it." Did he ever smile? "It's good exercise, and the rain's stopped. My first class isn't until nine."

8:04

As we pulled into the carport another wave of fatigue rolled over me. In one motion Jeremy killed the engine and was out of the truck.

I shut my eyes.

My neighbor had done the hard part for me. I only had to walk up the stairs and open the door. I didn't know if I could get out of the truck, but I had to get out of the truck. Jeremy opened my door, his hand outstretched. I took it. The ground rocked and my head spun. He helped me to the stairs, his steps close behind me as we ascended. We crossed the deck to the French doors. Still holding the banana, I turned the handle and pushed the door open. It wasn't locked.

"Get some rest." Jeremy dropped the keys in my hand.

The stern set of his mouth softened and the kindness in his eyes cut through my brain fog, allowing me to truly see him for the first time. Dirty blonde hair and a healthy tan made his face almost boyish, despite the fact he was certainly older than me. A manicured five o'clock shadow circled lips that appeared fully capable and equally ready to curse or bless.

"Be sure to lock up, Mrs. Rojas."

"I will, thanks."

"You're welcome. See you this afternoon." He turned and hurried across the deck, disappearing down the stairs.

I didn't see him that afternoon. I woke up on the couch to Anna kissing my face.

"I just got home, Mama." She bounced on the balls of her feet, the trauma of the ride to school ancient history. "Can I have my hour of TV?"

I blinked and hugged her close. No headache this afternoon. "Not yet. Talk to me baby, how was your day?"

"Great!" she chirped. "Miss Mary's here talking to Cici. She brought me back home. Can you make me a peanut butter banana?"

I gave her a long look. "To make up for the one you didn't eat this morning?"

She was suddenly sixteen years old. "Mom, I thought you were about to throw up in the car. How was I supposed to eat a banana?"

"Okay, you win." My body ached. "Did you get to see Christina or Mr. King today at school?"

"Yep." Anna plopped down on a barstool. "Well, Mr. King said hi to me at lunch. He said you were resting and that Miss Mary would take me back home. I didn't see Christina today. Can she come over this weekend?"

"I'll ask." I passed her the banana. Even though I'd only used a butter knife, my hand shook as I set it in the dishwasher.

Cecily and Mary came in from the deck. "Hey Shug, I'm so sorry about this morning. Mary just told me that Mr. King drove you back home because you weren't feeling well?"

I sat down on the barstool next to Anna. "Yes, what's left of me." I forced a smile. "I need to call my doctor and sort out my sleeping medication. According to the internet, you're not supposed to stop hydroxyzine cold turkey." I rubbed my shoulder, trying to relieve the tension in my neck. "I got strung out last night stopping it like I did." I didn't want to ponder whether or not I would sleep tonight. I caught Mary's apprehensive gaze. "You were a lifesaver, Mary. It was very kind of Mr. King to take me home, especially given the state I was in."

"Jeremy worked at the West End fire station every summer

throughout high school and college," Mary explained. "I thought it would be best for him to drive you back. If something serious happened, he has some medical training. I hope it didn't make you too uncomfortable. I know you haven't gotten out much to know him very well."

"It's okay Mary. I was barely conscious as it was."

"And barely dressed," Anna interjected, licking peanut butter off her thumb.

"Anna Marie don't shame your mama like that," Cecily laughed.

"I'm not shaming her." She took a sip of water. "Just telling it like it was."

"She is like you," Mary chuckled behind me. "Mature beyond her years."

"She has no context for spouting statements like that," I muttered.

"Mama, what's context?"

"You'll find out sooner rather than later." I gave her a kiss. "I need to call my doctor."

My phone dinged with a message from Clint.

Clint Myers

How are you feeling?

Incompetent.

Surely not.

I ran out of my medicine.
Realized in a terrifying way that's a bad thing.

Sounds like a time and a half.
Please keep me posted.

Will do.
How's the deal?

What deal?

I miss your asinine sense
of humor the most.

In all seriousness, I'm going to
need you on this soon.
We're past the feel-good stage of this gig.
You have a lot of work to do.
What's your login?

I'll encrypt and email it to you.
Where are you?

Saipan
Back at the end of March.

Enjoy.

Have had my fill of enjoyment.
Looking forward to having you back.

Glad I can kill the vibe.

I flicked the messages away and found my doctor's number. The nurse practitioner answered and refilled my prescription for two weeks. It would be ready at the pharmacy tomorrow. I asked her about tapering the medication and the violent rebound effects I'd felt earlier in the day. She informed me hydroxyzine had no known rebound effects. Perhaps I was mistaking it for another medication? I informed her there was no other medication. She said she would make a note for the doctor and let me know. I never received a call back from her.

After dinner, Cecily and I opened the windows facing the deck. The cool of evening rushed in along with the music of the waves. She told me about her visit with Tyler and Kayla.

"He hasn't much time left." Cecily's eyes were the same color as the ocean she'd sunk her gaze in.

"Tyler and Kayla haven't seen Darius again?"

"No. But I'm sure he won't try to see them."

"Maybe not. Have you heard from him at all?"

"No. I was planning on texting him in the next few days, though."

Darius. We rode our bikes to Tastee Freez every Tuesday and Thursday after school to get ice cream.

My thoughts raced ahead of my mouth. "I'd like to see him again."

Cecily's hand tightened around her mug. "You would?"

"Yeah," I counted in my head… Three, four years. "It's been too long."

I put on makeup for the first time in a month and a half. Tonight, people I didn't know from West End Bible Church were coming to my house to pray for me, and I was certain I would cry off most of my makeup. I gave a withering glance at the tube of mascara. Anxiety picked at my thoughts. I took a deep breath and zipped my toiletry bag. "Well, I do know some of the people coming over. All they're gonna do is sing and pray for me, and then they'll go home."

"Are you talking to yourself?" Anna wandered into my room.

"Yes, baby."

"Adults are so weird." She rolled her eyes and threw herself on my bed. "I'm glad Christina's coming tonight."

"She is? Why?"

"She goes to Pastor Jason's church."

I had no idea. Christina's presence in my home tonight almost certainly guaranteed Jeremy King's as well. I shrugged, attempting to shake off my nerves and gave my daughter a kiss. "The more, the merrier."

"What are we going to have for dinner, Mama?" Anna wrapped her arms around my neck.

"I think Mary and Chris are bringing pizza."

"I mean what am *I* having for dinner?"

I gave her a look. "Pizza?" Another eye roll from my progeny. "You could try it, you know."

"Are y'all gonna talk about sad things?" She was a master of redirection.

"Probably. To pray about them. That's good, right?"

Worry crept into her eyes. "Is it okay if Christina and I go up to my room when y'all do that?"

"I guess so, love."

"Whew." She released my neck and hopped off the bed. "I do not want to see you cry anymore."

"Thanks, babe," I called dryly after her. "Me neither."

Cheerful knocking sounded on the French doors. Cecily sang out, "Y'all come on in!"

Mary and Chris bustled in with half a dozen boxes of pizza. The Hamadas arrived with them, and Jason was shaking Cecily's hand.

"I'm Jason Hamada and this is my wife, Lilly. Thanks for hosting us and letting us pray for you tonight."

"I remember you from Caleb's memorial service." Cecily's smile warmed the room. "Aimee has told me a lot about y'all. We're happy to be with you, too. It's been a hard couple of weeks, for both of us."

"I understand." Jason caught my eye as I left the shelter of the shadows in the hallway. "Hey, Aimee!" A grin spread across his face.

Lilly ran to me, her dark eyes filled with tears. "It's been too long." She embraced me. I couldn't control my emotions, and my own tears began. Lilly hugged me tighter. "It's okay. We're going to bring all of this before the Lord tonight, and he is going to answer us."

I nodded, sniffling. "I know. I just love y'all so much." I tried to smile. "Did the kids come with you guys?"

"Not tonight." She smiled, clasping my hands.

"I guess the last time I saw them was at Caleb's memorial service."

"Probably so. All the kids are growing up so fast." She beamed as Anna ran past us. Cecily and the Coles greeted more church members who poured into our small house. Jason bent his tall, thin frame over to give me a hug. "Are you sure you're sick?" he joked. "You look great!"

"Ha, the weight loss has been nice. Insomnia, not so much."

"I bet." Jason scratched his head. "So, for tonight, we'll have dinner first and hang out for a while. Nothing formal. After that, we'll worship and pray for you and Cecily. Does that sound okay?" His long, black hair flopped to the middle of his forehead.

"That sounds perfect. Thanks so much for coming over and doing this for us."

"It's a blessing," he said. "We're just happy that you guys are here now. How long are you planning to stay?"

The inevitable question. Lilly waited to hear my response.

"I'm not sure. We have the house for six months, through June. I'm unsure about where work will take me at that point." I caught a glimpse of Anna heading up the loft stairs with Christina, both of them holding plates in their hands. "I haven't been able to even look at any kind of screen for more than a few minutes at a time since I've been sick, and it's driving my co-workers crazy." I pushed Clint's last text out of my mind with a nervous laugh.

"You mean you're still working like this?" Lilly asked, concerned.

"Not really. Don't worry, friend."

"I'm going to make sure you're resting," she said, dead serious.

Our living room surged with people. It was already dark outside, and my eyes were having trouble adjusting to the strong overhead lights inside the house, which Cecily and I usually kept off. I made myself a plate with a couple of slices of pizza and salad and tucked it away in the fridge for when everyone cleared out.

"Did you get something to eat, sweetie?" Mary asked at my shoulder. Her presence brought instant peace.

"Oh yes, I did. Thank you for organizing all of this, Mary."

"Have you talked to your mom, recently?"

"Not for several weeks. You know how serious Mom and Dad are about sabbatical. And they've been planning this trip to the UK for years. I don't want to worry them."

"I know, but I'm sure your mom would like a short update on how you're doing. Maybe I'll write her an email."

"I think she'd definitely like that."

"Hey guys, let's go ahead and get started." Jason stood in the living room, corralling the company of what appeared to be at least thirty people in our living room. "Cecily, Aimee, why don't you ladies come sit here, in the middle." The room rocked slightly as I walked to the couch. Jason made eye contact with someone behind us. "Go ahead and start us off in worship tonight."

The notes pulled from the guitar strings shimmered as they reverberated around the room. Someone sang, "*Alleluia, alleluia, for the Lord God Almighty reigns!*"

Almost instantly everyone joined in, a defiant roar of light in the dark of a late February night. Every thought fled from my head, leaving it just as empty as our house had been only an hour ago. The music and voices rose, and I heard my own voice harmonizing with everyone else, united in worship. I slid off the couch onto my knees, still singing. I felt a small hand on my head. Lilly prayed fervently, kneeling on the floor in front of me. The melody changed.

"*Your love is devoted, like a ring of solid gold…*"

Cecily's clear, thin voice warbled behind me. I continued singing and felt more hands slip into mine and on my shoulders as strangers who—simply because they loved Jesus—were also brothers, sisters and intercessors. They prayed for me, Anna, Cecily and Darius. The peace came and I sang louder. We all sang louder. Then the song ended, and the guitar sang alone.

Jason lifted his voice. "Jesus, thank you for this time together. You are always with us, and you know our every need."

Murmurs of agreement and amens rippled across the room.

"We bring Aimee before you tonight. Please bring your healing to her body, Lord. To her mind. After losing Caleb, she's walked such a long, hard road. And now, she's facing the effects of this unexpected diagnosis. Father, we ask for your peace to fill her heart and mind. We ask you to take away her anxiety, and to restore her sleep. Father, we ask you to bring something beautiful and lasting for Aimee out of this confusion and loss, and that you would guide her with your eye upon her, teaching her the way that she should go. Reveal your good plans for her and Anna. Father, we ask all this knowing that you hear us and that you love us. Give Aimee rest, Lord."

The guitar was gentle and strong.

Jason pleaded, "Jesus, we also lift up Darius. God, he is far from you. We rebuke the hold that drugs have on him. We know that your will for him is life, and life abundantly. Right now, his feet are on the path to death. But Father, we pray that you would—as you did with Saul—blind Darius with the light of your love so that he is unable to be bound by any drug, any prescription, any high or satisfaction the world gives him. Please set him free, Father. And please give your daughter Cecily the wisdom and strength she needs to love her son through this."

Cecily sobbed and my own chest heaved in tandem with her grief.

Jason knelt on the floor by the fireplace. "Thank you for Cecily's willingness to take care of Aimee and Anna, Lord. Please bless her exceedingly for it. Please protect and sustain this family, Jesus. We pray for your restoration and abundance in their lives, and that they would be mighty daughters for you,

Father. That people who look at them would see you."

"Amen." I whispered. "Jesus."

"God, we bring our church and our city before you. Work your good will in Galveston, and fill us with your Spirit now, and every day."

Clapping and praise rippled through the room.

"This is how I fight my battles." The worship leader's voice sang a new song over Jason's prayer. Other voices joined in as Jason continued his supplication along with more shouts of amen and alleluia. I was utterly spent, but also completely filled to overflowing.

Lilly was still beside me, singing. *"It may look like I'm surrounded, but I'm surrounded by you."*

As we all sang, an unshakeable peace took root in my heart. The exhaustion and heaviness in my head hadn't left, but they were easier to bear. The guitar reached a crescendo, prompting applause and more shouts of amen, and then the time of prayer and worship was over.

Lilly looked at me, cupping my face in her hands. "God is doing something in you. Changing you. I can see it and hear it when you sing." She leaned in. "You are in the valley of the shadow of death right now. But remember: you're only walking through it, you aren't camping out. God is walking with you, and we are walking with you, too, all of us at West End." She looked over my shoulder and smiled. "I know Jeremy is for sure. He never plays those songs for us at prayer and worship nights, and they're some of my favorites."

I turned, still on the floor, and saw Jeremy King for the first time all evening. I was surprised to see what looked like anger dissipating from his face as Lilly's voice pulled him away from his thoughts.

His expression softened. "With something this heavy, I figured it would be best to dust off what's tried and true."

I rose to my feet. "Thanks for leading us in worship. Those

were some of my favorite songs, too."

He reached for his guitar case. "You're welcome, Mrs. Rojas."

"Do you think you'll be able to come to church this Sunday?" Lilly slipped her arm in mine and led me to the kitchen.

"I don't think I can yet."

"I understand. We'll be praying for you. And you know that if you ever need any help—anything—we're here."

"I know."

People who had entered our house as strangers gifted us their goodbyes and exited as brothers and sisters. I caught sight of Christina and Anna sitting on the couch, their heads bent close together over a picture book. My next breath stabbed at my throat with guilt. I hadn't even introduced myself to the child who had immediately and—if my instinct was right—joyfully become my daughter's closest friend.

Jeremy leaned against the doorframe with his guitar case in hand, talking with Chris. I curled my fingers into fists, surprised at the sweat beading on my palms. I'd asked CFOs for millions without a second thought, but in that moment having a clear-headed conversation with Jeremy King scared the crap out of me.

Nonsense. I could ask the man about a simple playdate.

"Excuse me guys." I met Jeremy's eyes, and instantly realized I'd been wrong. "Mr. King, Anna wanted me to ask if it would be alright with you if Christina could come over to play after school gets out tomorrow?"

There was no hesitation from him. "Sure."

Fear-shatteringly, breath-takingly wrong. His irises weren't Prussian blue, but a dynamic, inky iron gray, and in the span of his one syllable reply, he almost smiled.

"Tell me about Christina, love." I took the hydroxyzine as soon as the last guest left and was fighting to stay awake. Anna talked at light speed as she put on her pjs and hopped into my bed.

"She's really nice."

"What do y'all play?"

"Hide and seek, and she has some dolls we play with, too. Oh, and she has a Nintendo Switch. Can we get a Switch, Mom?"

"Um, we'll see. Do y'all ever play outside?"

"All the time. Christina grows flowers on her patio, and she has a shell garden on the side of the yard by the beach."

"What's a shell garden?" My eyelids grew heavy. "That sounds cool."

"She and her dad take walks on the beach and collect shells. Then Christina puts them in her shell garden where she arranges them into like, patterns and stuff."

"On the ground?"

"Yeah, on the ground. On the side of their house with all the flowers." She snuggled close to me. "Are we gonna stay here for a long time, Mama? I like having a yard."

She liked having a yard. "I'm not sure, baby. But Mr. David said we could stay as long as we want."

Her arms twined around my neck. "I really like it here. I like my school and living next door to Christina."

"I like it here too, love. Is Mr. Jeremy nice?" I was letting my daughter spend so much time with a man whose eyes I had only seen twice and had yet to see smile, and the level of trust I had implicitly given was finally catching up to my heart. But if Cecily and Mary trusted him…

"He's super nice. He doesn't smile a lot though."

I chuckled. "He really doesn't, does he?"

"Christina doesn't have a mom."

"She doesn't?" I knew this but was interested to know if Anna knew anything more about the absent Mrs. King.

"No."

"Christina doesn't ever talk about her?"

"No. But she's not sad."

I considered this, listening to nachtmusik playing from across the street. Selena was up tonight.

My throat tightened. "Are you sad about Daddy, love?"

"Sometimes. Mostly at night when we used to say prayers together." She wriggled under the covers. "Can I just stay in here and sleep with you tonight, Mama? Your bed is so comfy."

Tears spilled down my jaw, rolling into my ears. I fought to keep my voice even, hoping Anna wouldn't hear them. "Of course, baby."

"Mama." Her voice quivered. "Are you crying?"

"Yes, but I'm okay. Sometimes even if you're the one that's sad, I'm the one who cries."

"Why?"

"Because I love you." I hoped she understood, even just a little. I pulled her close, stroking her hair. I knew she was afraid the tears wouldn't stop; afraid she would have to sleep by herself upstairs in the loft while her mom cried in the lingering darkness. "Everything is going to be okay, sweet girl. I'm getting better, remember?"

"I know." She was still for a few seconds. "Mama, do you feel better enough to take me to Christina's birthday party?"

"Is her birthday soon?"

"Yeah, in a couple of weeks, when we have spring break. She invited me tonight when everyone was praying for us."

"I think we can go, sweet girl. We have to pray that my sleep gets better."

"Are you gonna sleep tonight?"

"I think so, love."

"Okay. Then I'll be quiet now."

Her breathing deepened and her body relaxed against mine. "Dreaming of You" drifted into the room from across the street. I closed my eyes, and dreamed about my own mother, half a world away.

"Hi Mrs. Rojas, it's nice to meet you." Christina King flashed me a brilliant smile and shook my hand, her hazel eyes stunning me. The color was her own, but their intensity was undeniably inherited from Jeremy. This girl had high expectations of me, and I straightened, wanting to measure up to whatever they were.

"It's very nice to meet you too, Christina. Thank you so much for coming over today, and for being Anna's friend while I haven't been feeling well. Please come in."

Long blonde hair in French braids, and several years older than Anna.

"It's so funny to be in a house that looks almost like mine but isn't." She grinned. "Daddy used to live here."

"Did he?"

"Christina!" Anna bounded down the stairs and ran to her. They hugged each other and held hands. My head swam as Anna's excitement mounted. "So, Mom, what should we do *first*?"

March

"Darius texted me last night."

Cecily and I sat on the deck after dropping Anna off at school. The air had grown warmer with the rays of the coastal spring sun.

I kicked out my feet, praying away a headache. The doctor had prescribed fourteen pills of hydroxyzine with my refill, and the fact that the medicine was working was undeniable.

Since I never heard back from my doctor regarding how to taper the dosage and avoid a nasty rebound, I asked the pharmacist on the island for advice. He recommended cutting the tablets in halves, then quarters to taper down dosage over the period of about two additional weeks to stave off rebound effects. I wanted to hug the man right then and there, but Anna—thankfully—dragged me to the nail polish display, containing my verbose expression of thanks as concern germinated on his face.

My sleep had also improved to four and five hour stretches, and the floor no longer felt like it was rocking. But the sleep given to me by the hydroxyzine came with an ugly cost. Taking the medication for so long nursed a skulking depression which creeped at the edge of my thoughts. Strangely, the sensation made me more empathetic to Darius than I'd been in years.

"What did he say?"

"He wants to have dinner, and to see you and Anna."

I considered the broken promises and unfulfilled *want to's* he'd spoken to us intermittently over the last decade. "Do you really think he'll come all the way down here? He doesn't have a license and it's a long way from town."

"Not having a license hasn't stopped him yet."

We were silent for a few moments, listening to the surf.

Cecily sighed. "It's my fault, isn't it?"

"What do you mean?"

"Who else is to blame for the mess he's in?"

"Darius himself, for one."

"But I knew it was happening. I knew he was taking more of his prescription than he should have after he was injured. I knew it for years and everything I did to try and stop him wasn't enough."

I tasted salt on my lips. "That's not true, Cecily. You confronted him many times."

"I didn't try hard enough. I didn't put enough boundaries around him to keep him from the people who were fostering his abuse. I didn't keep him accountable. Sam would have."

"Cici," I scolded. "There's no grace in saying that. Guilt is part of the enemy's game. You're one of the best parents I've ever known, and Darius has had more accountability than most. He's chosen to ignore it." A small flame of anger added itself to the blaze of pain in my head. "He's ignored it time and time again."

Seagulls cried, wheeling over us to see if there was any food to be had.

I wanted perfect, healing words to encourage her, but everything my mind could dredge up fell flat. "I don't think anyone who loves Darius will ever stop feeling like there was something more they could have done to have prevented him from reaching this point. We can't look behind us. We can only look ahead and pray that the right time will come, and the right door will open for us to speak to him. And for him to hear what we're saying."

"Well, he said he's coming the weekend after next." Cecily waved her hand toward the gulls, who subsequently beat a retreat out to sea. "We'll see what happens."

Our conversation weighed on me, clinging heavily to my body.

I sat on the floor of my bathroom, reluctant to take the hydroxyzine. Hating the need to sacrifice my mental health for the benefit of my physical health. It had started like this for Darius, tiny choices that carried huge consequences. The promise of relief at the hidden expense of addiction.

The pills clattered as the bottle shifted in my hand. I twisted the lid, but a sudden surge of nerves in my fingers broke off the safety tab, plastic snapping then skating across the floor. A dozen hexagonal tablets flew out with force, skittering across the tile around the toilet. A word I hated escaped my lips as I crawled around, gathering them up.

I examined the lid. It wouldn't lock into place anymore. I carefully set the bottle back on the counter after taking my medicine. The Bible was open on my bed, and I read a passage in Romans 13 I'd highlighted who-knows-how-many-years-ago.

The night is nearly over; the day is almost here. So let us put aside the deeds of darkness and put on the armor of light.

"Mama."

Sunlight pierced the shutters. "Baby?"

"Guess what today is?"

I didn't have to guess. "Christina's party?"

"Yesssss!" Anna vibrated with ecstasy. She clambered into my bed, snuggling close.

Ever since Christina had appeared at our door, hand delivering an invitation bedecked with butterflies, the party was all Anna talked about. Now it was spring break, and because Christina's birthday was in March, the King's had decided to host a cookout while everyone was out of school. Anna was over the moon.

"Mama, can I wear some of your eyeshadow?"

"No."

"Why, Mama?"

"Baby, Mama isn't even going to wear eyeshadow. It's a miracle that Mama's going in the first place."

I had tried to get out of it.

"I don't think I can go to the Kings," I'd confessed to Cecily the night before.

"It would be good for you to go, Aimee. It's just next door." Her use of my name instead of *Shug* denoted the strength of her opinion regarding the matter.

"But you're not going. Why aren't you going?"

"I don't like children."

"Liar."

"En masse."

"Speaking of, there are going to be so many people I don't know there. It's not just the Kings."

"More people for you to talk to, Shug! Besides, there were scores of people you didn't know at the prayer night a few weeks ago."

I rolled my eyes, realizing in the moment that Anna came by the mannerism honestly. "I didn't have to talk to them," I protested. "They're going to ask me what I do for a living. And what am I going to say? Nothing right now? Surviving? I've barely been able to keep my wits about me around the people I live with."

"Well," Cecily replied with a manic grin. "That's not entirely your fault, Shug."

Anna's elbow landed on my chest. "Mama pleeeease can I wear some makeup?"

"Not today, baby. You can wear your yellow dress though, if you want."

I got out of bed. What was I going to wear?

I looked at my phone.

Seventy-eight degrees and sunny, a perfect day.

I eyed the bags Maren had filled from the boutique on the Strand. Black cut-offs and one of the checkered flannels with a white tank top underneath. Monochrome. Done. Thankful for the blessing of salty air, I ran my fingers through my hair. It would have to do. Anna danced around the kitchen waiting for eleven o'clock to roll around, constantly popping up behind me to tap on my phone screen as I read aloud a Hardy Boys story, or to twist around to look at the clock on the microwave. When eleven o'clock came, she bolted through the French doors. I checked out the neighboring deck as I headed to the stairs. Forty or so people mingled around the outside of the house and on the deck. A large grill boasted something that smelled wonderful. Something I knew I wouldn't be able to choke down in front of anyone. The Wheeland Brothers cranked on the King's outdoor speakers, and children played on the ocean side of the yard near a piñata strung up under the carport.

"Anna!" My call stopped her mid-sprint. "Don't go on the street side of the yard, okay?"

"Okay, Mama!" She bounded into the throng of children.

It was strange to be at this house, the twin of mine. Inhabited by other people. Sheltering other, unknown stories.

The King's landscaping had sprung to life and gardenias perfumed the air, evoking memories of my grandmother's garden in Morgan City. I was on the deck now, unable to focus. People were everywhere. Carefree strangers who all seemed to know each other talked about fishing and March Madness. I panicked. There was too much to take in, too much light and noise. No amount of nostalgia dredged up by flowers could comfort me.

"Aimee!" Mary's voice rang out.

Relieved tears stung my eyes. That wouldn't mix well with a party, either. "Hey, Mary."

"It's so good to see you out of the house. How are you feeling?"

"Honestly, a little jittery. But it's okay." My laugh resembled a croak. "And I'm right next to my house, which makes me feel a lot better."

"I completely understand." The warmth in her eyes sought to appease my anxiety.

"I'm so happy you're here, Mary. I guess I didn't realize y'all would be at Christina's party. Is Chris around?"

"Yeah, he's up by the grill with the boys. It's mostly teachers and some of Christina's friends from school and their families."

I wasn't sure what to do or say next.

Mary rescued me. "I was just about to make some more lemonade. Want to come with me and see the house?" She smiled. "It's very different from yours."

"Sure." I followed her, eager to be somewhere less crowded.

The King's set of French doors were new and framed in black. Inside, white oak floors ran throughout the house. In front of the fireplace, an enormous sofa commanded the living room, wide and low with a sheepskin throw slung across the chaise. The mantel and the built-ins were modern and masculine in style, but it was what was on the shelves that arrested me. A hundred model ships lined them from floor-to-ceiling, appearing to float. Schooners, yachts, and huge historical vessels sailed across the wall on clear stands, lighter than air.

"A million boats," I said under my breath, remembering Anna's words.

"Jeremy's made all of them."

"They're beautiful."

To our left was the window wall I'd seen Christina walk

through our first day on the island. The doors were thrown wide open behind a live edge table. A sea of flowers in mason jars bent their heads over a birthday cake with ten pink candles crowning it. On the deck, a crowd had gathered around the grill. I turned back toward the kitchen, vastly different than ours. The cabinets were a deep navy—almost black—complimenting a built-in fridge and range that any commercial kitchen would envy. Butcher block on the island, white granite on the countertops and backsplash. Copper accents. Everything kept with a Spartan discipline, and again, swathes of cut flowers covered the island.

"It's really nice," I remarked. "I can't see our landlord springing for these kinds of upgrades."

"Probably not," Mary laughed. "Jeremy's put a ton of work into this place recently. He's a bit of a perfectionist."

"It shows."

A chef's knife and lemons lay on a cutting board. I wanted to look away from the knife, but a knot welled up in my stomach.

"Can I help with anything, Mary?"

"Sure, sweetheart. If you could just cut and juice the final few lemons, that would be great."

I took a deep breath and picked up the knife, concentrating on the sweet fragrance of the citrus. Mary exited the pantry with a bag of sugar. "You know your way around their kitchen, Mary."

"Oh yes." She shuffled around in a drawer for a measuring cup. "We've known the Kings ever since we moved to the Sea Isle neighborhood. My goodness, it's been over thirty years."

"Really?" While this explained her unreserved trust in Jeremy King, another question surfaced, distancing my thoughts from the blade in my hand. "Mary, what happened to Mrs. King? Isn't there any family here for Christina's birthday?"

Mary hesitated, appearing almost puzzled at my question and was about to reply as Jeremy, Chris, and another man entered the house. I slid the knife through the first lemon, halving it, and grabbed another.

Jeremy's eyes were bright, touching me momentarily as he strode to the pantry. "Welcome, Mrs. Rojas. It's good to see you out and about."

A brief pain stung from the front of my head to the back like lightning, but I said, "Thanks, Mr. King."

"Mr. King?" The tall stranger laughed, sauntering over to the island. "She obviously doesn't know you very well, man." He leaned toward me and said in a conspiratorial tone but loud enough for Jeremy to hear, "Feel free to call him Jeremiah, any time and all the time."

"Wrong," Jeremy stepped out of the pantry. "Only members of the PTO and enemies call me Jeremiah," he proclaimed unsmilingly, giving me a wink. "Mike, meet my new neighbor, Aimee Rojas. She's here for the ocean air with her daughter and aunt."

"Welcome to the West End, Aimee, I work at the middle school with Jeremy. Sixth-grade science." At six-foot three and built like a gladiator, Mike towered over me. I read in his loose smile someone who was easily pleased and persistent, all of which I supposed was useful when dealing with several hundred thirteen-year-olds. But I was grateful to slice the last lemon instead of shaking hands with him.

I forced my best smile. "Thanks so much, it's nice to meet you."

"What line of work are you in, Aimee?" Mike sidled close to me.

Of course it would be this question.

"I'm taking a break from work for the time being."

Chris piped up next to Mary. "Aimee's a Market Activation Manager for Valiant Oil. For Asia, right, Aimee?"

"Well, y-yes," I stammered. "I worked primarily in Southeast Asia and Europe before Covid hit. Technically, I'm the Director of Global Sales, now." I flushed, feeling like a phony, even though it was true.

"Impressive," Jeremy emerged from the pantry. His arms were

filled with three enormous bags of chips and a case of Topo Chico. Dismissing the conversion entirely, he said, "I think we're about ready out there. Y'all want to join us?"

Mike took the chips from him.

"Sure, we'll be right there!" Mary called after them.

"Let me help you with the lemonade, baby." Chris relieved Mary of the pitchers while I washed up at the sink.

"You doing okay, sweetie?" Mary asked.

"Hanging in there." *Barely.* "Rapid fire conversation is going to tire me out, I can tell."

"Anything to help you sleep." She rubbed my shoulder as we stepped out to the deck.

Children swarmed the table. Anna sat next to Christina. Hot dogs, hamburgers, all the toppings, enough sliced watermelon to sink a ship, and lemonade lined the table. The sea roared in the distance, knit with the sky in a sun-dusted haze hovering on the horizon. The light glared off the water, and I pulled my sunglasses from my pocket.

Anna piled food on her plate.

"Having fun, baby?"

"Yes, Mama!"

"Need anything?"

"Nah, I'm good," she replied, her mouth already full.

The adults milled around the deck, chatting between sips and bites.

Tension drew my shoulder blades together, and an unexpected wave of fatigue hit. Mary helped Jeremy at the opposite end of the table and—the only other people I knew—Chris and Mike talked to a woman with curly red hair in front of the dining room windows.

"Hey." I joined their little group.

"Hey there!" The bracelets on the woman's arm jingled.

"What do you do?" I blurted out awkwardly.

Chris gave me a sideways glance.

The woman's lipstick was the exact shade of her hair. "I teach at the middle school with Jeremy and Mike, but this is my first time seeing Jeremy and Christina's house. I didn't realize how beautiful it was."

"That's because Jeremy's about as sociable as an oyster," said Mike, grinning.

Chris' voice boomed with pride. "Jeremy did all the renovations himself. He's got a trick or two up his sleeves. I need to have him come out and help me with our house, once he's done with what he's currently got lined up."

The curls bobbed. "It's so nice to see islanders taking care of their homes and staying settled here. There are so many transients and executives coming from California and even New York. Did you know I saw a license plate from *Oregon* here the other day?"

I started to sweat.

"Just between us, my favorite style of home is more along the lines of the restorations going on in the East End. All the Victorian Era houses are so charming, but they're almost all being converted into vacation rentals by *out-of-state* investors."

A wave of anxiety rose, shifting my gravity. I shook my head, trying to get my bearings.

"There's a lot to be treasured on the island, for sure," Chris agreed. "You can hardly set your foot down on the island where some historical event hasn't happened."

"Literally." Mike narrowed his eyes against the sunlight. "After the big storm came through in 1900, there wasn't any room to bury all the bodies. They tried to tow the carnage out to sea, but the bodies washed right back up. They had to either incinerate or bury them right where they found them."

"Seriously?" The woman gasped.

It wasn't my head after all, it was my stomach.

"Dead serious," said Mike. "Who even knows what another storm like that could churn up." His eyes narrowed, scanning the gulf. "And hurricane season's right around the corner. Gotta make sure my stockpile of pork and beans hasn't expired."

I clutched my waist. "Chris, do you know where the bathroom is?"

"Sure do." He threw me a half-concerned smile. "It's the same place yours is, darlin'."

"Of course it is." My laugh hitched in my throat. "I'm still not a hundred percent with it yet."

In the hallway outside the bathroom, I paced back and forth, trying to rid my thoughts of waterlogged graves. I took a deep breath.

About twenty photos, all black and white, lined the wall in front of me. Many of the moments were candid, and several photos caught my attention. A recent portrait of Christina, the ocean behind her. A photo of a younger Christina—maybe three or four years old—on the beach, her chubby hands holding onto a line boasting a bass almost her size. Jeremy stood behind her dressed in waders, kissing her cheek and holding the pole. A candid portrait caught my eye. Four people stood frozen in time: a handsome man who was unmistakably Jeremy's father, his arm around a strikingly beautiful girl some years younger than Jeremy, and Jeremy himself, also younger and holding a tiny Christina, maybe six or seven months old. Jeremy's face was the only one of the four turned away from the camera, looking lovingly at the baby.

In the bathroom, I washed my hands and took a few silent moments to study my reflection in the mirror. Tired eyes with dark circles that refused to fade looked back at me. I returned to the kitchen. The cake had been taken to the deck and food from the grill had been brought in. I made myself a small plate and choked down a few bites alone at the bar. I finished just in time to see the last few guests making their way down the stairs for the piñata. All the children were brightly dressed, and I followed the cheerful colors downstairs. On the carport, Jeremy was already spinning Christina around, a blindfold over her eyes.

Her grin was huge, and she shrieked, "Daddy stop, stop, stop!"

He obeyed and held her steady, his laughter transforming the somber cast of his face entirely. "Okay young lady, go get it."

Something caught in my throat, stealing my breath. Caleb would never get to see Anna turn ten. I'd reconciled the facts with reality several years earlier, but sometimes grief washed in without warning, refusing to ebb.

"So, will y'all be here long?" Mike asked near my shoulder. I almost jumped against the arm he'd braced on the stilt behind me.

I blinked hard. "Four more months at least. My friend owns the house next door and I'm sure he'll let us stay as long as we want."

"Nice gig. Which munchkin is yours?"

It was Anna's turn to try to crack the piñata. Jeremy was spinning her.

I nodded toward them. "She's currently up to bat."

"She's cute. Like her mama." He gave me a loose smile.

"I actually think she favors my husband."

Mike glanced at my hands, but I kept them shoved in my pockets. His face reddened. "I'm sorry, I thought—"

The smack of the bat echoed under the porch and Anna whooped. She tore off the blindfold and groaned, seeing the piñata still intact. "Man!" Head hanging, she trudged over to me. "I didn't get it, Mama ."

"It's okay babe. Someone will bust it wide open soon enough."

She squeezed my arm and ran back to Christina's side.

My phone dinged.

"Excuse me." I glanced at Mike and walked around the corner of the carport.

I nestled into a patio chair at the far side of the garage, away from the crowd.

Clint Myers
Availability for the next two weeks?
Need to see you to go over the final contract.
This one will make us.

Back from the South Pacific so soon?

Shangri-La is severely overrated.

Can't we do this over Zoom?
I'd prefer not.

Maybe Friday the 23rd?

Send me the address.
I'll bring lunch.

I'm not ready.

I set my phone and sunglasses on the arm of the chair and rubbed my eyes. My thoughts scattered into the static of the surf and the wind. I used to share Clint's zeal for the sale, but now the prospect of shouldering the responsibility for anything related to my career dizzied me. The travel. The long days. The pressure. My breath scraped the shallows of my lungs, forcing the air to rush through my throat like sand down a shaft.

Footsteps cut toward me across the patio. I squeezed my eyes tight. If this was Mike, I would scream.

"Taking a breather?" Jeremy King eased into the chair next to mine, two chilled bottles of Topo Chico in his hands. He held one out to me.

"Something like that." My hand shook as I took the bottle

from him. I popped the cap. The water rushed into me, liquid relief. I focused on the tall grass dipping and swaying in front of us, revealing dunes and the blue beyond.

"I'm glad you could come over today." Jeremy's voice gritted like powdered sand. "No point in being so close to the beach if you can't get out and enjoy it."

"You live here. Do you enjoy it all the time?" The rudeness of my words shocked me. Heat crept up my neck.

"For the most part." On the beach, a solitary seagull hovered, the breeze lifting its wings. We watched it dive, beak gaping wide. "Having pleasant company helps."

"Forgive me," I said hastily. "That was rude."

He waved away my apology with the bottle in his hand. "It's alright. Children and piñatas are a lethal combination. Puts the edge on me, too. All the crying and screaming when the candy comes out."

"Crying? From the kids?"

"No, the piñata."

I turned to look at him.

He held the mouth of the bottle to his lips, waiting to drink. His eyes were laughing. "Sorry, bad joke."

I almost smiled. "I deserved it."

My phone dinged again.

Clint Myers

Counting on it.

I turned my phone on silent and flipped it face down.

"Don't think I've had the volume up on mine since 2003."

I laughed then. "Clint is—" Anxiety plucked my voice like a guitar string. "My co-worker is on my case."

"On a Saturday? I thought you were supposed to be on a break."

"He thinks I'm ready to jump back into everything. And what

day it is doesn't matter to him." I hesitated. "It used to not matter to me, either."

Jeremy gave no reply.

I hadn't made small talk in months, and my head reeled from the effort. I couldn't talk about myself anymore. Not like this. More gulls wheeled into view, crying. Studying the evenness of their flight steadied my nerves. They soared out of sight, over our heads. "Your house is beautiful."

"Thank you." Shyness shaded his voice, and he didn't offer any additional commentary.

I pressed him. "How long have you and Christina lived in the West End? David mentioned your family's been around for a while."

"Yeah, we've owned this house and the one you're in for years, until David bought your place at the end of last year. I moved out here permanently for work when the middle school was built about fifteen years ago." He took another drink. "Christina joined me soon after she was born."

I looked at him. "Joined you?"

"Christina was my sister's baby. I adopted her not long after my sister died."

The beautiful girl in the family portrait.

"What happened?" I blurted, perplexed at how my social skills had deteriorated to this point.

Jeremy drew his foot into the chair and propped his arm on his knee, letting the bottle dangle. "My sister, Julia, picked up Christina's biological dad at a dive bar down here. It was a one-night stand. He left before she woke up. She never knew his last name, couldn't track down any of his information." His eyebrows drew close together, well-worn lines on his forehead suddenly visible. "Julia was diagnosed with cervical cancer at her first OB visit to confirm the pregnancy. The cancer was rare for someone so young, and because her doctors initially gave her a good prognosis, she opted to defer treatment until the third trimester.

But after Christina was born, her body just didn't respond to the chemo like they said it should."

Brokenness was everywhere, inescapable.

"I'm so sorry."

"Don't be," he answered simply. "God gave me undeserved joy at the darkest moment in my life."

"*Beauty for ashes.*"

"Literally." The glass of his empty bottle rang on the concrete as he set it down. "And you?"

"Me?"

"*There is anxiety by the sea, it cannot be calmed.*"

"Jeremiah?"

"Yes." His lips softened into a smile. "But remember, don't call me that."

We sat in a shared silence for several moments.

"Aimee, you're getting better, and that's good. Just be gentle with yourself. Depression is hard to navigate, especially on your own."

"How do you know I'm depressed?"

"Your eyes. I've seen that same despair reflected in my own mirror before."

I looked away from him, toward the gulf. "There's a lot you don't know about me."

"Not yet." He stretched out his legs. "But it might help to talk about it. Helped me."

Something torqued, deep in my stomach. My strength in sales had always been listening to what other people thought and wanted, learning how I could best deliver. Saying the right thing at the right time. No one deserved my emotional debris, especially someone I barely knew. But Jeremy King had shared some of his pain with me, so if he wanted the dregs of my mind, I'd give them to him.

"I blame myself for letting my health deteriorate to this point. Physical health, mental health. I've let it slip so far over the past few years since my husband died. I thought I could do it all on my own. Helping Anna navigate a new school every six months because of my travel for work, while I was also trying to navigate my own grief."

I stared at my shoes, twisting my wedding band. In the nightmare, seawater had sucked and swirled around my feet.

Don't let go, Aimee.

"I feel like every decision I make will be the wrong one. I think about the things I used to do even just a few months ago for work, and for my friends, and my family. I can't imagine how I ever had the confidence to be that person. It's like everything I was, is gone. I know that there's good and beauty out there, but now I can't see it."

I looked him squarely in the eyes, wondering if I'd find any regret there for asking me to open Pandora's box. Unwavering iron met my stare.

"I'm having to hold on with everything God's given me, every shred of hope I have left, to remember that he loves me and how precious I am to him. That the future isn't impossibly irredeemable."

Jeremy's voice held a quiet certainty. "Nothing's impossible for God. And he's not going to let you go. He's with you in everything you're going through. Sometimes peace is a fight."

"Yeah." The gulls dove down again, close to the house. "I know I'm depressed, but I also know that I didn't feel like this until I started taking steps toward recovery. I'm sure the medicine the doctor gave me to help me sleep is enhancing the depression chemically, but it's so frustrating. It's like I'm trading one illness for another."

"How much longer do you have to take the sleeping medication?"

"Only a few more days." I laughed a little. "The morning you brought me back home from school, I had just finished taking it as the doctor prescribed. She failed to tell me about the rebound effects of insomnia and anxiety the medication could have if I stopped it suddenly. I'm tapering off it now. I should not have been driving that day."

"No, you shouldn't have."

"You were so calm. Like you'd driven that truck with a totally incompetent stranger in the passenger seat a hundred times."

"I have." The light danced in his eyes. "That was my first truck. David got it with the house."

I felt my face flush and my jaw slacken as my mouth dropped, involuntarily pulling to a smile. "I hope not always with an incompetent stranger."

"Rarely, if I'm being honest. But don't be so hard on yourself. You've made significant progress since then. And based on knowing your daughter, and the little you've told me, incompetent is not a term I'd use to describe you."

I didn't want to turn away from his gaze. He really meant it.

"Thank you. Thank you for taking me home then. And for listening to me today."

He shrugged. "That's what neighbors are for, right?"

It was the second time I'd seen him smile. I wondered briefly if he knew how disarming it was. "You've been so good to us, even though we hardly know you. You and Christina both. Anna adores her."

"They're angels. That reminds me." He pulled his phone from his pocket. "Let me give you my number. I foresee a lot of togetherness for those two when school gets out."

I tapped the screen of my phone, waking it up. "Sure, Airdrop?" Just because he was giving me his number didn't mean I was ready to share mine.

Jeremy's fingers scrolled, long and capable. I remembered the myriad ships floating in the living room.

My screen lit up. "Got it, thanks."

"Mama?" Anna's steps skipped across the concrete. Christina

followed close behind. "Mama, everyone's leaving, but can I stay and play with Christina for just a little bit?"

"I'm being a terrible host." Jeremy gave me a wink and one last smile before bounding up the stairs. Christina hovered nearby, anxious to hear my reply.

"Probably not, Anna."

Christina's disappointment was palpable.

"But hey, Mr. Jeremy gave me his number just now. Maybe I can text him and we can figure out something for later this week, okay?"

Both of their expressions brightened.

"Thanks, Mrs. Rojas!" Christina bounced with joy.

I rose from my chair, the blood rush catching up with my head as I bent over to hug her. "Happy birthday, sweet girl. Thank you so much for inviting us."

My head cleared. I took Anna's hand, and we headed to our cottage.

Chris, Mary and Jeremy conversed on the street side of the carport. Stoic, he raised a hand while Chris and Mary called out goodbyes.

Cecily looked up from her book as we came into the house. Exhausted, I leaned against the door and gave her a weak smile.

Her eyes gleamed. "Small victories, Shug."

My fingers hovered over the screen.

He had been kind enough to listen to me. Inviting him and Christina to dinner was the least I could do.

I hit send.

> *Hi Jeremy, it's Aimee Rojas.*
> *Thanks again for having us over*
> *yesterday for Christina's party.*

I think Cecily and I are going to
have the Hamadas and Coles
over for dinner sometime this week.
We'd love for you and
Christina to join us if you're free.
Please let me know if there's a
certain day that's better for y'all.

Several hours later, my phone dinged.

Jeremy King
You're welcome.
Thanks for the invitation,
but we're heading into Houston
on Wednesday to spend the rest
of spring break with my dad.
We might miss dinner if it's
later in the week, sorry.

Is Tuesday evening at 6 okay?

Works for us.

Great, see y'all then.

Thanks.

Some nights were better than others.

Monday night found me sleepless, even with medication. I turned on my nightstand light, refusing to look at my phone. The timestamp blazing on the screen was a mortal enemy I could only evade, not defeat. I reached for my planner and flipped through the pages. I counted: four more nights of the dosed down hydroxyzine, leaving me five extra pills, just in case.

Dinner with everyone tomorrow night.

On Friday, Clint was bringing lunch and work with him. Darius was supposedly coming on Saturday.

"More small victories to be had." I turned off the light. "Father," I whispered in the dark, "thank you." I prayed for Cecily and Darius. For small but steadily increasing hours of sleep. I even thanked Him for the depression and anxiety, turning over the many times co-workers and acquaintances had expressed struggles with it. I'd never been able to comprehend how they were feeling, but now I could. It was a gift. It was all a gift.

Several bars of "In-A-Gadda-Da-Vida" danced in the dark across the street, vanishing almost as soon as I heard them.

I fell asleep.

I picked up a spatula for the first time in months on Tuesday evening and cooked my mom's lasagna from scratch. Cecily concocted a decadent tiramisu, composing a symphony of coffee, amaretto, and sugar which would have me doing cartwheels all night if I were to cave and indulge in dessert. The Hamadas brought their children, Kate and Johnny.

"Remember me, buddy?" I knelt and met Johnny's eyes.

He shook his head. Then, throwing all caution to the wind, he clamped his arms around me and stayed by my side for a majority of the night. He perched on my hip as I opened the door for the Coles and Kings.

Jeremy carried a case of Topo Chico in his arms. "Mary said it was your favorite."

"Mary is never wrong." I smiled.

Chris and Jason carved huge slabs of lasagna for their plates. Lilly lovingly interrogated me as I picked at mine, asking about my sleep, my sick leave ending, and how Anna was doing in school. She nodded after every answer. "Good," she assessed. "God's still working. Be sure to give him the room he needs."

After dinner, the kids ran to the table with dominos shouting a cacophony of "chicken feet!"

My head whirled, excited and overwhelmed with all the activity. Johnny sat in my lap for the duration of the game, Christina on my left and Anna on my right. Round after round, the game progressed as daylight waned. Chris entertained the kids and me while Cecily, Mary and Jeremy dominated everyone with no-nonsense concentration. Eventually, Lilly plucked a slumbering Johnny out of my lap, and the little girls wandered over to the sofa, talking a mile a minute. Drawing a double zero one time too many, I bowed out of the game to wash the dishes. Whoops of joy and groans of disbelief ensued as Cecily emerged victorious. I pulled my pruning fingers from the soapy water and grabbed another pan to wash.

Jeremy joined me at the sink.

"Couldn't hang?" I smiled.

"Not with those two." He nodded toward Cecily and Mary, then picked up a towel and a pot to dry.

"I should've warned you, they're thick as thieves. Have been since they were kids."

"Really? They go that far back?"

"Yeah. Cecily, my mom, and Mary all grew up in Morgan City. They were best friends."

Mary and Cecily sat at the table, cackling like hens.

"Still are."

He took the plate I passed to him. "What about your mom? Do your parents live in the area?"

"They do, but this year they're on sabbatical in Cornwall. They're both professors at Houston Theological Seminary and take their rest seriously, as they should. No phone calls. Limited emails and texts. I talked with my mom several times before coming down to the island, but otherwise I'm not planning on disturbing them."

"I see." His brows drew down.

He hadn't smiled all evening. As he reached for a serving spoon, a warm, sharp scent rose from his shirt sleeve. Brown sugar and smoked bourbon.

I scrubbed a stubborn spot on a skillet. "I hope y'all have a good time with your dad this weekend."

"Thanks." He took the skillet from my hand. "You sleeping better?"

"The past couple of nights haven't been too shabby."

"That's good to hear. Christina and I have been praying for you."

I didn't get to thank him. Johnny, roused from his sleep, barreled into my knees from the side like a runaway train, knocking me into Jeremy. He caught my shoulders as Johnny latched onto my legs.

Johnny grinned at me with baby teeth. I dried my hands and picked him up. "Hey there, mister." I kissed the dimple on his cheek.

"I'm sleepy, 'Mee."

"Me too, John John. Let's find your mom." I glanced over at Jeremy and mouthed, "Thank you!"

He winked as he took up another pan to dry.

The dominos were cleared, toys in Anna's loft upstairs put away, and children wrangled by their parents. Outside on the deck, we exchanged hugs and kisses from the Coles and Hamadas as they left, and staved off Johnny's tears. He waved a sad hand over Jason's shoulder.

"I'll see you at church soon, buddy. I promise," I called.

"Night, Anna!" Christina gave Anna a squeeze.

"Have fun at your Papaw's!" Anna answered. "Bye, Mr. Jeremy!"

Jeremy appeared immovable in my doorway, but he stepped aside for Anna as she retreated into the house. "Bye, Anna." Wooden planks sighed under his feet as he met me on the deck. "Thanks for having us over."

"You're welcome." I shivered in the crisp air. Exhausted and ready to take the hydroxyzine, I was unable to muster another smile.

He cleared his throat and stepped into the moonlight. "I'll let you know when we're back."

I was surprised to find that my grin wasn't forced at all. "Can't wait."

After tucking Anna in and telling Cecily goodnight, I fell into bed, half-wondering about the sensation invading my heart. As I drifted into sleep, I put a name to it.

Happiness.

"Mom, what are you doing?"

Anna sprawled across my bed, peering over my shoulder as I knelt on the floor. With care, I set the small bottle of my last few hydroxyzine tablets upright, mindful of the broken safety cap. I zipped it, and the remaining weekly vitamin D capsules in an interior pocket of my carry-on suitcase. "We aren't moving again, are we?"

The concern in her eyes shattered me.

"No love, of course we're not. I just don't need these anymore. I'm done taking my sleeping pills, and I'll take my big vitamin D a week from today. I just took my dose for this week. I'm feeling better, remember?"

She sighed, relieved. "Oh good, I don't want to go anywhere else ever again." She didn't see my raised eyebrows. "You are a lot better, Mama. I can tell. And Darius is coming tomorrow!"

There was no way she could have possibly made the connection between my medicine being tucked away and Darius' visit. There couldn't be.

I forced myself to match her excitement. "He sure is! We haven't seen him in a long time, have we?"

"Not since I was five."

"Time flies, doesn't it little girl?"

"Yep, and I'm not little anymore."

"Oh, you're not, are you? Then I can't do *this*!" I picked her up and tackled her on the bed, tickling her, and loving the joy that escaped in her uncontrollable laughter.

"If I'd have known you were camped out this far from the Strand, I would have picked up something closer."

Clint came early. Seeing him dressed in a Tom Ford suit tailored to flatter his height and the breadth of his shoulders brought everything about my career rushing back. The fast pace. The camaraderie. The stress. At the foot of the stairs, he handed me a takeout bag almost as large as my suitcase and kissed my cheek. "Food's stone cold by now." He stood back. The mossy spheres of his eyes studied me.

Today, I'd upgraded my sweats for jeans and an oversized button-up, my hair slicked back into a low bun.

I was proud my voice hid the tremor that tightened my throat. "Don't worry. It's not beyond repair."

"How do you always manage to fix everything, Aimee?"

"Prayer. Vitamins. Sleep." I nodded toward the bag he'd brought from Darlene's Shrimp Shack. "And in this instance, an air fryer."

He gave me a cocky smile. "That's my girl."

"I'm still technically your boss, bucko."

He followed me up the stairs and through the French doors, sizing up the house. "Not a bad place. Not my style, though."

"Your style is decidedly hard to define, my friend."

He smiled and said nothing as he opened his laptop at the counter. "You look great. Missing the taste of closing the sale?"

I took two plates out of the cabinet. "I have no comment other than to say appearances are deceiving."

"Are you still sensitive to screens?"

"Only a little."

"Good." His monosyllabic reply signaled the end of the small talk. "We've got a lot of work to do."

Clint briefed me on the final draft of our proposal for the Philippines job and projections for the second quarter. We sifted through preliminary contracts given to us by accounting and requested amendments for our customer to view. My brain was fried. Shirtsleeves rolled up, Clint was brewing himself a cup of coffee when Cecily and Anna came home from school.

"How was your day with the West End Bible ladies?" I asked.

"Great, Shug." Cecily's eyes flicked from Clint to me, then back to Clint.

"Clint, why are you here?" Anna scanned his hands for a phone, surprised not to see one. "Shouldn't you be at work?"

"I'm always working, Anna. But it doesn't mean…" He sank to his knees, pulling a small velvet box from his pocket and handing it to her. "… I'm not thinking about my favorite girl."

Her eyes grew wide as she opened the box.

"South sea pearls for a pearl above price," Clint murmured. Anna turned the box toward me, revealing two golden pearls perfectly sized for her ears.

"What do you say, baby?" I urged her.

"Thank you, Clint!" She gave him a joyous smile and hurtled up the stairs to the loft.

"You'll spoil her."

"She deserves far more than I can give."

Witness to the interaction between the three of us, Cecily chimed in. "Some of us would be happy to take whatever you've got." She eyed the French press. "Especially if it's caffeinated."

"It is." Clint's smile lit the room.

"Bless your heart." Cecily was charmed by Clint, as every woman was.

I shut my laptop. "Clint, this is my aunt, Cecily."

He had her in gales of laughter in the blink of an eye, and learned more about her in thirty minutes than I imagined my uncle had been able to garner in three months of dating.

Clint glanced at his watch. "I should be on my way."

I walked him to his car. The Ferrari SF90 Stradale he'd paid for in cash shone like onyx between the stilts on the carport.

I nudged him. "She looks well."

"My pride and joy. Wouldn't have gotten her without you."

"Give yourself credit where it's due." I turned to face him. "I'm really proud of the work you've done. And so thankful. You know I wouldn't have been any good to you on this contract. And based on what you've told me today about your back and forth with the customer, it seems like they're a tough crowd."

He opened the door and tossed his briefcase in the passenger seat. Digging his hands into his pockets, he demurred, leaning against the coupe, taking me in for a long moment. This was a test. We did this sometimes, mentally sparring to see if one could better the other at reading subtleties and body cues.

He was ready to empty his pockets and beat a retreat to Houston. If I read him right, he was thinking about how he'd beat the boss of whatever video game he was currently playing.

His shoe tapped the driveway. "Easy, actually."

I was immune to the power of his nonchalant posture and intent gaze, but others weren't. From his tone, I knew the negotiations he referred to took place outside of the boardroom.

His chest heaved as he let out a heavy breath. "I just wish I had your steadiness. Despite what you think, I need you, Aimee. You're the calm in my storm."

I crossed my arms. "Your flattery doesn't go unappreciated, but surely, you're joking. I'm just now getting my wits back."

He changed topics, a tactical move. "You like it down here, don't you?"

The subtle vibrance in his voice always made it difficult to disagree with him. I went along with the shift in conversation.

"Anna does. And the pace of life affords me the space I told you I needed in New York."

We stood arms-length apart, reading each other for a moment more. He wore his perpetual air of ease, but there was something wound up inside him, tense and indiscernible.

I broke first.

"You don't have to stay in the storm, Clint. You have so much to offer outside of sales. It would do you good to slow down and really make time for someone. For anything besides the job."

"If I didn't know you as well as I do, I'd give you the same advice. But I don't need to, do I?" His mouth curved into a sly smile as he slid into the driver's seat. His eyes captured my astonishment. "Whoever he is, he should understand he's damn lucky."

I was dumbstruck. "Clint, there's not—"

"Now the only thing left for me to care about is my Stradale. And as far as I'm concerned, that's fine with me." He revved the engine. "Talk soon."

I waved and let out a long breath, watching him drive down the street. "Bless his heart, indeed."

I was ready for her questions.

"Aimee, have you and Clint ever—"

"No."

"Then is he—"

"Not that either, Cici."

"Then why does—"

"That's how he operates."

The aquamarine clouded over. "So, it's just—"

"Yes."

"With everyone?"

"Just about."

"With you, too?"

"Not seriously. He knows better."

"Hmmm…" She was silent for a moment. "That's a shame. He's so nice. And nice looking, too." Cecily grabbed a yogurt cup from the fridge.

I shot her a look. "Cecily Fontenot, you already have two grown men to worry about. Do not add another to your plate, especially that one."

"Well, fine, Shug. Besides, I happen to know someone else who can't keep his eyes off you and I'm hoping you'll actually do something about him."

Cecily was in rare form.

I decided to join her. "Amos Guerrero would be quite the catch, wouldn't he?"

Cecily almost choked on the spoonful of yogurt she'd just eaten and cackled uproariously. "Horrors, Shug!"

Darius Fontenot
Heading ur way.

Cecily and I exchanged glances as both of our phones lit up with Darius' message.

"Guess I'll start cooking," she said.

Dinnertime came and went, and there was still no sign of my

cousin. I loaded the dishes into the washer. "I'm gonna run an errand, Cici."

"Okay, Shug." Cecily sat scrolling on her phone at the bar, unsettled and unsure of what the next hours would hold.

The doors at Guererro's slid open noiselessly. I beelined to the freezers at the back of the store. Darius could roll up to the house at any minute. I both wanted him to and dreaded it.

Mint chocolate chip. It had been our favorite growing up. Didn't smell and taste jog memory the strongest? Maybe a sensory tie to the past would be able to draw some of the poison of the present out.

I picked up the pint and held it in my hands, scratching off frost with my fingernails as I walked to the counter. Amos stepped out from the back office.

"Hey, Aimee! How're you doing?"

I couldn't help grinning. "Wonderfully, Amos."

His amiable face beamed as he scanned the ice cream and looked past me. "Did you come here by yourself?"

"Sure did!" I was seven years old.

"At night?"

"Yep!" Maybe five.

"Well bless God, you are feeling better! I told you some of our sunshine would help."

"It's helping a lot. And everyone is so kind down here."

"Especially your neighbor, and his precious Christina. I bet she and your Anna are just having a ball."

I handed him cash. "They are. I'm sure they'll be inseparable come summertime."

He nodded. "You know, I bet you're good for Mr. Jeremy, too. Poor guy usually keeps to himself even though he's never met a stranger. Maybe you could look after him too, some, hey? These days we just all need to look out for each other, you know?"

"I do. I'm sure we'll all take care of each other." I remembered Jeremy's own words spoken at Christina's party and repeated them. "That's what neighbors are for, right?"

"Of course! You have a good night, Miss Aimee. Enjoy that ice cream."

"I will, Amos. See you!"

I made the three-minute journey back to the house. An older model Corolla I'd never seen before was parked under the house in our carport.

Only a small jolt of pain crossed my head, front to back as usual. I grabbed the ice cream and flew up the stairs to the doors.

His back was to me and he sat on the barstool, making Anna laugh.

I took a deep breath. "Hey, cuz!"

He turned around and stood up. Darius. But not the same Darius I knew. His smile slid up his face, the way it always had, but he was thinner than the last time I'd seen him.

"Aimee *cher*, it's been way too long. Where have you been, traveling so far from home?" He pronounced my name the French way and hugged me close, the stench of cigarette smoke clinging to his clothing. I hugged him back, hard, and kissed his cheek.

"Too many places." I handed him the bag from Amos'. "Guess what I got us just now?"

Studded with impenetrable clouds, his eyes were the same sky blue, but his mouth carried an unfamiliar downturn I wasn't familiar with.

"Mint chocolate chip, no way!" His laugh was the same, contagious. "I'm ready for some now. Momma, get us some bowls down and we'll take care of this in no time. Anna *cher*?"

"Yes, yes, yes!" She adored him.

My heart pounded like a drum.

Cecily got the bowls and joined us at the table.

Anna carried the box of dominos to the table. "Do you know chicken feet, Darius?"

"Sure do, Anna *cher*."

Darius kept his phone in sight, compulsively flicking his fingers across it every few minutes as we played. His ice cream melted in the bowl, untouched. He told Anna dad jokes until she was crying from laughter.

I caught Cecily's eye. She was crying too. I sniffed.

Darius laid down a tile, completing a set of three. "All of y'all got colds or something?"

"No, Dare." I wiped my nose on my sleeve.

"Darius, you won!" Anna shrieked. "Aren't you happy?"

Was he happy?

He didn't answer her question.

He left after spending two hours with us, promising he'd be back soon. The Corolla shot down the road like a ball from a cannon.

All night and into the next morning, I had fitful dreams of Darius wading knee-deep in the tangled growth of a swamp. Darkness stalked him, an adversary who wouldn't stop until it consumed him entirely.

My phone went off at 6:21 on Sunday evening.

Jeremy King
Just got back in.
Christina's jonesing for the beach.
Want to take the girls for a quick walk?

Sure, we'll be down in 10.

Can't wait.

Smiling, I set the phone down and called out her name. "Anna!"

The evening was cool, and the breeze was strong. Jeremy appeared oddly ragged and said little besides hello. He waded ahead of us into the waves. Watching the sun scatter its final rays across the clouds, he let the rolled cuffs of his pants get doused by the surf as high tide came in. The waning light and thin plane of water pooling across the sand as the waves rose and fell turned the beach to glass. Anna, Christina and I knelt together at the water's edge digging up bean clams. Our clothes got soaked and we laughed, watching the tiny clams upend and rebury themselves in the sand almost as fast as we could excavate them.

A gust of wind burst over the dunes behind us.

Christina cried out as a plume of sand caught her full in the eyes. "Ow! It really, really hurts." She put her hands to her face and started rubbing her eyes.

"Stop, Christina. Don't do that." I sat back on my heels and pulled her hands down gently, turning her out of the wind. "Hey, it's okay. The tears are good. Don't rub your eyes though, the sand could scratch them."

"It really stings!"

"I know, sweetheart. But listen, the tears are good, and they'll help wash the sand out. Let me see. Can you open your eyes for me?" She blinked. No redness. "I think you're alright, just keep them closed for a few minutes. Let's take a deep breath and wait for a little while, okay?" She leaned into my arms. Several grains of sand freckled her nose and cheeks, and I wiped them away with my shirt sleeve.

"Mama's right, Chris." Anna squeezed Christina's hand. "You'll feel better in just a few minutes, promise."

The direction of the wind had carried our voices away from him, and I felt rather than saw Jeremy watching the three of us huddled together. I turned, apprehensive to meet the concern in his gaze. What I saw instead locked me tight with a tenderness I didn't expect. An earnest longing rested on his face, intense and unconcealed.

"Is it gonna be okay, Aimee?" Christina looked up at me, blinking, and I took in the hazel kaleidoscope of her still teary eyes.

"Yeah, sweet girl. Everything's gonna be okay."

"The heavens are telling..." Haydn's chorus swelled in my AirPods as my feet broke through the surf. The week after spring break was unseasonably warm. The morning sky bloomed with clouds. *"... the glory of God. The wonder of his work displays the firmament."*

Although I continued to wake up with persistent headaches, the depression dissipated like fog from my thoughts, burning off during the morning walks I took along the shore after dropping Anna off at school.

I turned the volume down and reflected on the events of the past few days.

I had signed off on several of the proposals Clint and I reviewed the week before, happy for him to shoulder the responsibility of the Philippines project.

Cecily invited Mary and Chris over for dinner one evening. Afterward, Jeremy and Anna knocked on our door to ask if Anna had finished her homework, and to see if we'd all enjoy a walk to the pier on the bay side of the neighborhood for some night fishing.

The memory of that evening came back to me as the sun climbed through the clouds during my morning walk on the beach.

Christina had slung a small folding chair across her back and helped Anna with another.

"Have you ever been pier fishing before, Aimee?" Christina asked.

"I haven't, but Anna loves fishing with her uncle when we visit him in California. I'm sure she'll enjoy this."

It was a quiet weekday evening save for the distant rush of the surf. Christina and I fell into step trekking the peaceful street lined with beach houses while Anna chatted up Chris and Jeremy, jabbering a mile a minute. Several paces ahead of us, they paused at the highway. Jeremy looked to the left and the right before Anna stepped onto the road, instinctively reaching out his hand. Almost unconsciously, she took it. I'd been unprepared for the wave of emotion their small gesture produced in me. Christina stayed near me as we crossed the highway, and Jeremy kept Anna's hand in his as they walked ahead of us, talking. Anna smiled at him as if he'd hung the moon.

"You know, Dad's really my uncle," Christina said matter-of-factly at my side.

"I know, sweetheart."

She looked at me with evident pride. "But I'm really glad he wanted to be my dad."

The memory of those moments lingered in my thoughts throughout the rest of the week.

A line of pelicans flew overhead. I waded into the clear water, feeling ridges of sand fall under my feet and counting the weeks it had been since we were in New York. Since I had started taking steps to getting well. Ten weeks down, and five more pills to take until I was done with the vitamin therapy. Fifteen weeks in all. Even though it was mid-morning, the sun began to do more than simply kiss my skin, and I hurried back to the cottage.

"Getting hot, isn't it?" Cecily sipped her coffee at the bar.

"It is, and I'm about ready for a dip in the ocean." I poured myself a glass of water. "Be right back Cici, I need to take my vitamin for the week."

I moved the pile of dirty laundry off the suitcase and unzipped it, laughing at how many clothes I still needed to donate, and how Maren had done me a world of good during our trip to the Strand last month. I rummaged in the interior pocket where I'd tucked the bottles away, but my hand found nothing.

It was empty.

"Why would he steal vitamins?" Cecily paced the kitchen. "Why would he bother?"

"I don't know. Did he even go back to my room?"

"I can't remember, Shug."

I stared at the table, replaying the evening. We played dominos at the table. His ice cream had melted, untouched. Darius won the game and Anna got up and went to the bathroom, and then…

"He might have used my bathroom when Anna got up to use the one in the hall."

"So, he would have been in your room, then?"

"I guess. It happened so fast. I didn't think about him going back there. It's not like you can deny someone the bathroom. But how would he even think to look in my suitcase?" The truth surfaced from the deep, bloated with rot.

"He'll take anything at this point."

"I guess. I mean vitamin D pumps up your metabolism, that's partially why I've lost so much weight. I don't know what it would do combined with something else, though." I remembered the hydroxyzine. "He took the hydroxyzine too. The pocket was completely empty."

I knew she remembered the first day I had taken it, almost two months ago. "It's strong, isn't it?"

"It can be." The sick feeling hit me everywhere at once. I

needed light, something that made sense. "I'm so sorry, Cecily. I need to take another walk; I need some air and space to pray."

My phone dinged.

Jeremy King

Are you and Anna free tonight?

Cecily sat on the sofa, reaching for her Bible. "Me too. Do what you need to do to calm down."

Outside, the noon sky was cloudless, cobalt. The bright light sharpened everything. This time, the heat of the sun blessed me like an instant balm, thawing the tension I felt mounting in my chest.

Confronting Darius seemed impossible, even if he did show back up at my house. But the alternative of contacting the police was equally hard to stomach. I had to talk with someone other than Cecily about Darius, someone who wasn't so close to the situation and could be totally objective. I stood on the deck just outside the French doors, blindly watching an ant crawl across the weathered beams when it hit me. I wanted to talk with Jeremy.

Jeremy, who had just texted me during his break at work.

Jeremy, who was serious and uncomplicated, and loved his daughter and Jesus like I did.

Hungry for the soothing sway of the hammock strung underneath the house, I started for the stairs. A Tesla crouched on the carport underneath the King's house. The car was startling enough with its blood-red hue, but it was something else that made me stop dead in my tracks, frozen to the spot on the path between our cottages.

The beautiful girl in the King family portrait had just cleared the stairs, a load of clothing in her arms.

The movement of my blouse in the breeze caught her eye, and she waved at me with her free hand. I waved back at her like an idiot.

Effortlessly caught up in a bun, her jet-black hair accented her delicate features. She wore biking shorts and a cropped sports bra.

"Hi there!" Her voice was confident. Makeup, flawless. "Please don't worry, I'm not breaking and entering, this is my house." Although I could tell she had aged slightly in the ten or so years since the photo had been taken, her smile spoke of youth as she threw the garments across the hood of the car and came around to me, her perfectly manicured hand outstretched.

This was a dream, and I was talking to a ghost.

"Lauren King." She gave me a brief, appraising look as we shook hands. "I'm Jeremy's wife."

The sudden surge of pain threatened to split my head, but almost two decades of corporate mirroring kicked in before any kind of visceral reaction to her words could reach my face. This woman wore armor—albeit skin-tight—but I spotted the weakness in it almost without meaning to.

A malicious glint in her laughing eyes gave away that she was playing a game with me. The same game I'd played with executives many times over the course of my career. This woman was trying to sell me something. I hated this game. I didn't want to hear my name in her mouth; didn't even want her to know it.

"It's so nice to meet you." My own smile flashed brilliantly across my face. "Don't worry, I won't call the cops. We've only recently moved into the house next door. Still learning the neighborhood."

"Have you met Jeremy?" She brightened as she spoke his name. This was more than a game. It was chess, and she was a master.

Never mind the message Jeremy had sent me moments ago, or everything we'd come to learn about each other over the last few weeks. None of it made sense or mattered at that moment. I made my move.

"Only a handful of times. My daughter loves playing with Christina, though." All true. My head swam.

"Wonderful! Jeremy likes it down here more than I do. And of course, with *work* and everything…" She let the thought dangle, incomplete. "I just thought I'd head down to the island today to pick up some of my things he neglected to bring into town last weekend."

A bold move.

My laugh was throaty, commiserative. "Men are prone to make detrimental mistakes, aren't they?"

Her eyes narrowed slightly at this. Still smiling, she agreed. "Yes."

I blinked, noticing the keys in her hand. She was leaving.

"You have a beautiful day for a drive. Too bad you'll miss seeing Christina and Jeremy. We've really enjoyed having them as neighbors." I shaded my face from the sun with my left hand.

She didn't miss the wedding band.

Check.

She laughed then, a shimmering sound. If I wasn't listening for it, I wouldn't have heard the slight note of trepidation in her final words.

"Well, I have a lot of errands to run today."

Stalemate.

"I understand. It was very nice meeting you, Lauren. Take care." I waved and ambled down the path to the boardwalk at an easy pace, counting on the fact that she'd be watching me until the dunes hid me from her view.

"Lord, what does this mean?" I prayed out loud. "Something isn't right here. Actually, something is very wrong."

I picked up my pace once I hit the boardwalk. My headache intensified, and the tightness in my chest strengthened, twisting. I cared if Jeremy was lying to me. It bothered me that some woman who'd called herself his wife had played a cruel game with me.

"God, help me with this. I don't know what's happening. Again."

I was in the waves now, knee deep and fifty feet out. In the shockingly clear, shallow water, hundreds of silver fish, lithe and quick, encircled me, rising and falling in the waves.

Perfect and tranquil, the peace came.

Ask him. He'll tell you.

I was back on the shore now. The soft sand coated my feet, and vines splayed across the dunes, their purple flowers fully opened to the splendor of the day. I sat down and stared at the waves. A pelican plunged down as a hundred streaks of silver shot up.

The phone weighed heavy in my hand as I typed a response.

Jeremy King

Yes, we're free tonight.
What did you have in mind?

I waited a few seconds.

I just met Lauren.

It was really all I needed to say. All I could say over text. Somehow, I knew it was the only prompting he would need and that he would tell me the truth. The pain in my head subsided. I hugged my knees to my chest.

My thoughts dove back to Lauren King. Lauren King in the family photograph on the wall, not Julia King.

I was wrong.

Christina wasn't a newborn in the photo, and Jeremy told me Julia had died not long after she was born. But Lauren was his wife? I hugged my knees to my chest, unable to think anymore. The sun sank into my skin, feeding it needed rays.

The phone dinged as the waves thrummed against the shore.

Jeremy King
An early dinner on the Seawall.
Christina's been asking to
take Anna to The Spot.
I also wanted to make a stop
on the way back if you're up for it.

I waited.

Lauren's always had impeccable timing.
Interested to hear about your meeting.

Want to head out when
y'all get back from school?

Perfect.

I let out a long breath. I needed to lie down. Doing anything with Jeremy and the girls tonight would only prolong the unexpected stressors of the last couple hours.

I found Cecily in the oasis of the living room on the sofa, her Bible open in her lap. I didn't bring up Lauren King.

"Jeremy and I are getting dinner with the girls tonight. I might try to rest for a while, before I pick Anna up from school."

"Sure, Shug. If you feel up for getting out, that's great. I've been texting with Mary. She's invited us over for dinner, but I'll let her know it'll just be me."

I went to Cecily and hugged her. "I love you, Cici. We'll get through all of this, together, won't we?"

"In Jesus' name!"

"Amen." I called from down the hall and closed my door.

The air hung humid outside the open French doors, cool after the blistering heat earlier in the day. While I hadn't slept, resting in the calm of my room had still done me a world of good. Cecily was already at Mary and Chris' house and—I was sure—would process everything surrounding Darius' visit with them.

Anna pulled on her shoes. "Where are we going again, Mama?"

"To dinner at a restaurant on the Seawall. The Spot. I've been there before, a long time ago. You'll like it."

"Do they have chicken nuggets?"

"Yes. And lemonade, I'm sure."

"Yessssss!" She threw on her hoodie.

I typed quickly.

Jeremy King

Coming down now.

I turned on the porch lights and locked the door.

Ready for you.

Jeremy's brief reply did something astounding to my pulse as Anna and I went down the stairs. He got out of his truck to open the doors for me and Anna. The smile I greeted him with did nothing to change his frown.

"Hi, Mr. Jeremy," Anna chirped.

"Afternoon, Miss Rojas. Hop in the back with Christina."

He shut our doors and revved the engine, reversing.

"Daddy, can we listen to Jesus music?"

Wordless, he flicked on the radio.

"Ooooh this is one of my favorites!" Anna crooned.

Jeremy configured the stereo settings to where most of the sound would funnel to the backseat's speakers. The girls sang, enraptured.

He glanced at me. "Long day?"

"You could say that. The events of earlier today were unexpected to say the least, and I didn't sleep very well last night." I paused and threw him a sideways look. "Unsure of how I'll sleep tonight."

"You up for this?"

"Absolutely." I gazed out the window, watching the tide go out.

"Close your eyes if you'd like. Since it's Friday, there might be some traffic, and it could take longer than usual to get into town." *And since the girls are with us, I can't tell you anything just yet.* He may as well have said it out loud, the strain in his voice obvious.

I gave him a small smile. "Okay."

He winked, still frowning.

Taking his suggestion, I closed my eyes. My and Anna's favorite song came on the radio. The last time I'd heard it was more than a month ago, when I was paralyzed with fear and Jeremy was in the driver's seat, taking me back home.

"Mama, Mama, it's our favorite!"

"It is, love."

"I don't know this song," Christina said.

"Mama, can you sing along with it? Please?"

"Please Mrs. Rojas, then we can learn it!"

With no apparent objections from the driver, I began to sing along with the song.

> *Here is where I lay it down, every burden every crown...*
> *This is my surrender...*

Anna joined me and eventually Christina did too.

My eyes were still closed. With the slowing and jerking stops of the truck, I knew we were getting closer to town. As I sang, a weight fell off me, and I thought I could feel it falling from Jeremy, too. Prayed it would.

Even if it drew some kind of pain out of both of us, whatever he was going to tell me tonight might also work for our good.

It had to.

Traffic slowed to a crawl as we neared the Seawall. Jeremy had visibly relaxed, but a steely glint remained in his eyes throughout dinner. On the ride back to the West End, the girls chattered in the backseat, no longer paying attention to the music. We blew past Sea Isle.

"Daddy, where are we going?" Christina inquired.

"I thought it would be fun to take Mrs. Rojas and Anna to see SeaSplit."

Christina squealed.

"What's SeaSplit?" Anna asked Christina.

"It's Daddy's house he's building! And the best beach. But we're gonna sell it soon, right Daddy?"

His eyes reflected her excitement in the rearview mirror. "That's the plan, nugget."

We were already a mile away from Sea Isle, heading toward the San Luis Pass and the end of the island. Neighborhoods straggled behind us and the dunes rose up high against the sea on our left. Jeremy turned the truck into an unmarked gravel driveway, stopping to enter a code at the gate. The dunes on the fenced property crested with life. Flowers and a sweeping paddock of salt grass rolled across a plain. Anna and I both gasped. A dozen horses grazed in the westernmost field, golden hour light burnishing their coats silver and bronze.

I turned to Jeremy. "I'm being punked. You have horses. Beach horses?"

A smile begged at the corners of his mouth, but he refused to let it out. "The horses aren't mine, only the land. I'm leasing it to a rancher for the time being."

The truck rocked along the winding gravel driveway. As we

took a curve around a particularly large dune, I realized we were traveling parallel to the ocean. I'd yet to see any house. "How much land is there?"

"Just under sixteen acres."

I stared at him, dumbfounded. "I hope your acquisition of this place will be included in tonight's narrative."

But all my thoughts ceased as the driveway opened to a panoramic view of the gulf. Set back against the dunes to our left stood a large beach house on tall stilts. The house was long and wide, one and a half stories with floor-to-ceiling windows running across the ocean side, the roof pitched at a daring angle. The siding looked like stucco although I knew that was impossible in this climate. The decks on both levels were cedar, railed with black industrial cording. As we neared the house, a yard took shape with a patchwork of emerald turf, recently laid. Leading up to the three-bay garage underneath the house, huge rectangular slabs of concrete with mondo grass growing tidily in between the blocks formed the driveway and continued underneath the stilts in lieu of a carport.

Jeremy hit a button, and we pulled into the largest bay of the garage. Christina didn't wait for her dad to turn off the truck. She tumbled out, dragging Anna with her.

The garage was epoxied a gun metal gray, brightly lit and large enough to hold several cars and a boat or RV. An elevator stood at the ready in a corner near the stairwell.

Anna looked over her shoulder at me in disbelief. "There's an elevator in Mr. Jeremy's house."

"I can see that, love. A lot of newer beach houses have them down here."

Christina mashed the button for the elevator and the four of us packed inside. Questions hung in the air between me and Jeremy, multiplying somewhere over the girls' heads. Lauren King. This massive house. The scent of brown sugar and the soft pressure of his shoulder against mine. As the elevator doors noiselessly slid open, he gave me a furtive glance.

"This way, Anna." Christina grabbed her hand, and they took off at a gallop to the left. We followed them, turning a corner into a vast room which was both a great room and kitchen.

"Remember, Christina," Jeremy called to her, "be safe and gentle here. This isn't our house." Then to me, "There are still a couple of tools in one of the bedrooms."

He opened his phone, turning on the lights. Shed ceilings sloped up to enormous windows which commanded a stunning view of the dunes, wild and grasping for the waves.

Even though the heart of the house was empty, it exuded warmth thanks to the almost white bamboo floors which ran throughout. Some of the windows would pivot open, leading out to a large deck, not as wide as the ones at our cottages, but running the entire length of the house and partially covered in the center by a smaller deck from the second floor.

My gaze landed on Jeremy. Behind him, clerestory windows flanked the top of the kitchen cabinets, the golden cast of the sun's rays as it began its descent behind the house illuminating the room. The expert placement of every architectural detail was breathtaking.

Jeremy leaned against the unfinished island, the only solitary structure in the cavernous emptiness of the space, his arms crossed, eyes guarded. The girls' voices echoed somewhere over our heads.

"They're in the primary suite. It's the only thing upstairs. Down here, there's just this room and four bedrooms and a bath on either side. They all have the same windows, same view." His explanation sounded as hollow as the house, as if the place he'd intentionally brought us to was the very last thing on his mind.

"Wright and Jones would be jealous. The house is wonderful." It was true, but it wasn't what I really wanted to say, and he wasn't listening to me.

"What did Lauren tell you, Aimee?" An undercurrent of

something in his voice, I couldn't discern exactly what.

"She asked if I'd met you and told me she owned the cottage." I faced the iron in his eyes. "She told me she was your wife."

Hearing my answer, the unreadable expression in his eyes fully bloomed into anger. His arms tensed involuntarily, bringing his hands to the back of his head. He strode to a window near me and turned a handle which I hadn't noticed.

"Let's talk on the deck. There are a couple of chairs out there I brought over a while ago. The girls will be alright by themselves upstairs."

It was a beautiful evening. The house melded into the land-scape, tethered to the dunes but still reaching for the sea and the sky, both on fire as the sun sank. Two chairs had been flung to opposite ends of the deck, the one nearest us knocked forward by the wind. Jeremy pulled it upright, set it in front of me, and retrieved the other chair. He brought it close to mine and sat without saying a word. For several minutes I wondered if he'd decided not to tell me anything.

Ask him.

Now, as it had been my whole working life, my job was to listen.

"What happened, Jeremy?"

It was all he needed.

"My family has had a place on the island for at least two generations. My grandfather worked with Patrick Hanratty at GM, then moved to Houston and was a primary force in implementing CAD in the oil and gas industry."

"Oh." It was all I could say to someone who had very cryptically and hurriedly told me he was closely related to a millionaire.

"Grandad was a good man, but he spoiled my dad. Never made him work an honest day in his life. My mom and dad were high school sweethearts and got married young." He gave me a meaningful look. "Because of me."

"You had no control over that, but I'm grateful for it, nevertheless."

My words stirred something deep in the ether of his eyes and he continued. "Grandad set my parents up with whatever they needed. When I was young, they traveled a lot, and to their credit, I think they really loved each other. Dad occasionally dabbled in real estate and had the twin houses built out here in the West End after Julia was born. She was eight years younger than me. They'd bring us out every summer to the house you're living in now. Sometimes we'd even come out over Christmas break." His eyes clouded, a sharp contrast to the peace which pervaded the house. "Mom was killed in a car accident my senior year of high school. It was terrible for all of us, but it affected Julia and my dad the most. The three of us stopped coming out here together for a few years after that. When I could drive, I kept coming by myself in the summers during high school and college to work. Julia always joined me when school got out for the summer. Dad would drive down and drop her off. He didn't care if we were here by ourselves. That's when Chris and Mary really became more involved with the two of us. Especially me, since I was down here the most. I don't know where I'd be without the Coles. They were the first touch of Jesus I ever knew. And Julia…"

His voice grew tender. "I think you'd have liked her. She was compassionate to a fault and fearless, always looking for strays, wanting to bring home hurt animals from the dunes. She'd find rabbits, mice, crabs." He laughed, absorbed in the memory of his sister, remembering it like yesterday. The wooden chair he sat in groaned as he shifted his weight forward. "I don't know why I'm thinking of this, but there was one year, as soon as my college finals were done, Julia and I couldn't wait to get down here. I guess we needed each other and needed this place. It was the middle of May, but we had a late cold snap that spring and the temperature got into the forties at night. Julia always took a walk on the beach after she woke up, and one morning she came back to the house carrying a half-frozen rattlesnake. A baby." He looked at me. "Do you know much about rattlesnakes?"

"Not really. Only to avoid them."

"They aren't born with the rattle, only a button where the rattle will grow after their first shed. But a newly hatched baby is just as venomous as an adult. Julia must have been eleven or twelve, and she didn't recognize what it was. She only saw that it was alone and about to die." He ran his fingers through his hair, kneading the back of his head. Rubbing the memory raw. "The sight of it in her hands shook me badly. I didn't have a good grasp on my temper when I was younger, and unfortunately fear got the better of me and I killed the snake before fully explaining why. It tore me up to see her cry like that, but she was completely blind to the danger of it. Julia said even if it was deadly, she didn't care because it still needed help…

"I started teaching at a school in Houston when I graduated, and Julia grew up. But we still came to the island together every summer. Through those years, Julia kept up with a lot of the people we'd both known as kids down here."

He wiped his palms on his jeans, and it struck me that this was probably the first time he had shared this part of himself with anyone. "Before I gave my life over to God, I was into a lot of stuff I shouldn't have been. I exposed Julia to people and things she shouldn't have known at such a young age."

He glanced at me, gauging my reaction. Taking encouragement from my steady gaze, he drew a long breath. "Most of the kids she ran around with down here in the summers were part of an even wilder set than my old friends, bent on raising hell wherever they went. Lauren was one of them."

The base of my head began to throb where it met my neck.

"The summer before I moved down here permanently to start working at the middle school—the year before Christina was born—I finally convinced my dad to come with me, to help me rehab your house."

The fire in the sky had retreated, transforming into a dusky haze hovering at the day's edge. Placid, the sea stretched to the horizon, smooth and dark as smoked glass. Far out in the gulf, lights came on, flickering across the water.

Jeremy's quiet voice sounded over all of it. "I've always regretted asking him to come. Julia had Lauren and some of her other friends over at the cottages constantly. Given everything I knew they were into, I thought it would be better to have them close by where I could try to keep an eye on my sister. At the beginning of August, Julia left for her final year of college and things quieted down, and Dad decided to stay on with me even after she left. He said he wanted to stick around to help me with a couple of finishing touches on the house."

The sun had disappeared entirely now, the gold died out.

"It was October before I found out Dad and Lauren were sleeping together."

"Jeremy…"

A brusque smile. "That same week, Julia called and told me she was four months pregnant with Christina and had stage three ovarian cancer. It was ugly."

"How old were you?"

"I was twenty-nine then. Julia had just turned twenty-one. Dad was forty-eight. Lauren was twenty-three. You met her. Lauren's manipulative, could get anything she wanted, and almost always has. She wanted the lifestyle my dad's financial well-being could offer. And he wanted—" Jeremy faltered, caught between protecting the man who had raised him and the anger he still felt toward him. "He wanted to forget. Julia and I confronted him about his relationship with Lauren. We tried to fight it, but neither of them would listen. They were married on New Year's Eve in Vegas. At that point Julia had been given a good prognosis, but after Christina was born and she was shown unresponsive to the chemo and other protocols, Julia believed my dad and Lauren would take the baby in when…"

His mouth hung open, twisted by words still too painful to utter. "Julia was in hospice at the end, so thankfully I don't think she understood the scope of what happened next. Lauren convinced my father not to adopt Christina. Got him to believe that she would be a burden to their lifestyle." His sorrow was palpable, still raw. "Lauren's never wanted children, and dad was fine with that. I was already having to let Julia go, and Dad had chosen to let all of us go. I couldn't let Christina go, too."

Neither of us spoke for a few moments. The breeze blew salty and sweet. Cloud cover had blotted out any hope of stars, but I could see the twinkling lights more clearly now, shining from four different oil rigs. I was small. Jeremy and I were both so small on the deck, facing the vast inkiness of the ocean. I wanted to give him my hand. Trace the tiredness off his face with my fingers. I wanted to ask him what he needed. But I wasn't ready, so I did none of these things.

Instead, I said, "Why was Lauren here today?"

"I'm not sure. Last weekend, I mentioned to my dad that he and Lauren still had some things at the house and asked if he'd like me to bring them up the next time we came. Lauren made some snide comment about the cottage belonging to them and Christina and I living there rent-free, and why did it matter where they kept what belonged to them?" He pressed his hands to his eyes. "I've tried to forgive my dad over the last ten years. Since he's gotten to know Christina, he's wanted to become somewhat involved in her life. But Lauren is a different story. I've tried so hard to forgive her, forgive the venom she's injected into my family. But it's so hard. And she'll never forgive me for trying to keep Dad from marrying her."

I remembered how subdued he'd been that evening on the beach while the girls and I had blissed out, digging for bean clams. I propped my feet up on the railing and hugged my knees, not entirely trusting my voice. "I don't think forgiveness is linear. Often, it's circular— something God asks us to do again and again. And even more often, people refuse to be forgiven. It's an intimidating gift to give and receive."

A keening gleam of light shone across the gold band as I twisted it around my finger.

"Aimee."

His speaking my name suddenly made my heart race. The pain panned across my head—front to back as usual—and I fought to overcome it, focusing on his face.

"I've never been married." His eyes were clear, begging to be believed. "I'm named after my dad, Jeremiah, and he still owns the house I live in. As you know, he sold the twin cottage to David last year."

"Jeremy's wife." A half-blown laugh gasped from my throat. "Enemies and the PTO, right?"

"Yeah."

"Lauren referred to your dad as Jeremy intentionally to toy with me. Why? She doesn't know me."

"No, but she knows me."

Layers of meaning I didn't miss in those words, but still I asked, "How would being cruel to me hurt you?"

He sent his gaze to something far out in the ocean, maybe the lights that twinkled miles away on the rigs.

"Lauren's always felt threatened by anything that's good and beautiful. Sincere faith and conviction. Christina." Then he looked back at me, silently completing his thought.

A flush of heat rose along my neck. It was as if all the words we'd spoken bound us together in an intensifying gravitational pull. Lauren had only brought things to a head, whether she would ever realize it or not.

"She would go so far as to sabotage even the possibility of your happiness." It was a statement, not a question.

"Yes," he said softly.

I'd heard enough about Lauren King. "Lying Jezebel."

Jeremy's laughter rang out uncontrollably across the dunes, and from the depths of my stomach, my own laugh joined in.

"Mrs. Rojas, you keep surprising me."

I caught my breath. "I despise games that hurt others. Although admittedly I played along with her today. I believe I left her with the impression that I'm a happily married and disinterested shrew."

He glanced down at my hand. "Your wedding ring?"

I smiled.

"And are you?"

"A shrew? You tell me."

"No, Katherina. Disinterested."

"Disinterested in petty games? Absolutely. And if Shakespeare had named me, I'd have preferred plain Kate."

His smile, as it had at Christina's party, took my breath away.

"I don't think you were referring to games." The undercurrent in his voice pulled like a riptide, drawing me out to depths I hadn't attempted to swim in over a decade.

I took a deep breath, yielding to the current. "I find you very interesting, Jeremy King. Given everything you've just shared with me, I doubt I'll be able to sleep tonight at all."

"I'm sorry," he lied, grinning. "You're right, though. You do need sleep, and it's getting late. Do you want to see more of the house? Or we can leave now, if you're too tired."

"No, please. I'd like to see the rest of it."

Leaving the specters of the past on the deck, Jeremy was all business inside the house. "Living, dining, and kitchen, obviously." He surveyed the space with a critical eye and took me through the east wing of the house: a hallway with two bedrooms, each facing the ocean and looking over the dunes with the same, black-cased floor-to-ceiling windows connected by a Jack and Jill bathroom, exquisitely appointed. "Each wing is the same, mirrored."

We returned to the entry near the elevator bank. He led us

to the stairs; a series of solid wood beams that seemed to float against a huge window overlooking the pasture and the driveway, toward the bay. On the landing, French doors stood open at attention, guarding the primary suite. The entry gave way to an alcove enclosed on two sides by windows. "I envisioned this space as a studio or home office." Jeremy said.

Christina and Anna sat on the floor, playing a video game. Christina looked up, grinning. "I found my Switch, Dad!"

He tousled her hair. "Good, baby."

I walked into the bedroom. It didn't jut out as far as the alcove, but was a larger room enclosed on the ocean side by the same floor-to-ceiling windows as downstairs. A bed on the opposite wall would have the luxury of the sea and sky, endless and unobstructed. In the middle of the windows were doors that led outside. Open to the sky and private, an upper deck was sheltered by the two glass alcoves of the studio and what I imagined would be the bath. The oceanfront side of the bathroom was also enclosed by windows on three sides. An enormous freestanding ellipse of a tub overlooked the deck. Next to it, a marble dividing wall with a spa-grade shower faced the other windows.

"It's two-way glass in here," Jeremy said behind me. "And there are six acres on either side of the house. Of course, the beach isn't private. But it is a bit of a hike to get here from the nearest public access points."

I noticed the accenting tiling and header beams. "You did all of this?"

"A majority of the smaller work on the inside, yes. I contracted a buddy of mine for the exterior and the bigger things. The smaller fit and finishes I've installed myself over the last two years. Thank God we broke ground at the end of 2019, before lumber got to be insanely expensive."

I grinned wickedly. "Maybe I should go into teaching. How did you swing all of this, Jeremy? Not with your dad's help. After everything you've just told me, I can't envision you accepting anything from him."

"Hard work over many years. Smart investing and thousands of eighth graders. I bought the land after Ike came through in 2008, after the recession. It was perfect timing, and dirt cheap for what it was. I couldn't have afforded to build a place like this if I hadn't bought the property when I did."

"SeaSplit." All at once I understood the meaning behind the name and the allusion to the parting of the waters. "God made a way through when it seemed impossible?"

His smile told me I was right.

Excitement built in my chest. "It's wonderful, Jeremy. You'll make a killing when you sell it."

"Well." His expression grew serious. "After Lauren's shenanigans today, I have half a mind to move out of the cottage and hole up here for a while. I've been telling myself that fixing up the cottage and living there was acceptable, but now I think I'm done making excuses."

I didn't blame him.

"Maybe we'll move when school is out," he concluded, casting a critical eye over his handiwork as he leaned against the doorframe of the closet.

"It seems like SeaSplit's a special place."

"I've certainly sat on it for a long time. I always imagined a big family living here, enjoying it. Not so much like mine."

I didn't know how to respond to the bitterness in his smile, the weight of too many difficult years. I caught myself wringing my hands.

So did Jeremy. "I'm sorry. You're tired and it's been a long day."

"Yeah." I smiled, happy to see warmth return to his face.

"Well let's roll then, Mrs. Rojas."

We gathered the girls who—upon being drawn from their screen stupor—were shocked at how dark it was outside. The moon broke through the clouds, flying full and high in the sky, its beams rendering the silhouette of the structure impressive against the dunes.

As we backed out of the garage, I considered my favorite part of the house. "The windows, Jeremy. What if a hurricane comes through?"

"Automatic steel storm shutters. They're recessed and roll down like a garage door, top of the line. The first floor is also built several feet higher than the FEMA standard, and there's a massive generator connected to the gas line."

"And insured out the wazoo?"

"The wazoo."

Anna giggled. "What are y'all talking about?"

"Money." We answered at the same time, then laughed.

"Jinx!" Christina cried.

We pulled into the King's driveway, the same one where I'd encountered Lauren earlier in the day. The cottages looked different to me now that I knew more of their history.

An unwanted wave of exhaustion permeated my body, and Darius entered my mind through some wayward thought. I hadn't gotten to tell Jeremy about him at all.

"Let's see the Rojas ladies to their door, Miss King," he said, shutting the passenger door behind me.

Christina and Anna walked on the path ahead of us, their heads bent close together.

The grit in Jeremy's voice gently grazed my ears. "Today was a lot, wasn't it?"

I laughed as we came to the stairs. "You don't even know the half of it. But I'm glad it all happened. Thanks for taking us to dinner, and to see SeaSplit."

"You're welcome."

As he turned toward me in front of the French doors, I felt the tension in our hands—only then realizing at some point during our brief walk from his truck and up the stairs to my deck, they had met and interlocked. We let go of each other easily, simultaneously.

I half expected to see it, but watching hope and desire mingle with the iron of his eyes stole my breath, and the words tripped out of my mouth. "Tell Christina goodnight, Anna."

"Goodnight, Christina."

"Night, Anna!" The girls hugged each other, and I held out my arms to Christina.

"We had fun hanging out with y'all tonight, missy," I gave her a quick squeeze. "Sleep tight."

Jeremy took Christina's hand. "Night, Miss Anna Marie. Good night, Mrs. Rojas."

"Sweet dreams, Mr. King," I called after them.

I thought I could see a smile pull at the corner of his mouth before he turned away from me. "That's guaranteed."

Jeremy King
Thank you for thinking of us.
Hope you slept well.

It was a lot of fun, and I had a great sleep.
Thanks again for thinking of us.

My pleasure.

Darius
Hey cuz, I'm coming down for Easter weekend!!!

We'll need more ice cream.

"And I need to punch you in the face," I muttered.

How r u feeling?

                                        Much better.

Glad 2 hear it.
Love u.

                              Love you too, so much.

  It was true, and only strengthened, rather than lessened, my urge to clock him.

Clint Myers
  I'm submitting the bid now.

                              お疲れ様です

You know my Japanese is rusty.
But you're more than welcome.

Maren Williams
  How are you feeling, love?
  Paris is the same as always.
  Carbs, carbs and more carbs.
  You won't recognize me when
  I see you in May.

                              Feeling a lot better.
                          Bring me back something.
                                   Not too sweet.

How's your neighbor?

                                        Alive.

Tease.

                    He took Anna and I out the other night.

OUT out? I'm calling you
tomorrow morning, your time.

469-461-469x
Hey Mrs. Rojas, it's Christina.
Dad gave me your number.
He said he asked you after we
got back from church yesterday
if it was OK.

Hey sweet girl!
Yes, it's OK.

Can Anna come play in the
shell garden with me?

Sure, she'll be down in just a minute.

Thank u!!!

Jeremy King
I think Christina just texted you.

She did.

Is that alright with you?

Of course!

Standardized testing is this week.
I'm still at work.
Swamped.

Yikes!
Praying for you.

Allison Nance

Clint Myers

Inbox.

10-4

Jeremy King

Hope testing is going well this week.

It is.
Sorry I've been MIA.

Clint Myers
Amendments.
Approve.

K

Mary Cole
Cecily told us about Easter
brunch at y'all's place.
Anything special you'd like me to bring?

GUMBO!

Hahaha!

Jeremy King
Can't remember if I told you,
but Anna and I will be at my
dad's next weekend for Easter.

You didn't tell me.
You'll be missed.

So will you.

April

"You look better." Nat leaned close to the screen, trying to discern as much as he could from the pixels. "Had to make sure Clint wasn't just pulling my leg and that you were still alive."

"Thanks, friend. I'm feeling a lot better. Hoff's taken a machete to my schedule. I'm working ten hours a week now, and twenty in a few more. He doesn't want me to push anything."

"Oh." He cocked an eyebrow at me that matched the angle of his grin. "I know how many hours you're allowed on the grid."

"Ha." I rubbed my forehead. "Of course you do."

"I know *everything*." Nat's villainous cackle was cut short by a rogue snort which sent me laughing until tears streamed down my face.

"I needed a good laugh, Nat," I said, catching my breath. "How've you been? How's HQ?"

A handful of Hot Cheetos flew into his mouth. "Okay. Same old, same old. Business is booming. Everyone's freaking out now that y'all are so close to closing the big sale. What's it called? Leviathan?"

"Velez."

"Eh, close enough. They give these projects the hardest names to remember. Should just call it 'Install Number 234' instead."

"Sounds a little boring."

"Whatever. I'm just trying to enjoy the spring weather Houston gives us before it gets too hot. At least with the lighter schedule, you're getting to travel again."

"If you call sick leave in Galveston, travel, sure."

"Weren't you in Asia last month with Clint?"

I shook my head. "No, I've been on the island since the end of January. Don't you know that, Big Brother?"

He wrinkled his nose, half-annoyed with me as he clacked away on his keyboard.

"Honestly, I've barely left the house with the exception of the last few weeks."

"That's weird." Nat looked confused.

"Well with the anxiety—"

"Nah, I meant it's weird that you aren't traveling yet."

I held my breath, counting slowly. *Six, five, four, three…*

"I just thought you were already back on the road."

Two, one. "Maybe it was something Clint said."

"Maybe. Speaking of your right-hand man, he's been hanging out a lot with Janelle when he's in town."

I drew a blank. "Janelle?"

"Yeah, Janelle Terill. One of the girls in Sharon's squad. Your boy's lack of a personal life is the stuff of office lore, ya know."

Sharon was Hoff's secretary who had half a dozen administrative assistants at her beck and call.

"Really?" I wracked my brain. A vague impression of Janelle Terill came to me. Reserved with her shy smile and reluctance to make eye contact. Always at the back of the room and on the fringe of conversation. Also, pretty and stylishly dressed, which I imagined could garner at least marginal attention from Clint. But if he did ever land on a type, she wouldn't be it. "That's interesting."

"Opposites attract."

"Not as often as the adage would lead one to believe."

"Oh well, to each their own." He shifted quickly and looked

at one of his monitors. "Uh oh, 911 in purchasing. Gotta go, Aimee."

"Okay. Thanks for checking on me, Nat."

He smiled and waved before hanging up the call.

While it was still on my mind, I texted Clint.

Clint Myers

You took my advice?

I breathed deeply, thankful to be sitting on the deck of the house. Not traveling, not having to force any emotion to please another human for the sake of a sale. The list of things I wanted to share with Jeremy was adding up, and the weight of it on my heart both thrilled and intimidated me.

Clint Myers
She has her benefits.

Your sentimentality kills me.

You know me.

I did. What I didn't know was how much longer I could handle Clint. Maybe the break in our proximity had done both of us good. It was as if we were siblings and had finally gotten rewarded with our own rooms in an amorphous house we'd both occupied for the last three years. But the hard scratch at the back of my throat told me otherwise, that my relief wasn't centered around Clint and our relationship.

I didn't know how much longer I could handle my career.

I had worked so hard. Fought so hard. With both Caleb and then Clint backing me up the whole time. It would be selfish to give it up now. Foolish to throw away the promise of stability and comfort.

Comfort?

I blinked hard as if seeing my surroundings for the first time. The deck. *Not mine.* The house. *Not mine.* Anna's school. *Not for long.* My neighbor…

You can't survive, my love. Not this way.

Cecily's steps rang out across the deck behind me.

She perched on the edge of the chair next to mine. "Darius texted and said he was on the way here. He said he's staying the whole weekend."

My eyelids fluttered, taking in the lines of love and concern emerging on her face.

"He's coming now?" The breath I drew was shallow.

"Yes."

"Do you really think he'll stay through Easter Sunday?" I exhaled, rooting myself here in this chair, in this moment with Cecily. With the string of pelicans gliding on silent wings, mere inches above the waves.

"We'll see," Cecily answered wryly.

"Should we ask him about my medicine?"

"I don't know. What do you think we should do?"

"I have no idea. I feel like confronting him would only make him angry." We were silent for a few moments. "It seems like there's no right answer."

"And he'd just deny taking it."

"He knows what's right and wrong," I said. "Or at least he used to."

"He still thinks he's a victim of everything that happened with Sam, even though all of that was out of our control."

I said quietly, "Let's love him well this weekend, and not bring anything up. Even if it infuriates us. At least Anna adores him unconditionally."

"She sees him with the innocent eyes of a child."

"Isn't it amazing how that kind grace overlooks everything? Even the glaringly obvious. Anna still sees his capacity for good. Let's try to be at peace with him but keep a close eye on things.

Maybe the Lord can use a time of quiet to speak louder than we can."

"Do you still think Darius can change?" Cecily's voice shimmered with tears. "That he can really come back to us?"

My own eyes welled. "Oh, Cecily."

I wrapped my arms around her and held her as she leaned into my shoulder. The seagulls wheeling over the gulf echoed her cries.

Good Friday burst awake, brilliant and beautiful.

The King's carport was empty, and by the looks of it, Jeremy and Christina had already gone for the weekend. After my walk, I stood on the path between our cottages for a minute or so, pushing off the hurtful sensation that he hadn't texted or called to say goodbye.

"He doesn't owe me anything." I plucked a blossom from one of his gardenia bushes and buried my nose in the whorl of petals, childhood summers at my grandmother's house in Morgan City rushing back. "Not a thing," I murmured. I waited for my cousin in the hammock downstairs, brushing the flower against my lips.

Darius pulled up at 10:00 in the same Corolla he'd arrived in a few weeks ago. He was beach-ready, clad in swim trunks, a tank, and turquoise-tinted Maui Jims. Somehow, he also looked worse, like he hadn't slept a single night in the three weeks since we'd last seen him. He hopped out of the car with superhuman energy.

"Beat you to it, I bet, Aimee *cher.*" He held two plastic bags aloft.

"What's that, Dare?"

"Mint chip, cuz. You thought I'd forget?" He held a bag toward me.

"No." Something caught in the back of my throat as I smiled at him. I didn't miss the carton of Marlboros in the other grocery bag. "Darius, there's three half gallons of ice cream in this bag!"

"Now who has a bad memory? You think I'd leave us in the lurch? Before I busted my ankle, I almost made it to Eagle Scout, *cher*. Always be prepared."

Anna had heard the Corolla's backfire, and she ran down the stairs. "Darius!"

He was ready for her rush and caught her up in his arms. "Anna *cher*, you're so sweet." He kissed her cheek. "When I get married, I want five little girls just like you."

"Five?" Anna giggled. "That's crazy, Darius."

"Well sugar pie, *I'm* crazy so it all adds up, trust me."

I couldn't speak.

Anna bopped the brim of his baseball cap. "Darius, are you ready to go to the beach now?"

"Sure am. Lead the way!"

I swiftly interjected. "Hey baby, I see you've got your swimsuit on but I'm sure you haven't put your sunscreen on, right?"

"Not yet Mama, but—"

"Let me go pop this ice cream into the freezer and get my beach bag. Y'all go sit on the hammock for just a few minutes. Wait for me, okay?"

"Ughhhh… Okay, Mom." Anna's chilly answer could have kept the ice cream frozen.

Cecily was in the kitchen, packing lunch in a cooler.

"He's here." I threw the grocery bag on the counter and opened the freezer. "Anna's ready for the beach, and so is he. I'm going to grab my swim bag."

"Darius brought that?" Cecily eyed the ice cream incredulously.

I shoved the last half gallon in the freezer and slammed the door shut. "Yep."

"He doesn't come into the house by himself."

"Agreed."

I slung my beach bag over my shoulder and jogged down the

stairs. Darius was smoking a cigarette. Anna hopped out of the hammock as soon as she saw me. She grabbed Darius's free hand and pulled him to the boardwalk.

"Come on, Darius!"

"You don't have to tell me twice!" Darius smiled at me as Anna yanked him after her. For a split second, I doubted everything I knew was true: that he had a warrant out for his arrest, that he was a junkie, and was putting his addiction above everyone and everything he claimed to love. That he was slowly but surely unmaking his very soul in front of me. The pain was brief across my head as I followed them, my feet sinking into the sand.

Darius and Anna splashed into the shallows.

I dug in my bag. "Anna, sunscreen!"

She looked up and slowly began to make her way toward me across the waves. Darius flicked the butt of his cigarette into the surf.

"Jesus, help me love him like you do," I muttered under my breath. "Because I can't right now."

Of course, my prayer was answered. We all swam. Darius stretched out in the water near me on a boogie board, slowly turning an alarming shade of red.

"You might need some sunscreen soon, Dare."

"It's gonna tan up real nice, *cher*, don't you fret."

"I wouldn't be so sure of that."

He squinted at me from under his hat and a smile slid up his face. "What's that get-up you're sporting anyway? Haven't you got a bathing suit?"

"Not a single one to my name."

"With those shorts and shirt on, you're out here lookin' like the Amish. You're doing yourself a disservice, hiding yourself away. You look good, losing all that weight." He kicked back and closed his eyes. "Don't be afraid to show yourself off."

"And who would I be showing myself off for, exactly?"

"Beats me, *cher*. Anna's next daddy?"

"Heavens, Darius!" Cecily piped up from her floatie. Anna snorkeled nearby, her flippers drowning out our voices.

"Kids need daddies, Momma." He shot Cecily a meaningful look. "You and I know that better than most."

I laughed in spite of the pathetic irony. "I have to say there aren't a ton of options for me at the moment, Dare."

"What about your co-worker? Good old what's-his-name. Clive? Cliff?"

"Clint."

"Yeah, him."

"That's a hard pass."

"OoOoo… Too much history, right? Sounds spicy."

He always got me laughing in no time, flat.

"How about him?" Darius pointed to a portly man knee-deep in the waves with three children dangling off his arms.

"I'm pretty sure that's his wife under the blue umbrella."

"What are y'all talking about?" Anna kicked over to us.

"Let me go and ask." Darius sloshed toward the shore, hitching up his trunks and abandoning his boogie board.

"Darius Evans Fontenot!" I yelled.

He flashed me his goofy grin and shook the man's hand, saying something to him and pointing to where Cecily and I were floating.

"Jesus, help us," Cecily groaned.

"What's Darius doing, Cici?" Anna asked.

"Acting a fool," Cecily replied.

After chatting for a few seconds, Darius shook the man's hand again and continued walking to the shore.

"He just wanted another cigarette," I said. We watched him light up in the distance, then walk back up the boardwalk toward the house.

"You locked up, right Cici?"

"Yes, Shug."

"What if Darius needs to get inside?" Anna asked.

"He doesn't, love. We have everything we need out here." I caught Cecily's eye. "The key?"

"In the bottle of sunscreen."

"Really?" I could have made a huge mistake suggesting sunscreen to Darius.

"Well, I have two bottles in my bag. One of them is empty," Cecily grinned. "Been burned too many times and learned my lesson."

"Geez, Cici." Anna made a face. "Maybe that's why you never get a tan."

Cecily chuckled. "Anna Marie, you are joy itself. Joy!"

Anna grinned, the droplets of water from her kick showering down on us like diamonds.

Darius never returned, and we hauled our beach paraphernalia back to the cottage after another half hour in the ocean. Jeremy's truck was parked in his driveway. They hadn't left for Houston yet after all.

Cecily caught me staring. "Heard from him today?"

"No." Under my sunburn, the flush crept up my neck.

"I'm sure you will before they leave." She smiled, hoisting her floatie above her head as she turned to climb the stairs.

We found Darius on the deck, smoking.

"Glad y'all finally showed up." He waved a Dr. Pepper in his hand. "Keepin' a man away from the can for this long is criminal."

The sun had zapped all energy from my body, leaving me

pleasantly drained and relaxed after swimming in the sea. Darius returned to the deck, chain smoking and occasionally pacing back and forth on a phone call. Anna and I showered and retreated to the cool of my room.

"Wanna rest for a while, bug?"

Anna nodded. She fell asleep almost as soon as her head hit the pillow. I laid beside her and watched her breathe, the peace on her face healing wounds inside of me garnered from all of the nights I'd spent sleepless.

The vibration of my phone startled me awake. I flipped it over.

5:03

Jeremy's name lit up the screen.

Jeremy King
Are you at home?

Yes.

As I hit send, raised voices overwhelmed my thoughts.

Cecily and Darius' conversation surged down the hall in waves. I laid still, straining to make out their words unsuccessfully over the drone of the fan.

"Mama?" Anna stirred, waking. "Who's yelling?"

I reached for her, and she nestled in my arms. "Cici and Darius."

"Are they playing chicken feet?"

The phone vibrated against my hip. "I don't think so, love."

"Should we help them?"

"Not yet. Let's just lie here a bit longer. Okay, sweet girl?"

"Okay," she murmured drowsily, but I knew she was still listening to the crescendo of the conversation taking place in the kitchen. I held my breath, waiting for silence. At last, the argument subsided. I reached for my phone.

Jeremy King
*Christina and I worked on the
landscaping at SeaSplit today,
but we're going to head out soon.
Thought the girls might like to
tell each other bye.*

What about you?

I watched the question float up on the screen as I hit send. My head spun with how quickly I'd typed the words. For fifteen years, I hadn't flirted with anyone except Caleb.

"It's all quiet now, Mama. Can we go to the kitchen? I'm getting hungry."

"Sure love, I am too."

My phone vibrated again.

Jeremy King
*Pretty sure I'd never enjoy
telling you goodbye.*

The living room glowed amber as it did at this time every day. The air was scented with something sweet Cecily was concocting, but the tension mixed in with it could have been cut with a knife. Darius sat at the bar, typing furiously on his phone. Anna sidled up to him on a bar stool. "Are you gonna hunt for eggs with me on Sunday, Darius?"

"Can't, *cher.*"

"Why not?" The hurt and surprise in her eyes could have slapped him, but he didn't even look at her.

"I've got to get back to town tomorrow."

"You're not going to stay for Easter?" Cecily wheeled around from her ingredients.

"No, Momma. I told you earlier I have to leave tomorrow morning."

The mixer thumped on the counter as Cecily added chocolate chips to the batter. "You didn't tell me, Darius."

He exploded. "Damn it, Momma! Why do you think I'm lying all the time?"

My phone was in my hand. I didn't want Anna to see the fallout of this. Even before he was an addict, when he was young and in his right mind, seeing Darius angry was a rare sight. One I didn't relish. I was surprised to hear my voice, sweet and soothing as honey as I touched Anna's cheek. "Hey baby, why don't you go and tell Christina goodbye before she goes to her Papaw's for the weekend? I'll text Jeremy when Cecily's cookies are ready and y'all can come back then, okay?"

Wide-eyed, Anna nodded, concentrating on my face, trying to tune out the raising voices.

I kissed her before she ran through the door.

Jeremy King

Can Anna come over to say goodbye now?

Sure.
What about you?

Tied up rn.
I'll text you when it's OK.

Is everything alright Aimee?

Yes, I'm sorry.
I'll explain when I see you.

OK.
She's here.
They were loud now.

"—and you've gone and sold everything out from under us. I've got no place to call home, Momma."

"Home?" The edge in Cecily's voice was razor sharp. "You haven't truly come home for a long time Darius. I'm not sure if you ever will."

"What the hell does that mean?" His mouth downturned. "What do you want me to do? What are we supposed to do now?"

"We? I don't know what you're going to do Darius." Cecily spat out the words. "You don't have many options left. You've left everyone who loves you. You left me."

When he spoke, his voice was low. "Well now you know what it feels like. Just keep doing what you damn well want to, Momma." He dug his hands in his pockets. "I need to go outside."

I gave Cecily a quick glance, seeing the pain etched on her face, and followed Darius down the stairs. He turned onto the carport, restlessly pulling on a cigarette.

He looked at me, his eyes agitated and hair standing on end. For an instant he was five years old again, upset that the Hot Wheel he slept with under his pillow had fallen off our barge into the lake. A lime green truck with black lightning.

"Sorry 'bout that, cuz."

The sun drowned in the tall grass, melting it to bronze. I sank into the hammock. "Swing with me?"

He eased in beside me. One foot slipped out of its sandal and up beside my shoulder, and the other rocked us. He draped his arm over my legs, leaned his head back and closed his eyes, exhaling smoke.

A memory raced back to me as we swung. We played tag at the campsite where our families went every summer. He chased me around the tent, about to smack into the hammock we'd strung between two pine trees.

I turned and caught him up in my arms before he did.

"Darius, be careful!"

Eyes like saucers, he breathed hard in my face. Five-year-old boy breath. "You saved me." His long legs twined around my waist. He wasn't a baby anymore.

"Shit." Darius flinched in the hammock as ash burned his hand. He flicked the butt away. "Momma's accused me of the craziest things, Aimee cher."

"Like what?" I couldn't trust my voice to be steady.

"It's ridiculous. Things like, I'm spending too much time in the bathroom. Says I never told her that I've gotta go back to town in the morning. She's makin' stuff up and getting forgetful. It's kinda scary."

I would have laughed at the irony if I didn't think I'd cry first. "I hadn't noticed."

"I think she tries to keep it under wraps. She's so secretive now."

I wondered how it was possible to love and despise him so completely and simultaneously.

"Where'd Anna run off to?" His words slurred.

"She's next door playing with a friend."

"Sweet." His eyes softened as he considered this. I remembered his comment earlier in the day to Anna about wanting five daughters. He'd always loved children. In his younger days he had desperately wanted some of his own. The powder blue in his irises focused on me briefly, then faded away. He closed his eyes again, shutting everything out. He'd taken something. What was I supposed to say?

"Tired?"

"Nah, *cher*."

"Why are you doing this?"

He rubbed his forehead with the back of his hand. "What?"

I was losing him. "Why are you doing this to yourself? To all of us?"

"I'm fine, Aimee *cher*," he murmured.

Seagulls cried out, wheeling above the dunes in the dusk.

"Darius…"

I felt worthless. His destruction and dismantling of our family rent my heart, and I couldn't even confront him like Cecily had tried. I cared for him too much. Or maybe I didn't care enough. He was completely under now. I prayed, my foot rocking us on the hammock.

The flood lights came on.

My phone vibrated.

Jeremy King
We're coming over now.

Sounds good.
I'm on the carport in the hammock.

I studied Darius' slackened face. I wondered what he was seeing, and if he was truly asleep or trapped somewhere in between waking and death. I wondered if this would be the last time I'd see him—if I would be the last one to see him alive—if he'd even make it out of the hammock breathing.

Not knowing was the worst.

The King's garage door groaned open. Anna and Christina's voices sang through the air like birdsong. Their feet scuffled on the path.

Anna ran to me with Christina close behind her, smiling.

Jeremy followed at a distance, catching sight of Darius asleep and draped over me in the hammock.

"Is Darius sleeping, Mama?" Anna's hand hovered over his, then recoiled.

I suddenly didn't want any of them to see him like this.

I gave her my warmest smile. "Yes, baby. Can you take Christina upstairs real quick? I'm sure Cici's cookies are ready. Please give her a big hug and help her clean up."

The bait worked. Anna and Christina grabbed each other's

hands and pounded up the stairs.

Jeremy watched them go then continued walking toward me. "Sorry, I didn't wait for your text. I didn't mean to disturb you, but Christina and I need to head out soon."

After being with Darius all day, seeing Jeremy's face—alive and healthy—shocked me.

"It's okay, you're not disturbing anything. This is my cousin, Darius. He's spending the night with us tonight. Thank you so much for letting Anna come over for a bit. It was a little—" I shifted my legs, gauging his responsiveness. Nothing. "—tense over here earlier."

Jeremy considered this, taking us both in. "Is everything okay?"

"No," I said simply, gazing at Darius. "It hasn't been okay for a long time."

Jeremy fixed his eyes on me, iron glinting in the last of the sun. "I'm sorry."

"Me too." I tucked my legs up, sliding them out from under Darius' arm. Jeremy's hand reached out, steadying the hammock for me as I stood. He gave one last look at Darius, and we walked toward the stairs.

"Drugs, right?"

"Yeah. Opioids, benzo, prescriptions. Mostly downers." I considered the empty pocket of my suitcase. "Anything he can get his hands on."

The muscle in Jeremy's jaw jumped.

"Please don't worry, he's harmless." I corrected my statement. "Well, to everyone but himself."

Jeremy gripped the doorknob. His gaze swept me up and down, noting the line between my brows, sunburned shoulders, hands I couldn't stop wringing.

The breeze rose. Smoked sage and brown sugar. I could lose myself standing next to him.

He turned the knob and stepped aside, waiting for me to pass.

"If you say so."

Cecily and the girls were in the kitchen with glasses of milk and a plate of cookies. Busying herself with the last of the dough, Cecily fought bravely to stave off her emotions.

Anna swiveled on her stool. "Jeremy and Christina are gonna be gone all weekend, Mama."

"I know, sweet girl."

"But Daddy said we could have a movie night at our house with all of us soon." Christina chewed a huge bite of cookie. "You like popcorn right, Aimee?"

"I sure do."

Jeremy opened the fridge, grabbed two bottles of Topo and passed me one.

"Do you like scary movies?" Christina asked me.

"Not at all."

"Good."

"Mommy likes adventure movies where the good guys win." Anna licked chocolate off her finger.

"Always," I admitted.

"What's your mom's favorite movie?" Jeremy asked Anna, leaning confidentially across the island.

Straight-faced, Anna told him. "*Die Hard.*"

Jeremy threw his head back and laughed.

Even Cecily was drawn out of her thoughts and chuckled. "Anna Marie, you have never seen *Die Hard* before. I know your Mama wouldn't let you watch it."

"Of course I haven't watched it, but I know it's her favorite movie!"

Christina wriggled on her seat. "Daddy, what happens if the good guys don't win?"

He glanced at me, then back to his daughter. "The good guys always win, sweetheart."

I thought of the nightmare happening in the hammock just underneath us. Darius had been a good guy once, but I wasn't sure if he'd win now.

"You're a good guy, Daddy." Christina grabbed Jeremy's hand across the island. He gave hers a kiss.

"He sure is." The words flew out of my mouth.

He locked eyes with me.

"My Daddy was a good guy, too." Anna piped up.

I pulled her off her barstool and onto my lap. "Best of the best." I caught Cecily's eye over Anna's head. "Cici, Jeremy and I can handle the girls if you need to go outside."

"Thanks, Shug. I know we've had dessert first, but…" She took off her apron, wiping her hands on it. "… I think we'll just peck around for dinner whenever y'all are ready."

Jeremy interjected, "Please don't mind us. Christina and I already had dinner at our house and we're heading out in about ten minutes."

"Girls." I had ten minutes with him. "Do you want to play in Anna's loft before Christina leaves?"

"Yes!" Anna enthusiastically accepted. "We don't need any more adult stuff."

"We'll decide on a movie, Mrs. Rojas," Christina called as they clambered up the stairs.

"I think I'll just step outside for a little bit." Cecily closed the door softly behind her.

Jeremy took another cookie from the plate. "*Is* Cecily gonna be alright out there?"

"I think so. Darius will be out for a while."

The same look he'd given me on the deck reappeared. "When did it all start?"

"I wanted to tell you. It was almost twenty years ago, after Katrina. My Uncle Sam was an EMS responder. You've done something like that here, haven't you?"

"Yeah. I trained as an EMT."

"Did you know the leading cause of death for Katrina wasn't the hurricane itself, but the physiological toll it took on the residents after everything was over?"

"I had no idea."

"The stress my uncle felt—what we all felt—after the storm was unprecedented. Sam died from a massive heart attack several weeks after Katrina."

"I'm so sorry." He meant it.

"You don't say anything insincerely, do you?"

"I try not to."

I looked at my hands, wrapped around my half-drained bottle. He'd held my hand, when? Two weeks ago?

Darius.

I unclasped my hands. "Darius played soccer back then—was great at it. We all thought he'd get a scholarship. The spring after Katrina, he broke his ankle during a game. It was a really bad break, required reconstructive surgery and months of therapy. Darius was in a lot of pain, so the doctor prescribed Oxycontin. And then kept prescribing it. Sam's death wrecked Darius. Between his dad's death and his injury… Darius was fourteen and wanted to numb the pain of it all. And that was only the beginning. It's been a long, terrible downward spiral since then."

Jeremy scratched the back of his head, a sign I was quickly learning meant frustration.

"I'm sorry I worried you with my text. I knew Anna would be safe with you."

"You're very trusting."

"I trust you," I said.

He almost smiled. "As long as you don't trust unhinged family members, I won't worry."

I did smile. "Speaking of unhinged family members, how do you think this weekend will go at your dad's?"

"Who can say? Probably nothing out of the ordinary. We won't make it to an Easter service on Sunday, though. Dad and Lauren don't go to church." He threw his bottle in the trash and reached for mine.

I handed it to him. "I've been praying for them ever since you told me everything."

His expression changed, penetrating through me. "You're something else, Aimee Rojas. You know that?"

The door swung open wide as Cecily returned, flustered, but not alarmed. "He won't wake up."

"He's breathing alright?" Jeremy asked, straightening up.

"Yes, it looks like it. He's just in a deep sleep." She hesitated. "Or whatever."

Jeremy and I shared a look, a breath.

"Christina and I will get out of y'all's hair. Baby?" He called up the stairs. "It's time to hit the road."

"Five more minutes please, Dad?"

"Now, Christina."

General moaning and dissent preceded both girls down the stairs.

"Did y'all decide on a movie for whenever movie night happens?" I asked Anna.

"Not yet."

"Well, y'all can think about it over the weekend." Jeremy steered Christina toward the door, his hand in hers. "The cookies were great, Cecily. Have a Happy Easter, ladies."

"Have a good trip!" Cecily called from down the hall.

Jeremy stopped at the door and turned to me, his voice low. "If you need anything, please call me. We'll come back."

"I know," I nodded. "I will."

His eyes softened. "See you soon, Mrs. Rojas."

I closed the door but left it unlocked, suddenly very tired. "Let's have some dinner, Anna girl, and go back to sleep."

Her hand felt especially small in mine. "Mama, can we spend a night in the hammock sometime? Like Darius?"

My throat tightened as I knelt in front of her on the floor. I pulled her close to me and cried.

Darius, for once true to his word, left on Saturday morning after having spent all of Friday night unconscious in the hammock.

He kissed my cheek. "Love you, Aimee *cher*."

The stench of smoke made me reel. I held him close anyway.

His cheek didn't fill my palm. The skin stretched dry and taut underneath my hand, thin over the bone and stripped of health. Every moment stole permanence from him.

"I love you so much. Please take care of yourself."

His eyes swam and the boy I'd loved my entire life flickered out, vanishing like smoke in front of me. He drove away without saying another word.

I never gathered the courage to ask him about my medicine, and as far as I knew, Cecily hadn't either.

Resurrection Sunday burned hot and bright, a prelude to summer.

Shooing us from the kitchen after lunch, Cecily began meditatively washing the dishes, basking in the solitude of an empty house after a happy meal.

Mary and I sat under umbrellas splayed open on the deck. We could just see Chris and Anna turning off the boardwalk.

"She's making him re-hide the Easter eggs on the beach."

"He'd do it all day if she asked." Mary's rosy lips parted in a grin. "How did the long weekend go?"

Our afternoon at the beach, Darius' outburst, and Jeremy's resolute concern paraded down my list of possible replies.

"Oh…" I answered lamely. "It went."

"Well," Mary said. "There are only five more weeks 'til school is out."

"I'm sure you're ready for a break."

"This is much more than a break, sweetheart. This is the homestretch. Eight more months until I retire."

"Really? Congrats!"

"I'm so ready. Chris and I are going to buy an RV. We'll live out every cliché in our golden years."

I laughed. "Golden years? That can't be, Mary. You're barely fifteen years older than me."

"That puts me at fifty-two, sweetheart. Making you—"

"Please." I straightened in my seat with mock alarm. "Don't. How long have you taught? At least since I was five, I'm sure."

She squinted her eyes, calculating. "Let's see. Here on the island, from 1992 until 2013, then from 2014 to now. Of course that's not counting the years in Louisiana."

"That's a long time." I gave her a side eye, grinning. "I'm still not sure I've forgiven you for leaving Morgan City when y'all did. I know Mom and Cecily haven't. But I'm so glad you're here now."

"God has a plan for everything." Chin planted on her fist, she leaned into the heat of the wind.

I replayed her words in my head. "Why the break between 2013 and 2014, Mary?"

"Christina was born in 2013. I took the year off to help Jeremy. He wanted her to stay at home rather than going to a daycare, but he had to teach, so I offered to take care of her." She hesitated at the astonishment on my face. "He's told you she's adopted, hasn't he?"

"Yes, he told me everything. I just haven't put all the pieces together yet. But it explains why you and Christina are so close."

She turned toward me. "When we moved from Morgan City, the Kings were one of the first families we met down here. Our families were some of the first to build in Sea Isle. Jeremy was a firecracker, and Julia was still such a tiny thing. I think she was only one or two years old."

I understood then. Jeremy and I had both been handed opposite ends of a thread woven long ago which had wound its way around all of us. Now that we were both pulling on it, the tapestry of the past was unraveling, tragic and beautiful.

"After Eileen was killed in the accident, Chris and I tried to look after Jeremy and Julia when they came down in the summers without Jeremiah. Chris helped Jeremy get his summer job at the fire department, and when Julia found out about the baby…" Her voice trailed off. "Did he tell you about his stepmother?"

"Lauren?" I laughed at the thought of her as his stepmother. "I actually met her several weeks ago. She was here to pick up some clothes when Jeremy and Christina were at school."

Shock rippled across her face. "You met her?"

"It wasn't pleasant."

"I'm sure it wasn't. That woman's always had a poisonous tongue. It's wounded all of us in different ways over the years." A shadow crossed her face. "Jeremy told you everything?"

"If you mean about the lead-up to her marrying Jeremy's dad, and her insistence that they not adopt Christina, yes."

"Lauren and Jeremiah's affair devastated him. Then Julia's death and the baby… it was so much. Jeremiah was utterly captivated by Lauren in the worst ways, and he chose her over his family. I know Jeremy felt betrayed, but I also know that the Lord sustained him through all of it. It's the only way he's made it through." Mary looked away toward the blue of the sea. "That was a dark time, but the wounds of the past can't claim permanence in the present. God was working in Jeremy's heart long before then. Preparing him for Christina. For everything." Tenderness warmed her voice. "Jeremy had started coming to West End Bible with us while he worked here in the summers. Chris baptized him in the bay that final summer after he graduated from college. He's like a son to us."

I noted the lack of bitterness in Mary's voice as she talked about Lauren. "You've forgiven her for everything, haven't you?"

"Unforgiveness is even more poisonous than the original wrong done."

"Amen to that."

The light was blinding. I slipped my sunglasses over my eyes.

Mary took my hand. "I'm glad Jeremy confided in you."

"Me too."

"He doesn't open up to many people. He's devoted the last decade of his life to Christina, always putting her first." She paused. "Not that he shouldn't, but I've always prayed that he'd look after himself as well as he does her. He's sacrificed a lot."

My breath hitched in my throat. "He took Anna and I to SeaSpilt a few weeks ago, the same day Lauren was here."

Genuine surprise and wonder spread across her face. Her hand fell from mine. "Did he?" Her eyes were looking at me, but she was far away, thinking of something else. "He hasn't let me or Chris come out to see it yet."

Mary deserved my transparency, especially knowing first-hand the love she and Chris had poured not only into my life, but Jeremy's too. "It's stunning. You're right, he has sacrificed a lot."

"He told you everything at SeaSplit, didn't he?"

"Yes." I rubbed my hands in my lap, remembering how his hand had found its way into mine that night. "I think we feel something for each other."

The smile was huge on her face, and there were tears in her eyes. "I can't say I didn't see it coming."

"What? Mary Cole, are you instigating things?"

"Not at all. He asked about you after you had us over for dinner last month."

"Asked about what, exactly?"

"What I knew about you."

I laughed. "Well, that's only everything."

"I didn't tell him everything. You'll have to share that with him in your own time." Her smile persisted, brilliant. "But among other things, I told him that I love you dearly, and that you deserve to be dearly loved."

"Everyone does, Mary."

"I imagine Jeremy knows the truth of that statement as well as you do. Which, I suspect, is why he didn't ask me anything else."

If you need anything. His nearness had stripped the worry from my mind. *We'll come back.*

"There's something about him. I feel safe when we're together. Like nothing can hurt me."

"He's a good man," she said proudly. "Who loves a good God. I'll be praying for you as you spend more time together."

My thanks were taken away by the breeze.

"Sweetheart, I don't want to influence you or put ideas into your mind that shouldn't belong there, but I'll just say this. Jeremy isn't one to confide, and he's always been loath to share something that isn't finished and perfect. I've known the man since he was nine years old, and I haven't seen his eyes follow anyone around like he's done with you the last few times y'all have been in the same place together."

I looked at the gulf, still fidgeting with my hands. "I'm excited to get to know him more."

"I'm excited for you to get to know each other better. You have more in common than you realize. If anything, I think you would be very good friends."

"Good friends are hard to find."

"Unless they live next door," she grinned.

My phone dinged.

9:12

Jeremy King
Happy Easter.
Hope you had a good weekend.
Christina and I just got back in.

Happy Easter.
Thank you, we did.
How was your dad's?

He seemed happy to see us.
Christina had fun.
We missed being at church though.

Glad nothing crazy happened.
I'm sorry about church.
It was my first time at a
service since Christmas.

Praise God.
Glad you're feeling that well.

Me too.

I went to the window and pulled down the shutters. His truck was in the carport but the house was dark. I slipped back into bed, tugging the blankets close around my chin. The darkness soothed my eyes, and I could just hear Freddie Mercury singing from across the street over the drone of my fan. My phone lit up, ringing. Jeremy.

I shimmied deeper under the sheets. "Hello?"

"Hey. Sorry for the late call. I'm not enough of a millennial to text everything I'm thinking."

I laughed. "What's everything you're thinking?"

"If only there was enough time." I heard the smile in his voice and the surf crashing distantly. He was on his deck. "I wanted to tell you something and ask for your help."

"I'm intrigued. Help with what?"

"Let's start with your weekend first. How did things end up with your cousin?"

"He left yesterday morning. Alive."

"No trouble?"

"No. There weren't any more incidents between him and Cecily. Walking the line between outrage and telling him to leave the house immediately, or holding onto him and begging him to stay and get clean was more difficult than I ever imagined. It's easy enough to stop liking someone but it's another thing entirely to stop loving them."

He made a noise that was both humor and frustration. "You just perfectly encapsulated my weekend."

"You're scratching the back of your head, aren't you?"

He chuckled. "You are feeling better."

"It's your turn. Tell me how everything was at your dad's."

"I told my dad the cottage will be ready for him to put on the market by May." A marked silence. "Christina and I will move to SeaSplit once school is over."

"How long will you stay out there?"

"At least a few months. I'm hoping to list it by the end of the summer."

"You ready for all of that?"

"Yes. Going to Dad's this weekend gave me some clarity. Staying here in the cottage is blurring boundaries I've worked hard to establish and maintain over the past decade. There needs to be greater separation in some areas, so that I can try to restore my relationship with my dad in other ways. And no..." He searched for the right words, "unexpected intrusions into my personal life."

"Of course." Hot, I kicked the covers off. "That's completely understandable. I'm sorry it came down to this."

"Don't be."

"I guess that gives you a month and a half before your move, then?"

"Yeah. This week after work, I'd like to try to get SeaSplit habitable. That's where I'd like to ask for your help. I was wondering if you'd mind picking up Christina from school and if she could stay at your place until I make it back in the evenings?"

"Sure, Anna will love that."

"Thank you so much."

I heard familiar relief. No one wrestled with guilt like a single parent.

I laughed. "You're welcome. And just for future reference, I'm no good with power tools. I'm hoping Anna inherited at least a little proficiency for that kind of thing from her dad, because she definitely won't be getting it from me."

He laughed with me, then grew quiet. "A few months ago, when you weren't feeling well, and Anna would come over… sometimes she'd mention her dad to Christina."

His tender prompt tread all over my heart.

"Caleb." I said his name as if he was lying in bed next to me. "We met at a party in college and were married for twelve years before he died. We loved each other deeply."

I could have stopped there. Summing up a marriage in twenty words isn't difficult until a memory, a touch, a certain smell comes back to punch you in the gut and make you realize that no amount of tears, or time, or words could ever adequately describe what it's like to be completely tethered to another person, heart, flesh and mind—and then to lose it all.

But for Jeremy—and Caleb—I would try.

"Caleb was an engineer. Absolutely brilliant. For example, he barely spoke English when we met but was fluent several months after we started dating."

"Motivation." Jeremy laughed.

I did too, then I continued, "We got married young, right after graduating. We moved to Houston and were both hired by the same company on the same day."

"Valiant?"

"Yes. Work had us traveling all over the place, but most of the time we were able to work together. It was wonderful. We got to see more of each other. Not just time with each other; but we got to see how the other worked, what made us tick. What ticked us off. It made our relationship rich.

"Our healthy personal relationship paid off big, professionally. We were valuable to Valiant, and we truly cared about the company. But when I got pregnant with Anna, we made a promise: nothing would come before our family.

"We requested two months of parental leave after she was born, and after that, we'd both continue to work. We had progressed significantly in our careers, and at that point, our work took us overseas for months at a time. It was thrilling, and of course Anna came with us. We wanted her to see the world through a child's eyes. To be unafraid of anything and to see the beauty of what God has done in this world."

I paused for a breath.

Jeremy's voice sank in the static of the sea. "Go on."

"We alternately lived in Europe and Houston during Anna's early childhood. At the beginning of 2020 we were in Northern Italy for Valiant, setting up a satellite office onsite with a contractor outside of Milan." I turned on my side and adjusted the pillows. "Not many people think of Italy as industrial, but near Bergamo there are a lot of smaller contractors who work with the big guys in the industry. Anyway, I got the sales team up and going with Clint and was scheduled to leave earlier than Caleb for Houston. There's a large convention held in town every year in the spring, and I needed to prepare.

"When Anna and I left Italy, it was the end of January. Caleb was supposed to come back the first week of March. Of course we'd all been hearing about Covid, but even in Europe at that point, nobody cared. For all the months we were in Italy, Anna,

Caleb and I had been staying at a small family inn in Bergamo, typical of the area. The owner and his family adored us, and we adored them. Caleb stayed on with them after Anna and I left."

I stopped. The next words were always difficult to say, no matter how many lives they lived in my mouth.

"No one was ever able to tell me if Caleb got sick first or our host did. With all the international travel coming in and out of Milan, it would have been difficult to say. All I know is that they ended up in the hospital together, and that Caleb drove them there. High fever, terrible chills, difficulty breathing. He Facetimed me several times from the hospital. Our host passed away three days after they were admitted. A week in, Caleb didn't call anymore. Later, I learned he died on March 12, when concerts and sporting events were starting to get canceled here in the States. By the end of March, more than two thousand people died in Bergamo alone. The morgues were full, and everyone was afraid to help the locals. Afraid to transfer bodies. At first, I didn't know where Caleb's body was. I didn't even know who to call. I struggled with how to tell Anna. She was four."

The silence on the line swelled.

"Jeremy?"

"I'm here." Almost palpable peace packaged in two words.

"It was months before the US government would be able to get any reliable form of official communication from Bergamo. Caleb was technically classified as a missing US citizen, even though we'd had confirmation from the hospital that he'd died. In August, I was notified of his burial in the graveyard of a small local church. All his personal effects were incinerated. I didn't get anything back."

The best of Queen echoed from our neighbor's house.

Jeremy let out his breath slowly on the other end of the line. "Losing Julia and raising Christina has been difficult enough on its own. I can't begin to fathom the pain you must have gone through, losing Caleb."

My hand bunched the duvet tight against my stomach. "You're a really good dad, Jeremy." I was certain he didn't hear it enough; positive I hadn't told Caleb enough. "Christina doesn't understand the blessing of everything you've done and how you've loved her, but she will someday."

"Aimee…" His voice faltered. "Thank you. Again."

"You're welcome, again." I wanted to be with him. Touch his face. See if the stubble on his jaw would scrape on me like the grit in his voice.

"I want to see you, Aimee."

I held my breath. I was able to pin the exact moment ten minutes ago when I knew he'd be frustrated, scratching the back of his head, but I couldn't comprehend how he'd been able to read my thoughts over the phone.

"I wanted to talk to you about the next few weeks because I didn't want any of this to come as a surprise to you. The pace of getting to know you has been wonderful, and I'd hate to think I'm changing it somehow by asking, but I just want to make sure that you're…" He hesitated. "Is this okay? You're braver than I know, but you've also been through a lot, and I don't want to complicate things for you."

Silence thrummed in my ears as I waited for his next words.

"I always want to be honest—with everyone—but especially with you. I've spent most of my life waiting for God only knows what, but all of a sudden, you're here, and I think that he's answering a lot of prayers right now. Impossible prayers."

The ceiling fan overhead turned, cutting through the air but failing to change the play of light and shadow in my bedroom.

"Nothing's impossible, remember?"

His breath was sharp in my ear. "You're right."

"Jeremy—"

"The last thing I want is for you to think I'm taking advantage of you."

"That would honestly be the last thing I'd think."

"Why?"

His bluntness caught me off-guard and for a moment, I was an executive answering quickly and with authority, matching his forwardness. "I find it difficult to believe that anyone would want to shoulder my past and my marriage to Caleb—not to mention the sagging boobs and postpartum belly from the babies we had—only to take advantage of me." I stopped, wondering if I'd said too much for once. "If anything, you're the brave one."

"Babies?" I heard surprise and compassion in the way he asked it.

"I had a miscarriage five months into our marriage. Our first daughter."

Across the street, Freddie effortlessly scaled the octave.

"Maybe I should be the one asking if you really want this, Jeremy."

"Last month, you told me I didn't know a lot about you."

I couldn't hear the music outside anymore. "Yeah?"

"If they're a part of you, I want all of the unknowns, Aimee."

His words sank into me, and my eyes darted involuntarily, searching for the way my heart was transforming as if it was visible on the ceiling. "Do you know what you're saying?"

"Yes." He gasped out a laugh. "Although I didn't anticipate our phone call getting quite this deep."

"One thing leads to another."

"It certainly does. We can take our time."

"Go slow."

"Go slow. I'm moving, for Pete's sake." He exhaled heavily. "SeaSplit will have me running this week, but why don't we have that movie night Christina and Anna cooked up on Friday?"

"That sounds great."

"And… do you think Cecily might be up for watching the girls if you and I were to head out on our own sometime?"

"Just us?"

"I think we've earned some time to ourselves. We'll celebrate you feeling better."

My heart beat faster. "I'll ask."

"I hope you will. Good night, Mrs. Rojas."

"Good night, Jeremy."

The next week flew.

Anna and Christina played in the loft upstairs while Cecily and I put away the dinner dishes.

"Cici, I wanted to ask if you'd be able to watch the girls so that Jeremy and I could—"

"Sure can."

"I haven't told you—"

"Doesn't matter what or when, I'm available."

"Has he—?"

"Nope, I've just been anticipating this moment for the past three months ever since I laid eyes on the man. Now that the time is finally here, I'm ready to shout hallelujah!"

Cecily hugged me, sudsy hands and all, and for a reason too wonderful to comprehend, I began to both laugh and cry.

Clint Myers
Just sent you the final round
of invoices for the deal.

Thanks for the heads up,
I'll approve them ASAP.

We're closing week after next.
I'm putting together a customer
appreciation shindig in your neck
of the woods for Cinco de Mayo.

Well done.
I've had virtually no interaction with
these people, they've only seen my signature.
I doubt they need to see my face.

I do.

Hasn't changed much since the last
time you saw me, I assure you.
Janelle can't come?

Wouldn't be appropriate.

Where?

Grand Galvez.
Cocktails and whatever else they want.
I'll pick you up at 7.

That late?

Per usual.
You're getting rusty.

I'll put it down.

Bless you.

"Daddy did *not* like the countertops. And honestly, I didn't either. They were too…" Christina waved her spoon in the air. "Overstated."

"Really?" I set a bowl of strawberries on the bar in front of her and Anna. All the King's dishes were hand-thrown pottery, every piece signed on the bottom, the artist's name etched into the clay.

"Should they be understated?" Anna asked seriously, spooning the last of her macaroni.

"They need to be *right*," Christina asserted. "Yesterday, Daddy showed me a picture and told me the guys brought the wrong ones, not the ones he ordered. So, they're bringing the right ones today. Daddy took off work extra early to finish putting the cabinets in the bathrooms downstairs so they can install all the countertops at once."

Anna's eyebrows scrunched together. "But we're still having movie night over here tonight, aren't we?"

"Yep. Daddy's helping Andre's guys install the countertops right now. Andre's our contractor. Last night on the phone, Andre told Daddy that between all of them working together they could finish the job in three hours. Daddy told Andre they better, because he's literally waited decades for tonight."

Anna's eyes widened. "He must really like *Star Wars*."

"Oh," Christina said, mouth full, "he's wanted to show me *Star Wars* practically since I was born." She swung her legs as she sat on the stool, comfortable in the only home she'd ever known.

The French doors opened.

I hadn't seen Jeremy for the entire week outside of exhausted *hello's* and handing off Christina in the dusk of evening.

"Daddy!" Christina jumped off her barstool. "You're home early."

"Sure am, squirt. We're all squared away with the countertops." He hugged her shoulders and kissed her forehead.

"Are you ready for *Star Wars*, Jeremy?" Anna asked. "Christina said you were really excited for movie night."

"You have no idea, Anna Marie." He flashed a rare smile at her and gave me a wink. "I've got to freshen up and change, and then we'll be set."

The girls whooped with excitement.

He set his bag on the floor. "Christina, is your room all tidied up? You know the drill."

"Oh, not yet, Dad. Anna, come help me."

Abandoning their empty bowls, the girls skittered down the

hallway and turned into Anna's room.

"I've always thought it was sweet of you to give her the primary bedroom and take the loft for yourself."

"I like the view better from upstairs, and she deserves it. After all, she runs the place." A playful look crossed his face. "Are you ready for *Star Wars*?"

"I am." I leaned across the counter. "And to round things out, we have mac and cheese with a side of strawberries for dinner. How does that sound?"

Moving across the granite, his hands gathered mine. I watched my fingers lace reflexively through his, like we'd been reaching for each other for years.

"Perfect."

Anna spit her toothpaste into the sink. "But why did Leia's hair look like that, Mama?"

"I don't know sweet girl, I guess that's just the style in space."

"But she had ears, right?"

I gave her a funny look. "Of course she had ears."

"Well, I don't know. She could have been an alien pretending to be human."

I watched myself smoothing moisturizer onto my face and neck in the mirror. Only a few weeks ago, I'd felt alien in my own body.

"She's human, love. She just had a wacky hair style."

"Well, I would never do my hair like that." Anna hopped into my bed. "Are you sleeping better now, Mama?"

I slid under the sheets next to her. "I am, love. At least five or six hours a night every night."

"Do you still have headaches sometimes?"

"Sometimes. Not as much."

"Are you a hundred percent yet?"

"Mmmm…" I shifted my eyes to the side, thinking. "About ninety percent."

"Much better!" She wrapped her arms around my neck. "You know what I'd like?"

"Ice cream?"

"A sister."

I gave her a long look. "I'm not sure I'll be able to help you out with that, Anna girl."

"No, not one from your belly. One like Christina."

"Christina's a very sweet girl, isn't she?"

"Mama, you and Jeremy like each other, don't you?"

I turned off the light. "Yeah. We're friends."

Her breath dampened my cheek. "Do you love each other?"

"We care very much about each other and you girls, so yes. I'd say we do. Don't you love Christina and Jeremy, too?"

"Well, yeah, of course I do, but I don't mean like that. I don't mean like an 'I love everybody' love. I mean like I want to love only this person kind of love."

"You're a smart one, Anna Marie."

"Do you love Jeremy like you loved Daddy?"

The pause I needed to collect the right words took too long for her.

"Mama?"

"I could never love anyone exactly like I loved Daddy, baby."

"Oh."

Confusion and disappointment felled her voice. But then I heard the silence of the wheels turning in her head.

"What do you mean 'exactly?'"

"God made us all differently, bug. Because of that, we get to think of special and unique ways to love each person. I know you love being with me, so I try to give you the most of my time to show you I love you. You know I love seashells, so that's why you'd always bring some back for me from your walks with Cici when I was so sick. Remember?"

"I never thought about it like that." She was quiet for a while, and her breathing deepened, becoming more rhythmic. "Mama?" she asked suddenly.

"Yes, love?"

"Jeremy gives you the most of his smiles, even more than Christina. Maybe that's how he shows you he loves you."

"Maybe."

She said nothing else.

Listening to the distorted tune of "God Only Knows," I fell asleep beside her.

I shut my laptop and hit call.

"Hey." I hated that I sounded breathless.

"It's good to hear your voice."

"Likewise. What's up with the last few sales orders you had me sign off on? I had to make twelve corrections."

"Not sure. I'll get with accounting to have them revalidate everything before we hand them off."

"Alright, thanks."

"You're welcome." His silence was awkward, the familiar rhythm of our typically short exchanges regarding work altered somehow. "I have to run, Aimee."

"Sure. Talk to you later, Clint."

I was startled to taste blood on my lip as I ended the call.

Maren Williams
You don't know how happy
I am to see you next month!

Same, sister.
Are you still in France?

Yes, for the next two weeks,
then back to Nashville.
My wardrobe can't handle
how long I've been here.
I have to practically blindfold
myself to avoid the temptation
of my neighborhood patisserie.

I can only imagine.

How's everything on the island?

Great.
A lot to fill you in on.

Tell me!

It's too much for text.

I'm not buying that.
I will, however, overlook your
fallacious assertion for the time being.

Are you reading William Lane Craig
in your downtime, again?

One can always tell, can't one?

Always.

"Kayla called yesterday. I don't think I told you yet." Cecily's eyes dimmed with concern.

"No, you didn't. What did she say? How's Tyler?"

"He's not doing well. He's entered a hospice facility where they have twenty-four-hour care. Kayla said taking care of him at home had become too much for her to handle."

"Can she spend the night with him?"

"I believe so, but she's also gotten herself a different Airbnb near the facility. Her mother is coming to stay with her for the next few weeks." Cecily pressed the plunger on the French press and brought it to me at the table. "She said Darius texted and asked her about Tyler."

"What did she tell him?"

"Just that he was doing worse. He asked if he could come over again."

"She said no?"

"She didn't reply at all, and she never heard back from him."

I glanced outside. Cloud cover had saturated the morning sky, but the sun promised to eliminate the haze.

"He hasn't texted you?"

"No. I haven't heard from him in over a week." Cecily peppered her scrambled eggs, physically trying to shake out the weight of her thoughts. "Are you looking forward to your date tomorrow?"

I couldn't help blushing. "I am."

"Nervous?"

"Of course. I haven't been on a first date in almost seventeen years."

Notes of dark chocolate and citrus drifted toward me as she lifted her mug. "It's amazing, how much better you've looked and acted over the past few weeks. It's been a beautiful privilege to watch God work by using you and Jeremy to heal one another."

I'd grown accustomed to my eyes welling with tears on a whim, but never enjoyed it.

"It's okay, isn't it? That Jeremy and I are doing this?"

Cecily's hand closed over mine.

"Of course it is, Shug." She spoke the next words with the

delicacy of a surgeon. "You're not married anymore, Aimee. You're not betraying anyone's trust or denying anything from your past." Her hand was warm on my face as she wiped the tears from it. "You and Caleb built a beautiful life together, and that itself is the perfect foundation for whatever comes next with you and Jeremy King. You're only building onto what you had with Caleb and honoring it, not tearing anything down."

I swallowed hard. "Thank you, Cici."

"I love you, Aimee." She pulled me toward her and kissed my forehead. "And don't you forget it."

I opened my closet, thankful I'd finally hung the linen dress Maren acquired for me during our visit to the Strand. I held it up. Black with thin straps and buttons all the way down the front from the sweetheart neckline to the full skirt. Jeremy hadn't said where we were going, and I hadn't worn a dress in months. I tried it on and examined my reflection in the mirror. The dress fit me perfectly.

"Three for three, Maren," I muttered under my breath. The golden gleam of my wedding band glinted in the glass as I turned. I stopped and slid it off my finger.

Caleb and I bought our wedding bands several weeks before the wedding, giddy twenty-two-year-olds out of our heads with desire for each other.

"Regular, white or rose gold?" Dark, thick lashes framed his eyes, only making the gold in them shine brighter.

"Regular?" I giggled. "You mean yellow?"

"Technicalities, Aimee Lynn Broussard." He kissed me breathless in the middle of the shop.

"Says the engineer. I like the regular gold ones. I mean yellow gold," I laughed, giving the plain bands the briefest pass of my eyes. The gold I wanted most ringed his irises. "When we're old and wrinkly it'll remind me of how your eyes look right now, today."

"I can't wait to grow old with you." He kissed me again, handing his credit card to the jeweler who hurried away, smiling to herself.

My fingers closed over the ring.

I rifled through my suitcase, reaching for the bottom left corner where it stayed. The cover was compact leather, zipped shut and hardly bigger than my hands. Almost transparent pages shuffled in my hands as I opened the book.

His writing was in the margins. Small, precise block letters. All capitalized. Meticulous.

I flipped to the beginning and found the frontispiece, brushing my fingertips across it as I read:

This Holy Bible belongs to Caleb Fernando Rojas Rodriquez

On the inside of the cover was a clear vinyl pocket for a business card or ID. I slipped my wedding band into it, then slowly zipped the cover back up. I hugged the Bible to my chest; eternally grateful he'd forgotten to pack it before the last trip to Bergamo.

I bowed my head. "Jesus, be with me. Thank you for Caleb. Thank you for Jeremy. Be with us."

The phone dinged.

Jeremy King
Just sent Christina up.
I'm downstairs.

I dropped my phone back onto the bed. Jeremy had said he'd bring his, and I didn't want the distraction of mine tonight. I looked in the mirror once again.

Black dress. Minimal make-up on sun-slapped skin. Hair down. Lip gloss two shades darker than my natural hue. Small gold hoops in my lobes and a single diamond in one helix.

Sliding my feet into the never-worn wedges from the Strand, I grabbed my wallet and keys and slipped them into my pocket.

I ducked into Cecily's room across the hall. "I'm out, Cici. Thanks for watching the girls tonight."

She looked up, appraising me. The aquamarine sparkled. "Of course. Y'all have fun."

Christina and Anna were in the kitchen.

"You look really pretty, Aimee." Christina's eyes were full of unguarded adoration, and I blushed.

"You do, Mama." Anna agreed.

"Thanks, girls. Mind Cici, okay? And go to bed early, please don't stay up too late waiting for us." I hugged each of them and turned toward the door.

"We won't." Christina giggled then whispered to Anna, but not quietly enough for me not to hear, "I think Dad will kiss her tonight."

I was glad they couldn't see the smile which spread across my face.

I gasped as I stepped out, catching sight of the sunset. The sky was glorious. The sun hovered well above the horizon, melting clouds into molten gold across the sky.

"Thank you, Jesus," I prayed under my breath. I crossed the deck and headed toward the stairs.

Jeremy was waiting for me on the path between the cottages. He wore a well-tailored white shirt with two—no—three buttons undone. Sleeves rolled up to his elbows. Pressed khaki shorts. With one hand, he held the handle of a huge picnic basket. His other hand stayed buried in his pocket. I faltered, unsure if I could walk down the stairs.

But I did.

The wood hummed under my feet, and he turned to greet me.

The deep blue glow in his eyes mesmerized me, called me close to him.

He said: "You are beautiful."

Not, *you look beautiful or you're beautiful in that dress,* but the highest, purest, most mathematical statement of truth one can give in the formula of $X = Y$.

God is love.

I am Aimee.

You are beautiful.

He gave me no time to thank him. He offered me his arm and I took it, resting my hand in the crook of his elbow. "We're headed to the beach at SeaSplit, if that's okay with you. The chef is mediocre, but the view is killer."

"That sounds wonderful. And I don't believe what you said about the chef."

He tucked me into the passenger seat and drove. The windows in his truck were down, the air strong and sweet with salt. The waves crashed louder as the tide pulled back out to sea.

He glanced at me. "How are you feeling?"

"Good. Great, actually. I can't believe how much has changed in just the past few weeks."

"Me neither."

We were on the property now, navigating the long gravel road. The horses were nowhere to be seen as we pulled up under the house.

He parked on the driveway. "We'll stay outside tonight, I think."

I tumbled out of the truck before he could open the door for me.

The turf was growing together nicely, and the springiness of the grass begged me to take my shoes off. I tucked my wedges against the garage and met Jeremy as he came around the tailgate. Contentment radiated from his eyes, and I found that my hand was already in his as we began our short walk to the beach. Beyond the lawn, a boardwalk cut through the dunes, new since my last time at SeaSplit. The sand warmed my feet as we walked through the grass where the boardwalk ended.

On our left, Jeremy had built a makeshift fire pit out of large rocks and driftwood. A grill plate leaned against a pile of firewood. Behind all of this, between the pit and the grass, a blanket was stretched and anchored by four large rocks, facing the water. He dropped my hand and set the picnic basket down on the blanket.

"Jeremy, it's amazing. You didn't have to do all of this."

He gave me a glance over his shoulder and winked. "Wanted to." He picked up two pieces of firewood. "Have a seat. Crack open the basket and set us up with something to drink while I get the fire started." As I opened the hamper, he looked over at me and added, "Don't cry."

"You're getting too good at this." I said, not obeying his last words.

In the picnic basket, I found two of the hand-thrown dinner plates from the King's kitchen cabinets and silverware wrapped in spotless cotton napkins. Four bottles of Topo Chico almost frozen to the touch accompanied stemless crystal champagne flutes, also chilled. Ready for the fire, quartered golden potatoes, seasoned and already baked once, and marinated salmon were enveloped in foil. A teak bowl filled with strawberries and blueberries and a bar of Vietnamese dark chocolate followed for dessert.

I swiped my tears away. "Mediocre chef, my ass."

He laughed out loud at that. "Make no assumptions, Mrs. Rojas. You haven't tasted it yet."

The fire blazed, and I handed him a flute filled with Topo.

He sat down beside me. "To answered prayers, and your good health."

Our glasses clinked. The sky blushed fuchsia now, and the clouds towered high over the gulf to our right. Jeremy tended to the food on the grill.

Everything was delicious.

I told him so.

He waved the compliment away with his hand and opened the chocolate.

Another log went on the fire.

We talked for hours about absolutely nothing of consequence. After that, we talked about movies our parents let us watch as kids that we would never let our kids watch. How much simpler life was before the internet and unhindered connectivity. He told me about his students, why he both loved and hated teaching. I confided in him about my growing reluctance to throw myself back in the career I'd spent over a decade building.

I finished lamely, "I don't know if I want to continue in sales. At least, not in the oil industry."

"What drew you to it in the first place?"

"Back then, it was fun. I enjoyed meeting all kinds of people and hearing their stories." It was terrifyingly easy to smile at him. "Still do. But I don't know. The industry is different now and I find myself wanting to invest in something more meaningful."

"Those sound like valid reasons to consider a change."

"Thanks. In any case, work is coming to me next weekend. Clint let me know that we're hosting a customer appreciation event at the Grand Galvez for the most recent account we're closing."

"You don't sound very excited about it."

"These things always end up devolving into some kind of debauched frat party, no matter where in the world we host them. There's too much booze, inhibitions become loosened and with stress and high stakes eliminated from the equation, seedier activities take place."

"Definitely doesn't sound like an environment you'd go for."

"I had Caleb with me then, and he didn't enjoy attending events like that either. We had a system down for bailing out early. I'd start slurping my drink really loudly if I was ready to leave, and he'd kiss my shoulder if he was ready."

Jeremy's gaze caressed my bare shoulders. "What if you were wearing a sweater or blazer or something?"

"He had another more subtle yet highly effective way to let me know he was ready to head out."

A smile pulled at the corners of his mouth as he studied the shifting movement of the fire, watching the sparks explode and fly into oblivion. "Speaking of social events we dread, I have to go to Miami at the end of May for a week-long mathematics continuing education seminar."

"That sounds terrible. And you'll be so busy with the houses. Is it mandatory?" I asked.

"Unfortunately, yes. That's why they have it in Miami. Makes the tedium go down easier."

He laid beside me on his back, feet to the fire. "Talk about frat party vibes. You'd never believe how teachers can behave outside the classroom."

"Not your scene?"

"Not in a very long time, thank God."

The warm breeze picked up, perfumed with the scent of impending rain somewhere offshore. From where I sat, I could just see the glint of lights on the oil rigs winking across the water. The heat of the fire was heavenly against my outstretched legs.

"Are you going to stay in the cottage past June?" Jeremy asked, eyes closed.

"I don't know. I haven't told David anything either way. I'm sure he'll need to know soon, though." A twinge of anxiety hurtled through my head. "I think about how many places Anna's had to call home. How many schools she's attended. I know the constant moving will wear on her as much as it has on me, sooner or later. She really enjoys being here on the island."

The surf soothed, washing ashore. The hem of my skirt had folded on itself in the sand. Jeremy's hand found and unearthed it. His fingers followed several inches of the silk binding, thumbing it back and forth like worry beads.

"And so do I. But I'm not sure what's next, Jeremy. There are so many unknowns. Isn't that bad for someone who's thirty-seven? It's not like I could have even anticipated a Plan B after everything that's happened over the last few years."

He rolled onto his side and gazed up at me. "You remember what I said about your unknowns?"

"Yes," I said quietly.

"I wouldn't sweat it. God is in your corner. None of it has been surprising to him. Besides, you're an intelligent woman. I'm certain anything you put your mind to, will prosper." He rolled onto his back again and rubbed his eyes with the heels of his palms.

"What time is it, Jeremy?"

Suddenly, lightning cracked the clouds in front of us, scorching the night sky.

He jumped to his feet. "Time to go!"

Thunder rolled across the waves, clashing with the sound of the surf. I threw the things we hadn't finished back into the basket, and Jeremy used the teak bowl to douse the fire with sand as the first heavy rain drops landed on our shoulders. Everything, including the blanket, found its way back into the cavernous picnic basket. Jeremy caught it up and we sprinted through the grass back to the boardwalk. The rain pelted us, and the lights on the truck flashed as Jeremy unlocked it. We slammed our doors at the same time, winded and laughing at each other in the dark.

"Nothing like cardio after dinner." He turned over the engine, his face illuminated by the glow of the dash lights.

"Are you soaked?" he asked.

"Not completely, but definitely damp."

"Ready to head back then, Mrs. Rojas?"

"Sure."

He turned on the heater and navigated the highway back to Sea Isle as the rain hammered down in relentless sheets.

"I'm glad we don't have far to go."

"Me too," he agreed. The torrent kept his eyes on the road, but a quiet joy emanated from him, filling the interior of the truck. Twinkling lights strung underneath the King's deck beckoned us to take refuge from the storm. His truck rolled into the carport, sudden silence deafening in the absence of rain pounding against the roof. We wouldn't make it to either of our stairs without getting drenched.

12:04

Jeremy eyed the clock on the dash, then me.

"Want to try and wait it out on the porch for a bit?"

"Why not?"

As I stepped out of the truck, I realized my wedges were tucked safely against the garage at SeaSplit. The familiar sound of music drifted from across the street, cutting through the rain. Defying the fury of the storm, "Neon Moon" couldn't have been clearer if Brooks and Dunn were on a stage in front of us.

"Every night's a party for them." Jeremy ran his hand through his sopping hair, standing it up on end.

"Seems like it. I had to buy a box fan to drown out the bass the first week we were here. How does Christina sleep through it?"

"That girl could sleep through nuclear warfare. And you? I'm certain it's not conducive to a good night's rest."

"Decidedly not."

"But the good Lord turns nuisances into blessings." His hand found mine for the second time that night. I couldn't decide which, but I was confident the way he was looking at me would either make me fly or faint. "Want to dance?"

I put my other hand on his shoulder. "Despite the persistent mean mug, you're really a glass-half-full person, aren't you?"

"Truth be told, I'd prefer the whole bottle. But I've learned to be resourceful with whatever I get." He spun me out and drew me back again, holding me close.

We said nothing and I relaxed in his arms. The rain kept coming down and the two-step eventually changed to a waltz, a song I wasn't familiar with.

"I don't know this one."

"It's new. Pat Barrett, "Shelter."" He lowered his head and spoke softly against my hair. "Sorry you're up so late again. I thought we'd make it back in before the storm blew in tonight, but I guess we got distracted."

"It was wonderful."

"Being distracted?"

I wanted him to know. "Being with you." His arm tightened around me, and we danced slowly, taking in each other's touch and listening to the persistent pulse of billions of drops of water. An enormous luna moth guarded a dark corner of the ceiling, shielded from the downpour.

"I have to confess, you're not the first girl I've danced with down here." His jaw flexed against my temple.

"Really?"

His voice rumbled through me, somehow louder than both the storm and the music. "Really. I spent many sleepless nights on this driveway, trying to get Christina to fall asleep. Trying to calm my own heart. I felt so out of my depth and alone. And foolish for trying to raise an infant by myself. I cried out to God so many times down here, told him that I'd made a mistake and begged him to help me. I thought of his silence as an absence, that he wasn't going to answer my prayers. But now, ten years later, I'm on the same driveway in the middle of the night, thankful to be awake. I was so wrong. I wanted an immediate answer to prayer, but in the waiting, God gave me something better."

"He's good like that."

We weren't dancing anymore. I saw my hand resting inside his shirt, like it belonged there. He'd spoken evenly enough, but his heart pounded underneath my palm. I didn't want to leave him. I wanted to follow him into his house, lie down beside him, and fall asleep in his arms. Nothing more. The thought as it played out in my mind hit me with force, both astonishing and yet entirely unsurprising.

"Rain's not gonna let up for a while. We'll both have to run for it. Should we say good night, Mrs. Rojas?"

"I don't want to."

As soon as the words left my mouth, I realized how they sounded underneath the weight of his empty house. He made no move to let me go but instead glanced down, his tact buying several seconds to reply.

"Aimee—" He began, then said something I knew he hadn't intended to ask at all. "Where are your shoes?"

Appeasing the urge I'd had for weeks; my fingertips brushed the sandpaper stubble up his jaw. I let my lips sweep his cheek—inhaled the scent of rain and brown sugar and smoke on his skin—kissing it before I answered near his ear. "On the carport at SeaSplit."

I knew I would never forget the look on his face as I turned and—taking his suggestion— made a run for it.

Sunlight spilled through the shutters I'd left open before tumbling into bed, waking me up. I yawned down the hallway and into the living room before Anna, a rarity. Cecily was curled up on the sofa, cup of coffee in hand. My wedges perched on the countertop, a miraculous apparition from SeaSplit. Beside them, a bouquet of gardenias in a hand-thrown vase. A small envelope with "A" scrawled across it in a looping, careless line leaned against it.

"Those were on the deck outside the door this morning." The smile in Cecily's voice was obvious. "Looks like you had a good time last night, Shug."

"It was lovely." I picked up the note. "He cooked for me on the beach at SeaSplit, and then we had to run for the car because of the rain. Tried to wait it out by dancing to the neighbor's music in the carport but failed miserably. We broke my curfew."

"Sounds romantic."

"It was."

I opened the envelope.

I hope you'll accept my sincerest apologies for keeping you out so late. However, please know I've paid my dues, as our last few moments together kept me up all night.
X, J

I was grinning like an idiot.
Cecily chuckled. "A very good time."

"Did he kiss you, Mama?" Anna rubbed her eyes.

"No, love. Is Christina awake?"

"Dang it," she yawned. "No, she's still asleep."

"Want to help me make some chocolate chip pancakes? I bet the smell will convince her to get her out of bed."

My daughter's eyes lit up. "Yes!"

Clint Myers
Check your inbox.

Clint's text sent me to my laptop after breakfast. Anna and Christina devoured the chocolate chip pancakes with delight and sat on the couch, enthralled with *Garfield*. Back at my desk in the bedroom, I culled my emails.

It's already time to ESign?

Yes.
You're still technically the lead on this.
After your OK it heads to Hoff's desk.

It's Saturday.
I'll review it on Monday.
This folio has to be airtight,
and I need to check the invoices again.

The clock told me it was 9:36. "And I was having a pleasant morning."

I tried to evade the nagging guilt of being absent for the entirety of this sale. Even though my fingerprints were hardly on the deal, I still felt compelled to do my due diligence. The file was hundreds of pages long, and I began my review. Clint had done an excellent job closing the sale and landing Valiant's biggest customer to date. An hour passed as I continued skimming the document. Order of sale. Purchase orders. Commission compensation. The usual legal jargon. The contract was solid. I opened up Valiant's internal invoicing system to double-check the purchase orders. Perused the numbers. I squinted, trying to ignore the beginnings of a migraine which rose like a specter from the combination of staring at the computer too long and the angel's share of a late night.

My door opened behind me, letting in the sound of Anna's footsteps.

"What d'you need, baby?" I asked absentmindedly, not looking away from the screen.

"That's a loaded question coming from you, beautiful," Jeremy replied.

I whirled around in my chair. He leaned against the doorframe, arms crossed and somehow impossibly more attractive with minimal sleep and in a paint-stained Henley than he'd been last night.

"Hi. Thanks for returning my shoes. When did you go back to SeaSplit?"

"Right after you left."

"In the rain?"

"Let's just say I felt highly motivated. I dropped them off this morning and then got in a couple more hours of work at the house since Christina was over here."

My phone dinged.

Clint Myers
Call me now.

I flipped it over as I stood.

"Busy?" he asked.

"No, annoyed."

"You don't look annoyed."

I leaned against the doorjamb opposite him. The house was quiet.

What do you need?

He frowned. "What did you say?"

I realized I'd spoken aloud only after his back straightened off the frame and his arms uncrossed.

My heartbeat steadied. I asked the question.

"What do you need, Jeremy?"

Vulnerable.

"You're sure you want me to answer that?"

I couldn't focus anymore. I drank in his eyes, his mouth, the way he smelled like just waking up and brown sugar and sweat.

I nodded.

One of his hands landed like a sigh on the small of my back, guiding me to him. Our foreheads kissed; his nose brushed mine. His other hand cradled my head, tilting it to the left. The room rocked and I closed my eyes.

His lips moved gently by my ear. "I needed to tell you good night, Mrs. Rojas. Didn't get the chance last night."

"You've told me good night before."

"Tonight, then," he whispered, the heat of his mouth burning against my neck.

The phone dinged.

"God willing, every night," softly on my collarbone.

Dinged again.

The silk strap of my camisole slipped down my shoulder as he kissed it. He made me forget how to breathe.

I opened my eyes and saw light dancing on my bed, scattered by the fronds of the palm trees whipped by the wind outside.

"Jeremy," I managed.

He understood—either the fear or desire in my tone, I'm unsure which—and let go of me. We stood, watching and wanting each other for far too many seconds.

He cleared his throat. "The girls are playing outside with Cecily. I'll join them and get Christina since you've got a full plate this morning. Someone really wants to get a hold of you."

His rare smile flashed, daring me to reconsider every shred of self-control I'd mustered.

"But your phone's blowing up. I can see why you're annoyed."

"Jeremy King."

He took a step toward me. His fingers climbed my arm, sliding under the fallen strap of my camisole. He brought it up over the swell of my shoulder, securing it in place.

"Thank you," I murmured.

"The pleasure's all mine."

"No, it's not. Trust me on that. And while I'm thinking of it,

I'm having a very difficult time reconciling your definition of 'slow' with mine."

He blushed. "Should I spell it out?"

"I thought you were a math teacher."

"Am I? Looking at you scrubs my memory."

"Yep. I'm sure you know all about lines. Angles. Improper fractions."

"Tangents. Seriously, now. You're working?" He took my hand and led me down the hall toward the kitchen.

"Yeah, Clint's on my case to sign off on the biggest fish we've landed in Valiant's history. I'm neck-deep in this sales order."

A thought crossed my mind.

"Speaking of reconciling… would you mind looking over it with me sometime? I'm not sure if I should chalk my trepidation up to nerves or residual brain fog, but something just seems off to me, even though everything adds up. Accounting's put it through the wringer, and I've had to make more corrections than I'd like."

"Happy to, as long as it's okay to have someone outside the company look at it."

"Sure. It's just math."

"'Just math.' Tell that to my kids at school." He let my hand go. "Why don't you and Anna come over tonight and I'll give it a look? I'd ask you over for dinner but we're only having cereal."

"What kind of cereal?"

"Cheerios. Cornflakes. There's oatmeal. And fruit."

"I love oatmeal and fruit."

"Then come." He opened the door and stepped outside. "And I can tell you good night."

Clint's name lit up the screen of my phone.

"It's Saturday. None of the execs will be looking for this until

Monday morning. Why are you in such a huff?"

"Call me impatient." He exhaled heavily. "I miss you."

"No, you don't. You just want my digital Hancock on this doc."

A deep laugh from him. "You're right. I want it back for Hoff to sign by nine on Monday at the latest."

Silence between us on the line. I could hear birds singing. He was sitting on his patio.

"Are you smoking? You quit."

"Would you be angry if I was?"

"You don't need me to tell you what you already know."

"You're sounding much better."

"I'm feeling much better." I rubbed my neck where Jeremy had kissed it. "How's Janelle?"

"Still asleep."

Information I neither wanted nor needed to know.

"I'll be at your place at 6:30 on Friday."

"Alright. Sure you don't want to take Janelle along with us?"

"You don't need me to tell you what you already know." A deliberate undercurrent of intimacy shaded his voice. "See you then, Aimee."

He hung up.

"Jesus," I implored, and began to pray.

"Everything looks fine."

Jeremy pecked on the keyboard, absorbed in my laptop. "The program you're using is an older one and I'm guessing it's a little glitchy because you're having to log-in to the network remotely. But other than that, math is math, and everything checks out."

"Thank you for taking a look at it."

I loaded the final bowl from the King's cereal dinner into the dishwasher. "Whoever did the accounting before this final draft of the sales order was way off. There was an obscene amount of adjustments I needed to make."

Anna and Christina rushed down the hall from Christina's room.

"Mama, Chris and I wanted to ask y'all if we can have another sleepover tonight?"

"Tonight? After the sleepover you just had last night? I don't think so, love."

"But Mama—"

"Aimee," Christina tried to sound consoling, "we can have it over here. You can have a break this time."

"I don't—" I began as their protests spilled onto Jeremy and me.

"Girls, we'll have another one soon," Jeremy promised, his voice slightly raised. "I didn't sleep well last night and I'm sure you two didn't get a whole lot of sleep either."

"Why didn't you sleep well?" Anna asked, concern crossing her face. Her voice lowered and she glanced at me suspiciously. "Did Mama get you sick?"

Christina turned to her and hissed, "But you said she told you they didn't kiss?"

"Ladies." Jeremy put a hand on each of their shoulders, and I blushed furiously. "We are all tired. I didn't sleep well because I have a thousand things on my mind. I assure you both, I'm not sick. I feel great."

"Daddy, then please can we—"

"Christina King." His voice was stern but still contained a hint of playfulness. "School's almost out for the summer and I'm certain there will be plenty of time for sleepovers. Tonight's not the night."

A twinge of pain jogged across my head. David. I needed to call him as soon as possible to ask about extending our lease.

"We've got lots to look forward to, girls. And Maren is coming in two more weeks," I reminded Anna.

"Oh, I forgot!" She turned to Christina, her eyes brightening,

"You'll love Auntie Maren."

"Please let the adults talk about it." I eyed both of them, "Maybe we can figure something out for the weekend after next when Maren's in town. Alright?"

Anna considered my offer. "Deal." She grabbed Christina's hand in hers. "Can we play on the deck?"

"It's fine with me if it's okay with Jeremy." I looked at him.

"Go ahead."

They took off through the French doors.

"It's like they haven't been with each other for the past twenty-four hours straight." I closed my laptop and sat beside him. "They're really good friends. I don't know what Anna would have done these last few months without Christina. It's all been such a gift."

"It has," he said quietly. "Your work event at Galvez is next Friday?"

"Yeah, at 7." My conversation with Clint this morning seemed like years ago. "Clint called me after you left earlier today. I'm not looking forward to it. He's picking me up at 6:30, like old times."

A smile made its way across his face. "Sounds like a stand-up guy."

"It doesn't bother you?"

"Of course not. It's your job. And," he scratched the back of his head, "between your town crier and mine, I'm certain to hear all about who's kissing who."

"I'm so sorry about that."

"No need to apologize. I'm trying to be transparent with Christina, too." His hands were near mine on the bar, but he held me with his gaze instead. "I'm going to start moving things out to SeaSplit this week after school. Christina will come with me. I know you need to dedicate more time to this big contract you're closing."

"Thank you for looking at it with me tonight. Typically, I'm able to catch discrepancies before they pile up. I'm not sure why it happened so much this time. I know not being able to handle blue light very well for the past few months hasn't helped at all."

I caught him looking at me as if I was a candle in an infinitely dark cave. "What?"

"You're being too hard on yourself. You're very good at your job. And what's more, you care."

A smile trembled on my lips. "I do."

"Precious soul. You're tired. And so am I."

I scooped up my laptop. "Anna and I will head back home now, I think."

"Come on, then."

He stood and I followed him. The model ships sailed into view, still gracing the shelves on the far wall.

"Will you pack up everything this week?"

"Not too much, I'll leave some of the larger pieces to stage the place for when Dad lists it. We'll mostly pack tools and personal things this week." The wood of the stairs groaned, complaining as we went down together.

The girls squatted in Christina's shell garden, creating tiny worlds.

"Anna Marie," I called, "It's time to go back home."

Her head whipped up. Seeing Jeremy and me hand in hand, she smiled brilliantly and tugged Christina's arm.

"Chris, look!" she cried with unbridled joy. "It's happening!"

I sat at the desk in my room.

The glow of my bedside lamp was warm, but the cool light of the computer drew me in like an insect about to be zapped. I had forbidden any thought of Jeremy to enter my mind, intent on concluding my review of the file Clint had sent me more than twelve hours ago.

A nebulous uncertainty nagged my confidence. "Is this pride..." I murmured, "or fear?" Both vices had tripped me up to the point I'd sunk earlier this year, stripping my field of vision down to a narrow and lonely track.

I scrolled to the very end of the file and briefly skimmed the sales notes. The chronology started with today's date, records of the validations and corrections I made that morning. I scrolled down farther. Invoices sent to customers. Normal. My yawn almost split my head in two.

"I need to go to bed." I rubbed my eyes. My hand hit the mouse clumsily, sending the cursor tumbling to the very end of the sales notes.

Rojas, Aimee L. Initialized 12 February 2023.

"I'm fairly certain the only thing I was initializing in February was a nervous breakdown." I said to myself. I scrolled up and counted silently. Scrolled down and counted again. I hadn't miscounted. The sales notes were stamped with my name forty-three times between February 12 and the first weekend in April.

I reached for my phone and found his name, pressing call.

"Yo."

By the looks of it, Nat was at Whataburger waiting for the clock to strike 11.

"Breakfast taquitos?"

"You know it. What's up?"

Anger threatened in my voice. "Nat, how do I trigger an internal audit?"

"Someone rubbing you the wrong way?" Clint's voice shattered the morning's calm to shards. The sun rose directly in front of me over the water, and I stopped ankle-deep to pick up his words more clearly above the gentle morning surf.

"No. I'm doing the due diligence you asked of me."

"By requesting a formal audit on our own file? The week it's due. The week we're closing."

"You said it first, Clint. I'm a trying person, and I don't appreciate my name being smeared on a file that's undergone so many revalidations, especially when I've barely touched it."

"God, Aimee. You gave me your credentials your first week back in Texas, don't you remember? Of course your name is all over it. I was covering for you."

Honestly, I hadn't remembered.

"In any event, this many revalidations on one file looks careless. Our work has to be better than this, especially on paper."

"Maybe if I wasn't undertaking the roles of two people, you'd be more satisfied."

"You could have asked me—"

"Asked you what, exactly, Aimee?" His words lacerated me. "You were incoherent the last time you were actively on the job. You could hardly get yourself dressed."

"Then you should have asked Hoff instead. He would have given you my clearance in a heartbeat." I hadn't raised my voice like this in a very long time. "All you had to do was ask. You could have kept Brooklyn and Griffin on the project to pick up your slack. Reassigning them was your decision, not mine."

He doubled down. "So you triggered an interdepartmental audit without the courtesy of consulting me about it first?"

"Apparently you've forgotten, so allow me to remind you." I hated hearing the ice in my voice, hated pulling rank on him. "I don't need to consult you regarding necessary measures that ensure we're delivering the best service to our customers."

His voice dropped. "After New York I heard nothing from you for weeks."

"And I'm sorry, that's my fault. But please don't—"

"Do you think it was easy for me, watching you suffer after Caleb died? Having Anna ask me if he'd been with me on a long business trip when quarantine ended?" His voice broke. "For the past three years, I've been at your side. Are you really telling me this is the level of trust I've gained?"

I fought in vain to keep the tremor out of my voice, upset it was there in the first place. "It's an audit on a file, Clint. Not your performance. If anything, this will come back to haunt my record, not yours. Why are you making this personal?"

"With everything we've been through, how can it be anything but personal, Aimee?"

My throat tightened. The warm air hovering over the gentle waves did nothing to assuage the sudden chill washing down my back.

"This is going nowhere." His tone turned opaque. "I shouldn't have called."

"No." I forced my reply like air through a bellows.

"Talk to you soon."

He ended the call.

Angry tears wet my face. I swiped them away, desperate to eliminate any trace of the last five minutes. The grass whipped my legs as I stalked through the dunes toward the boardwalk. For reasons I couldn't quite explain, I thought of Julia King walking the same path, carefully carrying death itself as she brought the hatchling rattlesnake to her brother's house in the early hours of the morning.

"Kayla called again, Aimee. Her mother is going back home for a work function next week, and she asked if I would be up for spending a few nights with her. What do you think?"

I stretched, thankful for Cecily's intrusion into the black hole of emails I'd set into motion.

"Not this weekend, right?" I was woefully unprepared for a corporate fête and apprehensive about seeing Clint in a mere four days, especially after this morning's exchange.

"No, next Friday through the Wednesday after. I thought with Maren coming into town, it could all work out nicely."

I smiled at her. "Of course it will, Cici. You're always working things out nicely."

The doorbell rang, and Cecily and I looked at each other in surprise. I opened the door to a young man carrying what appeared to be an entire rose bush in his arms.

"Delivery for Aimee Rojas?"

"That's me." I stepped forward, relieving him of what could have filled half of Eden.

"Have a good one, ladies." He grinned and sprinted down the stairs.

Cecily radiated with excitement. "Looks like things are getting serious between you two, Shug!"

"Hmm. They are beautiful." At least three dozen fully blown roses boasting the color of a Tavel rosé reposed on the bar, nestled in ivy tendrils and fir. The humble bouquet of gardenias hand-cut from the garden next door peeked around the lavish arrangement.

"This doesn't look like Jeremy."

I plucked the envelope from its holder.

"Surely it's not from Amos Guerrero?" Cecily asked half-jokingly.

"Surely not."

We read the note together.

Please forgive my behavior on the phone earlier today. I was severely out of line. Looking forward to seeing you on Friday.
- CM

"He must have messed up," Cecily remarked.

"Big time," I murmured, straining to quiet the silent alarm sounding in my heart. "He knows I hate roses."

Clint Myers

The audit is complete.
No revisions needed.
Thank you for bearing with me.

Excellent.
See you on Friday.

May

J eremy King
*Christina and I are going
pier fishing with Mike tonight.
I'll miss you.*

*That sounds infinitely
more fun than my plans.
I'll miss you too.*

*Please let me know when
you get back from dinner.*

*I will.
It will be late.*

Doesn't matter.

:)

The other dress Maren purchased for me did, in fact, fit more than my leg. Sleeveless and constructed of black guipure lace with a provocative amount of stretch, it hugged every curve and ended just below my knees. I unearthed my Louboutin's from the depths of my largest suitcase and checked the mirror.

Hair up in a loose French twist. Perfume from my favorite shop on the Italian side of Lago Maggiore strategically applied to pulse points. Well-defined lashes, brows and lips. Diamonds in my lobes. No helix. I only vaguely recognized the woman staring back at me with a full face of makeup. She'd been wildly successful and—of her own volition—painfully overworked the last few years.

"Mama?" Anna came into my room and stood beside me, slipping her hand in mine. She examined our reflections side by side. "Are you and Jeremy having another date tonight?"

"No, baby. I'm all dressed up for a work dinner I'm going to with Clint. I'm sure he's almost here."

"All the way in Houston?"

"No love, here on the island, at a hotel called the Grand Galvez. You've seen it, we've driven by it before. It's the big pink building that looks like a palace with palm trees everywhere, all the way at the end of the Sea Wall. Remember?"

"Oh, yeah." A strange look crossed her face. "You're coming back tonight, aren't you?"

I followed the plump curve of her face, brushed the hair out of her eyes. "Of course, love. This isn't a trip. We aren't going anywhere tonight. Just down the road." I kissed her cheek before we made our way down the hall. "I won't get home until very late, but I'll be here when you wake up."

Cecily looked up from stirring her soup on the stove and smiled. "Be safe. Anna and I will get lost in a good book. We're almost done reading *The Secret Garden*. I bet we can finish it tonight."

"You think so, Cici?" Anna's joy wrapped around the three of us.

"Sure thing, Anna Marie."

I plucked my clutch from the entry table.

"Love y'all. Please don't stay up too late," I called, blowing them a kiss as I left.

I glanced at the house next door. Lights off, Jeremy's truck gone. The air was still. Clint was waiting for me, parked on the street, leaning against the passenger door of the SF90.

He straightened to his full height as I came into view. "Perfection."

"Thank you."

He was very close to me, barring the door. His eyes arrested me, asking a question. "Bygones?"

"Bygones," I conceded, allowing him a small smile.

He opened my door and gave me a passing kiss on the cheek as I slid inside. He rounded the hood and sat beside me in the cockpit. The Stradale snarled as Clint quickly sent it into first gear, then second. Neighborhoods blurred together as the sun sent its dying radiance across the sky behind us.

"Why couldn't Janelle come?"

"Didn't want her to."

"So that's over already?"

"Destined to fail." He sounded genuinely happy.

Unhindered by any traffic he drove fast, maneuvering the car with astonishing speed and skill.

"I'm sorry."

"You're not." A smile slipped across his face, and he glanced over at me admiringly. "Love becomes you, Aimee."

"Then I'm certain I've been disappointing you the last few years."

His laughter rolled, filling the interior of the car. "It's impossible for you to disappoint me."

"You're joking."

The emerald flashed in my direction. "I'd never lie to you." The car tore through a yellow light. "Tell me, what's he like?"

"Who?"

"The one who put life back in your eyes."

I remembered Clint's parting words to me the last time he

was on the island; the information he'd been subtly attempting to prod from me over our last few conversations. I knew he wouldn't be satisfied with a few paltry facts, but I also didn't want to share my feelings about Jeremy with him.

So instead, I said, "He's a single dad, raising his dead sister's daughter all while fending off personal attacks from a manipulative stepmother who's worked hard to make his estrangement from his father permanent."

Clint's eyebrows raised. "And?"

"He's taciturn and intense. Strong. Took me a minute to figure out that his persistent frown was more from carrying his past by himself for so long, than ill-will."

"Sexy. What else?"

"He teaches eighth grade algebra and lives in the house next door."

He laughed. "Of course he does."

I was done talking about Jeremy. "What's the plan for tonight?"

"Tech and specs with the old man for you. General fraternizing for me."

"The usual, then." I flipped the visor mirror up, checking my reflection. "Please not too late, Clint."

"Dance card already filled for later this evening?"

"Yes, by my bed."

I sneezed and opened my clutch only to realize that I'd forgotten to put any tissues in it.

"Your cologne would fell a redwood, Clint."

"Glovebox," he said, cheerfully coaxing the car to soar along the green-lit seawall.

"Thanks." In the glovebox, Clint's wallet and a small box of tissue laid directly in front of me. As I pulled one out and brought it to my face, a tiny breath mint fell into my lap, rolling against my clutch.

"What's his name?"

I almost didn't catch the wistful note in his voice as I turned the mint over in my lap with my finger.

Hexagonal. A star like an asterisk on one side.

"Jeremy." As I spoke, all the oxygen in the car seemed to vanish. "Jeremy King." I shifted my legs so my clutch covered the pill.

We pulled up to a light, now halfway to the hotel.

I was blind and stupid. Darius hadn't stolen my medicine after all.

"Now that surname would suit."

His words didn't really register but I forced my best smile as if I'd heard him anyway. "I suppose at this point, nothing's impossible."

Dominating the room, gargantuan chandeliers set the Founder's Bar awash with scarlet light.

The gallery glowed, flanked by candlelit windows, and a Latin groove band in the alcove of the bar made the atmosphere sizzle. I floated across the checkered mosaic tile, keeping my hand on Clint's arm as if my life depended on it. If I didn't hold onto him, if I wasn't charming and unshakable Aimee Rojas, Director of Sales for Valiant Oil and Gas, I would immediately run, taking any chance of knowing what my prescription was doing in the glovebox of his car away with me.

"Ready?" He smiled then introduced me to the customers: five well-groomed men of varying ages whose names I immediately forgot, and a young blonde whose skirt was shockingly short for a business dinner. Her eyes never left Clint.

Clint ordered a bottle of Glenfiddich Grand Cru for the table and drank it neat.

"Club soda with lime for the lady," he added, nodding toward me.

I chatted with the oldest man about the upcoming project with Valiant, clutching my soda to mask the tremor in my hand.

I tried not to think about the hydroxyzine wrapped in the

tissue inside my clutch. Tried not to think about the night on the bathroom floor when I broke the bottle's plastic safety lock and how it never shut correctly after that. Tried not to envision Clint cursing, picking pills from the Ferrari's floorboard after they'd certainly spilled out of the glovebox.

The old man made a joke, and I laughed. My eyes darted to Clint.

He was confident and in control with the blonde pressed close to him, his arm stretched across the top of the circular booth, his last comment producing a spate of raucous laughter from the men.

"This hotel's an art deco fever dream." My conversation partner waved his drink aloft. "Wish my wife could see it. She'll need me to describe it in great detail when I get back to Houma."

What do you need? Clint had sat on the couch, gazing at me as if his life had depended on my answer.

I laughed again, my mind in overdrive, demanding I put the pieces together now. "My family's originally from Morgan City."

"Is that so? What brought you to Houston?"

"The thing that brings everyone to Houston. Work."

"We'll try our best not to discuss work tonight," he demurred. "Do you live in Houston?"

"No. I've been living on the island for the past five months. I'm working remotely."

Not remote enough. He'd taken what had helped me sleep.

"Do you have anyone waiting at home for you here in Galveston?"

"Yes, I do. My daughter."

He'd given her the pearl earrings that same day.

For a pearl above price.

"Oh, wonderful." Houma man was delighted. "My daughter is a junior at Centenary."

"I'm sure you're proud." I beamed at him. "What's her major?"

"Economics."

"Bless her heart. Arithmetic is my Achilles heel."

"I can't believe that, as esteemed within Valiant as you are."

"You'd be surprised how far an iPhone calculator can get you."

"Mercy!" Scotch singed the air as he laughed out loud.

The taste of lime bit my tongue as I sipped my drink. "Anyway, we aren't supposed to be discussing business matters. My apologies."

"This is true. How old is your daughter?"

"Eight. About to be nine."

"That's a precious age." He eyed me shrewdly over his glass. "You're a single mother?"

"Currently, yes. My husband passed away from Covid several years ago."

Set against the riotous frivolity of the holiday unfolding around us, the sorrow in his eyes was instantaneous and unexpected.

Death makes being human painfully simple at times.

"I'm so sorry for your loss. And please, do forgive me. I'm an old fool to pry into your personal affairs."

"No need to apologize." I smiled. "Your interest is welcome."

"Alright, dear." His leathery hand patted mine, then reached for his drink. "I hope you don't mind my asking—you do remind me so much of my daughter, after all. You said 'currently.'" He took another sip of Grand Cru. "Is there a lucky prospect lined up for you?"

"I believe so." The thought of Jeremy was like manna in the wilderness. "I've been seeing a kind man who has a daughter of his own."

"Not your partner here, then." He grunted, catching Clint's eye from across the table and raising his glass in a salute. To me he muttered, "That's good. Clint Myers is a pit bull. He hounded me for months negotiating this deal."

"I'm sorry. He can be maddeningly thorough. Was there an issue?"

I glanced at Clint. He couldn't want the drug for himself. The steadiness of his hands, the carefully chosen words. Clint always had to be in control. Always. The amber swirled in his glass. I'd never even seen him affected by alcohol. Nothing moved him. Except…

"Numbers." The older gentleman took a sip and shook his head. "Mr. Myers berated me over our invoicing software more times than I care to count. Said a glitch existed in our software your accounting department kept having to manually reconcile. Not sure how, our system is top of the line. So new I can barely get a handle on it myself, and I've been in accounting for almost forty years. Can't tell you how many times I've told him everything'll add up alright."

At the old man's words, every one of my untethered thoughts about our work on the project fell into place. Clint stood in the shadow of my memory, watching me shake as my confidence swirled like snow in a globe. The numbers hadn't added up, even as far back as New York. Before our bid had won.

It wasn't me.

Get well. I can't do this without you.

His eyes were all over the blonde, but it would have been naïve of me to think his ears weren't on our conversation.

"Clint doesn't let anything get in his way."

His eyes cut to me, an expression I couldn't quite read crossing his face for a moment.

The blonde slipped something into the breast pocket of his jacket, and he turned back to her attentively.

"I'm getting too old for this business," Houma man was saying. "Between you and me sugar, you should get out while you're still young. The culture of this industry will eat you alive, even as it's in its final gasps."

I lowered my voice and raised my glass. "Between you and me, sir, you've voiced my sincerest hope and desire."

He grinned. "Cheers!"

His glass met mine, the impact threatening to shatter them both.

I had to get away from Clint. My urge to run was too strong.

The man from Houma had excused himself and retired to his suite, thanking me for the pleasure of my company and wishing me the best. After three glasses of Grand Cru, the blonde cut an unsteady path to the restroom.

Clint claimed the seat beside me.

My heart hammered as anger and fear jockeyed for position.

"Enjoying yourself?" I asked.

"Immensely. Audacious hussy gave me her room key."

My out.

I let bitterness seep into my voice, hoping he'd recoil. "Little does she know the ice omitted from your drink is reserved for your heart."

He took a sharp breath and studied me. Another test. I couldn't let him see my shock or confusion. The only thing I could let him see was the hope that somehow I was wrong, even though I knew I wasn't. His eyes bore a hole through me, and I failed to hold his gaze.

The blonde emerged from the bathroom, fighting to keep her balance.

"I'm tired, Clint, and she's coming back. Make your choice." I silently prayed he'd stay at the hotel with the girl, prayed I wouldn't have to endure another car ride with him. Tense and distracted, I slurped my dwindling drink.

"Look at me."

Frozen by the tone of his voice, I obeyed. Luminous eyes that had known my thoughts, at times even before I did, glinted hard and calculating. I didn't recognize him anymore, and for the first time ever, I was afraid of him.

And he knew it.

His touch was featherlight along my jaw, and I barely flinched as his lips grazed my cheek and met my ear. "What's in your head, Aimee? Your thoughts have been spinning all evening."

Then, as I made no reply, "Never mind. The girl's expecting me to stay, but honestly, I'm feeling a bit masochistic tonight. I think I'd derive more pleasure driving a woman who's in the thick of despising me back to her home. Now, do your part Aimee. Make them believe you really want me to."

His words seeped into my mind like poison, contaminating it. I closed my eyes, praying I wouldn't wretch. Terrified, I felt the smile unwittingly pull at the corner of my mouth in full view of the blonde as Clint's fingers slid from my face down my arm and found mine, pulling me up with him as he stood. I knew exactly what our exchange had looked like, and seeing the faces of the customers, I knew they'd bought it.

I shook hands with the men and even the blonde who stared daggers at me.

Clint slipped his hand around my waist as we turned and walked out of the bar to the foyer.

Well aware our guests were still watching us, he pulled me close to his side and said carelessly, "You know I can't resist a hard sell." He kissed my shoulder and before I knew what was happening, his fingers skated down my backside, expertly finding a part of me I never thought he'd touch.

Anger overtook fear as I flushed with rage and walked faster, falling out of step with him as we cleared the doors.

The valet bowed over the ticket Clint gave him and ran off.

"How dare you."

I tore my phone from my clutch and opened Uber. I wasn't going anywhere with him. The mariachi music drifted up from the gardens below, disjointed and out of place.

"How dare I what?" His gaze fastened on me as he drew a cigarette from his breast pocket. People passed us by on both sides of the entryway, drunk and laughing because of the holiday, unaware of what he'd done to me. He smiled through the smoke. "How dare I grab your ass when I've had your back the past few years?"

"How dare you use me! How dare you behave like a lascivious pervert with a friend who trusted you. You've always had my back, and I've never doubted you until now."

"Believe me, I'm sorry to let you down. It's out of necessity at this point. Rest assured, I don't want you, but I sure as hell needed you." The steel in his voice dared me to ask him for more, and for some vile reason I knew he wanted me to.

"What are you talking about?"

He flicked his cigarette into the driveway. "Feigning ignorance is the singular item that doesn't wear well on you, my girl. You think I can't tell when you're faking it?"

My phone buzzed in my hand, affording me a few precious seconds to think.

Lindy is three minutes away.

I looked back at him, breathless and nauseated, the old pain radiating from the front of my head to the back.

"Why did you steal it?"

He laughed in disbelief. "You don't really have to ask, do you?"

"Why did you steal my medicine?"

The beautiful smile had begun to reappear on his face, but my question caught him off guard, a spasm of shock snuffing out his humor. "At the time I thought it was necessary. I hadn't counted on the boon of your being lovesick over a total stranger or I would have left well enough alone."

"You wanted me to be unwell?"

"I wanted you safely sidelined. You said it yourself, Aimee. I don't let anything get in my way. And I refuse to let you of all people get in my way. I've had to hurt you tonight and over the past few months to do just that. Hear me when I say I don't want to have to hurt you again, or anyone else that's dear to you."

I cut through his threat. "Anyone else dear to me? What if it's you, Clint? Don't you think I care?"

His resolve wavered at my words, but he pressed on. "I'm not sure I know what you care about anymore, Aimee. And until recently, I don't believe you did either. You've been in a dry, desolate season but suddenly you meet Jeremy King, and you're ready to get yourself wet again."

He'd weaponized his words, and every syllable found their mark.

"You want him more than anything, don't you?"

I hated his crude assumptions. Hated that he was right.

"Why are you doing this?"

"God, it's true isn't it? You wouldn't be nearly so offended if you hadn't already made up your mind to give him the privilege first." His verdant eyes flicked away from me to the Ferrari crawling along the curb to meet us. "You've already taken your wedding ring off for him. I'll wager it won't be long before you take everything else off, too."

Neither of us was prepared for how quickly or how hard I slapped him. But it brought us both to our senses. Speechless, Clint stared at me, his eyes filled with shame and regret. I didn't have to take his verbal assault anymore.

The valet bounded around the hood of the car and dropped the keys into his hand. "Here you are, sir."

The phone flashed in my hand.

Lindy is arriving now.

I leveled him with my gaze. "Understand that you've accomplished more than you set out to. In addition to shaming the memory of one of your closest friends, you've completely lost another." I controlled the tremor in my voice. "If I even ever was one to you ."

"Miss Aimee?"

A voice sang out over the raucous noise of the crowd from across the driveway and I turned, catching sight of a colorfully dressed woman standing beside a pristine turquoise Dodge Neon. She couldn't have been taller than four foot five.

"Aimee—" Clint's voice groped for me.

"Lindy?" I stumbled toward her, refusing to turn back to him.

"Miss Aimee, it looks like you just told that fine man good-bye." She held the door open for me. "Get in the car baby. I'll fly you out of here."

I crawled into Lindy's car. The coconut scented Little Tree dangling from her mirror dipped and swayed as the Neon made the curve down the Grand Galvez's long drive.

The Ferrari roared angrily behind us, but I didn't dare turn around.

I sank deeper into the cushion of the seat as Lindy whooped loudly. "Sure wish I could kick a man to the curb like that!"

The Ferrari screamed to the right, gunning toward the Strand and the mainland.

Lindy turned onto Seawall Boulevard, stepped on the gas, and flew.

"D'you make it back, baby?" Warm and thick with sleep, his voice sounded like home.

I struggled to speak. "Jeremy?"

"Where are you?" He was instantly awake, his voice shot through with concern.

"My room." Breath refused to stay in my lungs. "I wish you were here."

"Meet me outside." He hung up.

I ran down the hallway and out the door barefoot, still wearing the dress Maren had bought me. The moon was full and very high in the sky. He was on the path between the cottages, and I went to him like a magnet.

His arms locked around my shoulders. "You're safe. It's going to be okay. Are you hurt?"

"No." I thought about it. "Not like that."

"Tell me what happened, Aimee." Worry laced his voice.

"I found some of my medicine in Clint's car on the way to the hotel. I thought Darius stole it, but he didn't. I was so scared. We had cocktails with the customers, and I told Clint I wanted to leave, and he—"

I knew I had to tell him.

"He kissed my shoulder as we were walking out of the hotel and then he touched me."

"Touched you?" Jeremy's body grew rigid against mine.

"Like Caleb used to when he was ready to leave, like I told you…" I still couldn't catch my breath.

One of Jeremy's hands buried itself in my hair, his fingers cutting pathways through my panic. "Breathe."

I laid my head against his shoulder. "Clint knew what we used to do. That it would hurt me in more than one way."

"He will never touch you again."

The depth of resolve in his voice shouldn't have surprised me, but it did.

"Before I found the medicine he asked me about you. He knows your name, where you live. I told him everything." Hyperventilation threatened to overtake me again. "Everything."

"Good," he said evenly. "Now he knows how to find me."

"He said such horrible things about us. About you."

Jeremy's thumb met my cheek—the same one Clint's lips had marred—and gently wiped away the tears they found there. His touch melted away the darkness which had dogged me all evening.

"Clint started to tell me about something with work too, something terrible that I think I've been dancing around for the last few weeks. Tonight, everything started to make sense."

"With the sales order you showed me?"

"Yeah." My breathing evened out.

"Let me pray for you."

I nodded, wordless.

Jeremy's voice held freedom and the fervent confidence of someone who knew he'd be heard and answered. He prayed for healing and protection over me. He asked for justice and wisdom moving forward. He prayed for Clint.

"In Jesus' name."

"In Jesus' name." I echoed.

"Feeling better?" I heard the smile in his voice.

"Yes. But I'm so tired."

"Mmhmm…" His thoughts were elsewhere. "Aimee?"

The distant music of the waves soothed me like a lullaby. Jeremy's hold on me loosened, and I looked up at him, trying to make out his expression in the dark.

"There's nothing we can't face together in the light of day. You know that, right?"

I could have stood in the unknown with him all night. "Yes, I know."

His tone held urgency. "Your house has an alarm system. Will you turn it on once you're back inside?"

"You bet your sweet life I will."

As I climbed the stairs, the breeze carried his laughter away from me, somewhere out across the dunes to waves that gleamed like leaded crystal in the moonlight.

My phone rang less than an hour after I fell asleep, its glaring light sending slumbering shadows to cower in the corners of my room. Nat's name blazed across the screen.

"Nat?"

"Aimee?" He gasped for breath, hurtling down the stairs in

the parking garage next to our office downtown, his video call looking like a scene straight out of *The Blair Witch Project*.

"You're not gonna believe this."

I sat up at the edge of my bed, flicking on my lamp. "Try me."

"How are you?"

Jeremy called before the sun had fully risen, beating me to the punch.

"I talked with Nat an hour ago. He found something. I told him about last night with Clint. We have a Zoom set up with Hoff, Sharon, and our CFO Kevin at 9.

Silence on his end for a moment. "Take the call over here. Bring Anna when she wakes up. I'm making breakfast."

Anna was thrilled at the prospect of seeing Christina so early in the morning.

"Can I stay in my pjs?" Anna asked.

"Yep."

"Mama, you look pretty." She tilted her head to the side. "But your face is also, like, blurry."

"I didn't take my make-up off last night, bug."

"Oh. You should do that next time."

I brought my laptop and headphones.

Gardenias scented our walk up Jeremy's stairs.

Christina lolled on the sofa, playing her Switch while he busied himself at the stove.

"That smells delicious."

He caught my eyes, unsmiling. "Stress cooking."

"Stress appreciating." I plugged my charger into the outlet under the bar and slipped my AirPods into my ears.

"I'm going to sign in now."

"I'm going to keep praying."

"He left here just before midnight," I said.

Kevin's wire-framed glasses dropped to his desk with a clatter. "Where is he now?"

"We don't know," Sharon answered. "Since it's Saturday, he hasn't come into the office. There were no swipes on his security card for the parking garage or the building. The police haven't gotten a warrant for the CCTV at his townhome yet, but they said his passport hasn't gotten any hits either."

"And he hasn't accessed the network remotely," Nat offered.

"Son of a bitch can't be too far away," Hoff growled.

Jeremy solemnly cleaned the dishes at the sink in front of me. He caught me staring at him and winked.

Hoff's tone blasted through me like a shotgun. "Repeat everything you told me this morning Nat, so Sharon and Kevin can hear this pile of horse shit for themselves."

Nat straightened his glasses.

"Basically, when Aimee flagged the final sales order last week, it triggered an internal audit, not only for accounting, but for my department in IT as well. As you all know, accounting and sales work very closely together. While sales generates the numbers for each project, accounting has to balance and approve them, so—"

"We're all familiar with Accounting 101, Nathaniel. Get to the point," Kevin snarled, hot with impatience.

"Yes sir. The forms that sales uses to submit invoices for accounting have been in our system for years. They're very basic, but the encryption is failsafe. They're impossible to hack. However, someone's created an invisible duplicate of the form. Think of it like a digital carbon copy, one form stacked on top of the other. So, when any errors are corrected, the copy or template on top appears to be validated. However, the carbon copy underneath still shows the overage. Accounting sees the copy on top and verifies it, thinking that everything looks good. But what actually gets processed by the software in accounting is the copy underneath with the overage error still on it."

"All of the invoices you've seen have been overages, not short pays?"

"Thus far, yes sir."

"What's happening to the overages once they're processed?" Hoff asked.

"I'm not a hundred percent sure sir, but it looks like they're being directed to an external account not affiliated with Valiant. Depending on how sophisticated this hacker was, the IP address is most likely running through what could be hundreds of thousands of VPNs and will take several days to trace."

"How much has been funneled out so far?"

"Based on the invoices I've audited this morning, $800,000."

Kevin and Hoff both let out a series of obscenities, and I flinched.

"But those are only from invoices dating from today back to last week's monthly cut-off."

"We have multiple checks and balances in place to ensure a breach like this cannot possibly happen. Who signed off on these invoices?" The fury in Kevin's voice threatened to shred my eardrums.

"I did, Kevin. I'm the only one who can." My voice was clear and unshaken.

"Then what the hell are you doing on this call, Aimee?"

Despite my head throbbing, I heard the steel I used during the toughest negotiations in my tone. "I initiated this call, Kevin."

"Clint threatened her—" Nat tried to cut across his anger.

"Hoff, what the hell is she doing on the call? Do you realize what a liability—"

Hoff minced no words informing Kevin about the exact manner in which he could shut up, and then said to me, "He's right, Aimee. We have to end this call immediately and go through the appropriate channels to square everything away. Nat, freeze Aimee and Clint's access to the network. Hell, freeze all our accounts that carry fiscal access, including mine. My signature is attached to any contract over ten million. Until we can get an outside party to go through digital forensics, we're all in this shitshow together."

My head was splitting. I desperately needed sleep.

Hoff concluded, "I need to call the board. I'm signing you off now, Aimee. You're too close to this dumpster fire and I don't want you to get burned. Keep your phone on and with you at all times. I'll have Sharon forward you info for the appropriate party to contact, should you hear from Clint." He paused before ending the chat. "Chin up, Rojas."

I nodded dumbly and my screen turned black.

Earlier in the week, Christina and Anna had played as I'd helped Jeremy pack. They pretended to be florists, filling half a dozen mason jars with gardenias and lining them up on the kitchen windowsill.

I stared at the flowers, unseeing, as Jeremy's hands met my shoulders.

"Jeremy."

His breath escaped his lips as they pressed against the back of my head, warm.

"I think my career just ended."

"I'm so mad I could spit, Shug. I could just spit."

I'd left no word or detail out of the previous night's events at Galvez and concluded with the morning's impromptu meeting. "Believe me, I know how you feel."

Livid, Cecily sloshed beside me through the waves. Anna ran ahead of us on the beach, collecting seashells.

"But he never lied to me."

In the sleepless hours between seeing Jeremy and Nat's call, I read back through every email, every text message, and replayed every conversation in my head. "Every single interaction he's had with me over the last few months was calculated. He manipulated my feelings the whole time. It was a long sale."

"To be more sympathetic toward him?" Cecily's voice dripped with scorn.

"No, to appear more repulsive. He took advantage of how sick I was to get me into the exact position he wanted. First, it was little things. Subtle poking at my relationship with Jeremy. Then his ridiculous assertion that I needed to consult him before conducting an internal audit by making it personal. By trying to make me believe that any of his feelings for me were true." The shame in his eyes haunted me, fresh in my memory. "He wanted as much distance between us as possible. He didn't want to hurt me."

"But he did," Cecily said firmly. "No amount of remorse changes the fact that every single thing Clint did was wrong, Aimee. Lying or not."

"I know."

"What did Jeremy say about it when you saw him last night?"

Remnants of a thousand broken seashells littered the beach.

"He prayed for Clint."

Cecily gasped. "The integrity of the man. I would've hopped in the Jeep and hunted him down. Still have half a mind to."

"Oh, Jeremy was furious." Shrouded in shadow, I'd hardly been able to make out his expression in the dark, but I remembered how he'd tensed against me as I told him what Clint had done. "He more or less vowed Clint would never touch me again. The way he said it, I believe him."

"Jeremy King doesn't seem like the kind of person I'd want to cross. But I'm very grateful for his care of my darling niece."

"Me too." The smile I gave her ached. "You know he and Christina are moving at the end of the month?"

"Yes, Mary mentioned it to me." Her voice softened. "What are your own plans, Shug?"

"I need to call David about extending the lease. I keep forgetting."

"You think you'll stay on the island?"

The constancy of the waves seemed taunting today, reminding me that their transience was infinitely more stable than my own. "I'd like to."

"It'll all work out, Shug. It has so far."

Briny air filled my lungs. "Jeremy will be busy this week. He's getting his classes wrapped up and grades turned in. Then there's field day and some middle school PTO barbecue on top of getting the house packed up. He wants to hand the cottage over to his dad next week."

"I don't think you have to worry about him going far." She smiled at me confidently. "Anyone can see how much he cares about you." She spied Anna, crouching in the water ahead of us. "And Anna, for that matter."

I chewed my bottom lip. "I've only known him for two months."

"When has truth ever been constrained by time?" Her eyes caught mine, sparkling.

"Never." The surf licked our feet. "That reminds me, Maren's coming in next weekend."

"Yes, and I'll leave to go see Tyler and Kayla on Friday morning."

"I don't know how you've had the capacity to care for everyone, Cici."

"We were made to love, Shug. To love God and love others." She ran her hand across her forehead. "Which reminds me of something. I think I'll stay here on the island and look for a place to buy. There's a realtor Chris and Mary want to introduce me to when I get back from my time with Tyler and Kayla."

"Really? That's great. You like it down here that much?"

"I do. I love the community here, and being by the ocean is a big bonus."

"A new start," I said.

"Yes, a new start."

"How are you doing, Aimee?"

"Better. I finally got some sleep last night."

The waves boomed in answer to the bright call of dawn. Salt clung to my legs after the water washed back out to sea.

"I need you fully back on the job. I know you're not in town, but I need you to run things from Galveston like I know you can."

I smiled to myself. "I'm assuming there's new information since I'm not benched anymore?"

"Yes. We got the preliminary report back from the powers that be." Hoff's voice was grim.

"What did they find?"

"A portion of the missing funds in an offshore account with Clint's name on it, and several other things I think should remain vague at the moment."

"The less I know, the better?"

"Exactly. You, me, Nat, and several of the managers in accounting will give a deposition. We testify, and the more honest we're able to answer, the more damning the evidence against Clint will be."

"Alright. When is the deposition?"

"Last week of May. I'll have Sharon send you the details." His chair groaned as he swiveled. "Come dressed to kill, Aimee. Someone's getting lynched and it sure as hell isn't going to be one of us."

A pelican soared, then abruptly halted mid-flight, plummeting headfirst into the waves.

"Heard."

A beep sounded in my ear.

"Sorry Hoff, just a sec."

I held the phone away from me. David. Calling about the cottage. I sent his call to voicemail.

"Hey, I'm back. What else can you tell me?"

"Only a few things. You want the good or the bad first?"

"Good."

"With the exception of Clint and Janelle, we're all cleared. But only just."

"Janelle?" The weight of something akin to a truck rolled onto my chest. "What about her?"

"The poor girl broke. Everyone at the office knew she and Clint were, well…" He cleared his throat. "Obviously because of their relationship, she was a person of interest. The police asked her some routine questions and she lost all composure. Confessed to giving Clint Sharon's credentials and clearance level so he could access accounting and funnel the money out. Because of her involvement, the board has filed criminal charges against her as well as Clint. As much as I hate to admit it, I still can't wrap my head around what he's done to the company. To all of us. And that girl. She's got a lifetime of misery ahead of her now, thanks to him. It's worse than knocking her up. And do you know what that son of a bitch promised her in exchange?"

I didn't have to guess. "He didn't promise her anything, did he?"

"Not a damn thing." Hoff let a thoughtful silence dangle over the line. "How did you know?"

"Because I'm certain she loved him, and he made her believe he loved her too." I shut my eyes tight, preventing the tears from spilling out. "She was wrong."

When he finally spoke, his voice was kind. "You two were close, weren't you?"

"We were."

"Then I hate to tell you, but there's one more thing you should know."

"This is the bad part, isn't it?"

"You could say that. At this point I feel it's necessary for your security."

The surf tugged at my feet. "Hoff. What is it?"

"The police found Clint's car parked on the fifth floor of a garage downtown. They were tipped off by local security."

His Ferrari. The only other constant in his life, too ostentatious to go without notice for long.

"They found his phone in the car. He put it through a hard reset. Wiped clean."

My breath deserted me. "Which garage? The one next to the office?"

"No, Aimee. One in downtown Galveston. On Market Street."

"What?"

"Two blocks from the Strand. And based on the footage from the garage cameras, it's been parked there since last Friday evening."

All thought escaped my mind.

Hoff concluded, "Clint might not have left the island."

I told the three people closest to me.

Cecily verged on hysteria. "I can't leave, Aimee. Knowing that he could be here on the island somewhere is maddening."

"He may not be here at all, Cecily." I tried to sound like I believed it. "This is just another power play to keep me afraid. Maren will be here right after you leave on Friday, and Jeremy's next door. He's not going to let anything happen."

She cast me a doubtful glance. "If you're sure."

"I am, Cici. Tyler and Kayla need you right now, and you need to be with them."

Anna immediately knew something was wrong.

"Mama, ever since you went to have dinner with Clint you've

been different."

"How, love?"

"I don't know. You just seem really sad."

Telling Anna the truth had never failed me. "I am sad, baby. Clint's not working at Valiant anymore."

"He's not? But he loved working. He loved you."

Her innocently spoken words lashed me like a whip. "I know, baby, I loved him too. He was our friend."

Wasn't he?

"Why did he leave?"

"He made a big mistake. One that Hoff and the owners of the company couldn't overlook."

I dreaded telling Jeremy.

Anna and I rocked in the hammock, waiting for him and Christina to come home from field day.

"They're here, Mama!" Anna jumped up and ran to greet them.

Christina hopped out of the truck, ready for Anna's hug. They rushed up the King's stairs together.

"Only a few minutes today, ladies." I called out after them.

"Hey, beautiful." Jeremy's door slammed shut.

"Hey." I fell into him, completely disregarding his mud-speckled clothes, saturated with sweat. The breeze sighed underneath the house and the patio lights strung across the rafters swayed unevenly.

"You don't mind the dirt?" he asked, a laugh catching his voice.

"No," I murmured against his shoulder.

His arms changed from curves around my waist to right angles, pushing me back so he could see my face. "What's wrong?"

"Hoff called me this morning. The police found Clint's car in a garage near the Strand. They said it's been parked there since Cinco de Mayo."

"We have nothing to fear from Clint Myers."

"I know."

He drew me close again. "It's been five days. He has no reason to see you, no reason to come here. With every local and even some federal authorities on his tail, he's the one who's on his back right now. As far as we're concerned, it's business as usual, right?"

I swallowed hard. "Right."

"Let's talk it out. Two more days of school. We'll have the girls' sleepover on Friday. Dad's realtor is coming over on Saturday to take photos and list this place. Then we'll tackle the week after. And by then it'll be two weeks since Cinco de Mayo."

The sleepover had completely slipped my mind.

"Jeremy, you're moving out on Saturday. You don't have to have Anna over, it's too much."

He released me.

"Please let me take some stress from you. Your best friend is coming to see you, and you could use some frivolity. I can be put out for a night."

In the sunlight, I saw a peppering of gray sown in with the blonde climbing from his jaw up to his temple. Concern framed his mouth.

I blinked, committing to memory his solid determination in the still of the moment. "I don't deserve how good you're being to me."

"This isn't about deserving." He traced the curve of my mouth with his eyes. "Besides, I've been short on romance recently. Hopefully this makes up for it in a small way."

"Given everything the past few days have thrown at us, offering me a girl's night is highly romantic. Don't convince yourself otherwise."

"Do you have any plans for this next week?" he asked.

"No. Why?"

The heady scent of gardenias carried us up the stairs. "Nothing concrete yet. Just promise me you'll keep your schedule open."

"Alright."

"Dad!" Christina appeared at the top of the stairs, breathless. "We're out of toilet paper."

The next two days flew with hours on the phone, piecing together the shattered morale of Valiant's sales department and saving the Philippines bid Clint had worked so hard to take.

I pushed the possibility of him showing up unannounced at the cottages to the far reaches of my thoughts.

On Friday evening, Christina knocked on the French doors at 5:30 sharp.

"Anna, are you ready for our farewell party? It's our last night in the house! We'll do manis and pedis first, and then makeovers. I still have my toiletries in the bathroom. Then, Daddy said after dinner he'd make us popcorn while we watch *Garfield*."

I smiled, remembering Jeremy's rendition of how his evening would go.

"Chicken Caesar salad and passing out upstairs after I make sure the girls have brushed their teeth."

Anna threw on her butterfly backpack, thrilled for the very first sleepover outside her home. She turned to me, eyes bright. "I'm ready to go!"

"I'll walk y'all outside, love."

"Okay." She clung to my arm, leaning in for a kiss.

Christina danced with impatience on the deck. "Come on, Anna! Daddy's waiting for us at the carport."

They both waved at me, then scrambled down the stairs hand in hand. The sun shone high in the sky, its light blinding me after emerging from the darkness of the house. A brief but intense pain surged behind my eyes. I shaded them against the brilliance of the day and watched the girls run across the walkway between the twin houses. Jeremy stood underneath his house, power washing the driveway. He'd pulled his truck into the open garage, and the big American flag which usually hung on the street side of the house had been relieved of its duty, rolled up and lying on the picnic table.

He shut off the power washer and called out to the girls.

"Y'all ready for some dinner and *Garfield*?"

Squeals of excitement as they ran out of sight under the house to the stairs. Jeremy looked up at me and lifted a hand in salute.

"Have fun!" I waved.

"Will do!"

I turned to go back into the house, but the distant roar of the waves called to me. I looked over my shoulder at the sea. The air shimmered and danced as the grass, sand and boardwalk inhaled the heat. The farthest waves exhaled diamonds under the relentless rays of the sun. I breathed it in like a balm for my lungs, ignoring the nagging thought that today would be the last time Jeremy would be next door.

"Vitamin D is good for me." I sank into an Adirondack chair, stretching my legs and taking in all the beauty.

Earlier in the day, Anna helped me gather the ingredients for my pizza night with Maren. I made the dough for the crust, pounding it with my fists after stomaching all the corporate rage from the mainland I could handle. I leaned back and closed my eyes, soaking in the peace I felt about Anna spending the night with the Kings, seeing Maren; grateful that some things hardly changed at all.

"Bless tonight, Father," I prayed.

A car door slammed, and Maren's voice skipped under the house as she dismissed her Uber driver. I rose from the chair and felt a big, stupid grin stretch across my face as she cleared the top of the stairs.

"Hey sister!"

"Hey friend!" She embraced me, laden with a Trader Joe's grocery bag and her overnight backpack. Then she pushed me away and studied my face.

"You look so much better." She cupped my cheek. "Stop crying."

"I am not crying." I wiped my eyes. "I'm just happy you're here."

The house was brighter now that she was there.

"Make yourself at home. You're in Cici's room since she'll be in Houston for the next few days. I changed the sheets on her bed. I think the mattress is even better than mine, you'll love it."

"Sweet!" She headed for her bedroom.

I turned on the oven and pulled our pizza toppings from the refrigerator. Marinara, arugula, pepperoni, Italian sausage, grilled chicken, parmesan, burrata and olives bathed in oil.

Maren blew into the kitchen. "How's your neighbor?"

"You never beat around the bush."

"You're just so *obvious*."

"He's wonderful in every conceivable way."

"That's sickeningly delicious," she grinned. "Have y'all made out yet?"

"What? No."

"He's taking too long."

"Too long? It's only been two months, and as far as I'm concerned, he's not taking anything I'm not wholeheartedly giving him."

"Where's Anna?"

"She's next door, spending the night with them. With his daughter, Christina."

She arched an eyebrow. "Really?"

"The King family," I said, tearing a fistful of basil, "has been a blessing for all of us."

"Praise God." She removed a small bottle of champagne from her grocery bag and tucked it into the refrigerator.

"Hey, you know I'm still off that right?"

She cocked her head to the side. "Of course you are! It's all for me. This," she said, lifting out a bottle of sparkling cider, "is for you, love."

"You're the best. And ridiculous. Are we celebrating something?"

"Dummy, of course we are. We're celebrating your return to the land of the highly functioning, if not living. And that's not all. We have matching jammies as well. But that's for later after we have dinner, and after I kill this bottle of Chandon. I'm still staving off jet-lag."

We devoured our pizzas and drank our respective bubbles. We sat on the couch binge watching season three of *The Great British Bake-Off*, hooting at the hosts and drooling over everything on the screen.

Maren sat across from me, curled up in the corner of the massive couch. "How're you holding up?"

"Great." My empty glass landed with a clink on the coffee table. "You haven't asked me anything about Clint."

She peered at me. "Why speak of darkness when there's so much light?"

"Just curious."

"You told me all there is to tell over the phone last week. He's a lying cheat and scoundrel who felt you up last time you saw him."

She unwrapped a dark chocolate peanut butter cup and popped it in her mouth.

"He recklessly dismissed one of the best parts of his life." She gave me a significant look. "That's you, love. And he's most likely in some god-forsaken land that won't extradite, never to be seen again."

"You really think so?'

"With every fiber of my being." She took a sip of champagne. "And good riddance. What I can't believe is that Jeremy King hasn't asked you to marry him yet."

"Maren!"

"Hush, love. You're radiant with the same glow you had after you first met Caleb, and that tells me everything I need to know. It's inevitable."

"You haven't even met him."

"Don't need to. His coming into your life is a direct act of the Lord and we will be thankful!"

"You've drunk your champagne too quickly my girl." I smiled. "It's all going to your head."

"This is still my first glass, and I've been nursing it for hours. It's warmer than a bath. Kind of disgusting, actually."

"Speaking of hours, what time is it?"

She checked her watch. "11:30."

"Oof, an hour past my bedtime."

"We're living large tonight dear. Oh! That reminds me." She hopped off the couch and ran down the hall. She returned carrying a black box tied with a wide, blush ribbon.

"A souvenir from Paris. Decidedly not sweet, as requested. I got myself a set too."

As I unwrapped the box, the fragrance of lavender flooded the house.

A delicate black camisole hung by its straps on my fingers. At first, the lingerie appeared opaque. I turned it. In the right light, it was completely sheer, leaving nothing to the imagination. The matching black shorts scalloped at the sides, promising minimal coverage.

"Who am I wearing this for again?"

"Yourself, love. Jammies like these are for you."

"I stopped wearing stuff like this way before I was pregnant with Anna."

"Wear it again! That set is one-hundred percent silk, lighter than air. Breathable. Barely there. *Mademoiselle* assured me. Count this gift for you, as therapy for me."

"Did you bring yours?"

"Yes, and I'll be donning them as soon as you say lights out."

"I make no promises about wearing this tonight, or anytime soon," I laughed. "But you're precious to think of me. Lights out."

Maren threw a smile in my direction and headed to Cecily's room. "Night!"

Taking the box, I stopped in the kitchen to grab a bottle of Topo Chico and turn on the dishwasher before flicking off the lights. In my room, I tossed the box with Maren's gift onto the ottoman in front of the wingback chair by the bay window and sat on my bed pulling my Bible toward me, opening it to Psalm 63.

> *Because your love is better than life.*
> *My lips will glorify You.*
> *I will praise You as long as I live,*
> *And in Your name I will lift up my hands.*

"Jesus, thank you for giving me back myself. Thank you for this peace."

I turned down the covers, and for sheer frivolity—as Jeremy put it—slipped into the weightless lingerie, killed the light, and by the grace of God, instantly fell asleep.

The sirens were far away at first then came closer, screaming directly outside my window.

I was out of bed, running to it and pulling down the shutter. Two police cars parked rakishly on Jeremy's carport. Policemen running up the stairs. An ambulance. More flashing lights shrilling down the road toward us.

Anna. *Jesus.* "Maren!" I screamed.

The phone flashed in my hand.

2:56

Maren slammed against me in the dark hall. "What is it?"

"I don't know, I don't know. It's next door. Anna." My breathing came in sobs.

I was at the front door, tearing it open and running across the deck and down the stairs, barefoot.

Maren was hot on my heels.

We flew across Jeremy's driveway.

Two EMTs ahead of us sprinted up the steps.

We were almost there when someone wrenched my wrist from behind, stopping me just short of the stairs.

I turned around ready to swing but the policeman was prepared and caught my hand.

"Let me go!" My voice splintered. "Let me go, my daughter is in this house. She was having a sleepover with her friend. What's going—"

"What's your name, ma'am?" The officer's voice cut loudly across mine.

"Aimee Rojas. Aimee Rojas. My daughter is Anna. Anna Rojas."

The words could only spill out.

Maren spoke up. "Officer, please let us up. Or bring Anna down, if…" She faltered and didn't finish the sentence.

The policeman clutched his radio. "Casey, there's a woman down here, Aimee Rojas. Says her daughter's inside."

Seconds that seemed to last an eternity.

The radio crackled. "Send her up."

The officer let me go. "Take care ladies, it's not pretty in there."

What did that mean?

Jesus have mercy.

We pounded up the stairs that were the twin of mine, the fragrance of gardenias sickeningly sweet as I gasped for breath. Another officer met us at the open French doors and allowed us inside.

The ships floated, waveless, on the far wall, but the air was acrid with a familiar smell I couldn't identify. Nothing seemed even remotely out of place, until I saw Jeremy standing between two officers in the kitchen, shirtless.

Handcuffed.

There was blood on his hands. Blood all over his sweatpants. Blood on his face.

Nothing is impossible.

"No."

The floor seemed to shift underneath me as I remembered our words, too hastily spoken.

My mouth and hands tingled, numb. "No, no, no."

Jeremy's eyes widened as he caught sight of me, his unwavering stare alone keeping me on my feet and conscious, even though the sight of him terrified me.

He spoke without hesitation. "Aimee, the girls are alright, Anna is okay. Everything is going to be okay."

Nothing could have convinced me to believe him.

The officers' eyes passed between us as he spoke freely.

Two more paramedics dashed through the French doors behind us with a gurney and ran through the hall to Christina's room. Loud, urgent voices shouted, drowning out the shrill of a charging defibrillator.

"Where is Anna?" I didn't recognize my voice. "What have you done?"

The words fell from my mouth like stones, too heavy to ever take back. This was a nightmare, and every irrational fear I'd ever had was coming true.

"Mama!"

Anna and Christina peered over the railing of Jeremy's loft, then flung themselves down the stairs. Anna wore the same pajamas I'd packed in her bag. No blood anywhere. I sank to the floor and the girls filled my arms.

"Baby! Are you okay?"

Anna nodded, burying her face in my chest.

"Thank you, thank you, thank you." I prayed softly against her hair.

Christina clung to me, her eyes wild with panic.

Everything moved in slow motion.

Another officer came down the stairs, holding Jeremy's backpack and a hoodie he wore often.

The officer nearest Jeremy took his arm. "We'll need to take you to the station now, Mr. King."

Four officers flanked him on all sides, but as they passed us, Jeremy took a step toward us and spoke quickly.

The reek of sweat and blood on him was nauseating.

"Aimee, Captain Casey is in Christina's room. He's my friend. Talk to him."

His eyes were desperate.

"Everything's going to be okay, and we're going to get through this. Please keep trusting me. I love you. I'll see you and the girls tomorrow."

"We're stable, move *now.*"

The command coming from Christina's bedroom made us all look in that direction and my thoughts shifted, jolting with alarm.

I glanced back toward the French doors, but Jeremy and the policemen were gone.

The paramedics worked quickly, expertly maneuvering the gurney in front of us and out the doors.

The man on the gurney was gravely injured. His right pant leg had been cut, denim slashed open to the groin, and a large tourniquet applied on his thigh. What had been a white t-shirt was knotted just below the tourniquet, soaked through with blood. He was deathly pale and his eyes lolled half-open, swollen and unseeing. Despite the bag valve mask and heavy bruising of the left side of his face, I recognized him immediately.

It was Darius.

Sunday found me sitting outside on the deck, my mind as blank as the canvas of clouds strung across the sky. The glint of yesterday's diamonds had vanished, and thick fog crept across the water, impervious to the morning sun. I cradled a cup of coffee in my hands and closed my eyes, hoping for my phone to ring. Dreading it.

Maren's feet whispered across the deck

"Christina's passed out." Mug in hand, she curled up in the chair next to mine. "Is Anna still asleep?"

My voice cracked. "Yes."

"Have you heard from anyone yet?"

"No. Did you sleep?"

"Some. Christina is a gem. I think she didn't mind sharing a bed with me at all. You?"

"A little. It took Anna a while to fall asleep." Her body had finally relaxed into the curve of mine just as the colorless light of dawn began to break.

My eyes scraped shut, tender from all the tears I'd shed while speaking with Captain Casey. From tears that kept streaming down my face long after Anna stopped shaking in my bed.

I reached for Maren's hand. "I'm so thankful you're here."

"Of course, friend. All things work together for good." Her hand was warm. "Did Anna tell you anything the police didn't?"

"A little. It sounds like she and Christina had been asleep for a while but woke up when they heard Darius breaking the window."

The surf was strangely silent this morning.

"When she told me about everything that happened, she kept calling him 'the burglar.'"

"Who, Darius?"

"Yes. I guess she didn't recognize him in the dark, and she

said as soon as Jeremy turned on the lights, he yelled for her and Christina to get under the covers."

"Oh, love." The wind blew Maren's hair across her eyes. "You didn't tell her it was Darius?"

The bitterness of the coffee slid down my throat. "No."

She glanced away from me. "What was he on?"

"Who knows. The police notified Cecily, but I haven't heard from her yet. It must have been something hard to make him break into the wrong house."

The house next door, pristine and almost empty, ready to sell. Jeremy, power washing the carport and asking the girls about *Garfield*. It could have ended so differently.

"But then again, Jeremy cleaned things out yesterday. He took the flag down and parked his truck in the garage. And since neither you or I have a car, and the old truck is locked in our garage, there's virtually no difference between the two houses with all the usual landmarks gone."

I continued, "Anna said Darius—well, the 'burglar'—never made it to them. He went straight for Christina's dresser. Hers is exactly where mine is. She has the primary suite, same as my room. He fumbled around on the dresser looking for my drugs and the girls started screaming. That and the glass breaking must have woken Jeremy up. I don't think he's been sleeping much since everything that happened last weekend with Clint."

Maren pulled her hoodie closer around her.

"Anna said before she got under the covers, she saw that the burglar had a—" My voice broke. "—a knife."

Maren shifted in her chair. "That doesn't sound like Darius. Does he own one?"

"Besides the knife he got from Boy Scouts when he was ten, not that I've ever known. I don't know how much of the Darius I knew is left, though."

Stubborn pain scorched my forehead.

"It seems like it all happened so fast. Apparently, Jeremy

got around Darius somehow and managed to get him into Christina's bathroom."

"I heard Casey say the 911 call came from a child?"

"It was Christina. She has a phone. And she's smart as a whip."

I closed my eyes again. It was all too much, too unbelievable.

"Are you okay, love?" Maren asked. "I mean, none of us are okay with any of this, but you don't need to talk about it right now. I should shut up."

"No, I… it helps to hear myself saying it all out loud."

"If you say so."

We were silent for a few moments.

"Jeremy and Darius were in the bathroom. Casey said they fought with the lights off. Jeremy tried to get the knife away from him, but he couldn't get at it easily. Casey told me Jeremy said it was like Darius couldn't feel any pain, like he had super strength. Jeremy was holding off the knife with one hand and trying to knock him out with the other, when Darius slipped on the tile and fell on the knife."

A swell of tears flowed down my cheeks freely, unchecked.

"Jeremy used his shirt as a tourniquet. The paramedics told Casey that with all the blood loss, it must have nicked the femoral artery."

Maren sighed. "Jesus."

"Jeremy used Darius' knife to cut his pants and get at the wound, so his fingerprints are also on the knife. Casey was confident that forensics and self-defense would clear him of any charges, though."

"But they still handcuffed him?"

"The responding officers didn't know Jeremy. They broke in through the French doors and found them all in the back in Christina's room. When they saw him covered in blood, they drew their guns on him. Of course he complied. I think the girls were terrified."

"Of course. Lord."

My phone dinged.

Jeremy King
Casey's bringing me back home.
How is Christina?

I rubbed my runny nose and took a breath, then typed out a reply.

"Jeremy?" Maren asked.

"Yeah," I hit send.

The girls are still asleep.
Maren and I are on the deck.
Coffee?

I waited for his response.

Black.

"Casey's bringing him back now. I'm going to make more coffee."

I glanced at Maren as I got up.

She chewed her bottom lip, a small spark of whimsy in her expression.

I stopped and gave her a long look. "You know I know what you're thinking."

"Uh huh. But I can't decide yet whether my timing was wildly unfortunate or providential."

"At least one of us had better sense and decided to sleep in actual clothes."

"You keep it as cold as a morgue in there, love! I had no choice but to throw on a sweatshirt. I never could have predicted you'd end up half naked at a crime scene. Forgive me?"

"We'll see." I started toward the doors, the decking groaning under my feet.

She called out, "You heard what he said to you as he was being taken away, didn't you?"

"Yep." I threw my reply over my shoulder and went inside.

Of course I had heard him say it. It was the last thing I could remember thinking about before passing out from emotion and exhaustion beside my daughter less than two hours ago.

I ground the beans. Turned the kettle on boil. Opened the French press and dumped the grounds from my first brew. Poured fresh grounds inside.

Performing this mundane ritual returned some normalcy to the day. I rubbed my head. Just a small headache. "It's okay," I told myself. "Definitely no more coffee for me though."

Maren entered breezily through the French doors. "Jeremy's here, on the deck. I'm going to make breakfast."

"I hate you." I grabbed the press and a fresh mug.

She opened the fridge and blew me a kiss.

He was staring at the fog-shrouded gulf but turned around quickly when he heard my steps. The mug and French press rattled as I set them on the table. Jeremy stood far from me at the opposite end of the table, his expression flat. The blue of his eyes was fogged over just like the ocean and tired. Very tired. He had changed into gym shorts and a t-shirt touting Pantera's 1994 world tour. It looked like he'd been able to wash up a little at the police station, but it was impossible to miss the faint tinge of Darius' blood still on his feet and face, along his hairline.

"There's still blood on you."

He nodded, almost indiscernibly.

"How are you?" I asked.

"Overwhelmed." He exhaled heavily through his nose. "Thankful. Angry." His keys clattered on the table. Dark bruising cuffed his wrists.

The police had been afraid of him.

I had been afraid of him.

"Your cousin fought like a Berserker. Casey thinks it was angel dust. It was the best I could do to keep the knife away from me." A deep furrow emerged between his brows as he remembered.

The gravity of the night before welled up in my chest.

I could have lost all of them.

He cleared his throat and glanced back to the invisible sea. "I smell like jail. I'd like to clean myself up and take a nap before the day really gets going and Christina wakes up. If that's alright with you?"

His politeness was barbed, and I struggled to meet his eyes.

"She's welcome to stay here for as long as you need."

"Thank you," he said. "I'm going to take you up on that. I need to clean up the house this afternoon, too, hopefully before the realtor gets here."

His phone was in his hand, the distance between us greater than just a few plastic chairs and wooden decking.

"Casey gave me the number of a professional crew that handles stuff like this. He said the police have taken all the photos and evidence they need."

I shuddered.

"I'm going to try and get back over to town before the day is too far gone. I know a wholesaler for the window that was broken."

"Won't insurance take care of that?" I asked, trying to match his apparent preoccupation.

"I'm not waiting for them. I have to clean up the mess as soon as possible and get this place off of my hands."

"I'm so sorry, Jeremy."

"It's not your fault," he said simply. "I need to apologize too, before I go, if I may."

"Why?" I held my breath, afraid if I inhaled too deeply the sky itself would collapse.

"Last night I told you I loved you. I was feeling a lot of things at that moment, and I know you were too." He measured his words carefully. "What I said is true, and I don't think what I said, or the fact that it's true is surprising to you. I want to apologize because I shouldn't have told you I loved you last night. It wasn't the right time. I was shaken and didn't want you to be. Saying it while there was so much trauma unfolding around us wasn't fair to either of us, and I'm sorry."

The usually dynamic hue of his eyes was dull, flat and opaque.

"I don't expect anything from you, Aimee."

Cool, humid air flooded my lungs. "I was afraid it was all happening again."

He moved towards me involuntarily. "Again?"

"Losing someone." My voice shook. "I thought Anna was gone. And you were there, covered in blood and the police arrested you and I thought I was losing you too. It was the longest fifteen minutes of my life from when you left until Casey had the time to explain everything and told me you'd almost certainly be released."

My arms bound around my waist like a straitjacket. I watched the tears fall, splattering on my feet, unable to look at him, astounded that in months after everything I'd been through, I felt the most powerless in *that* particular moment.

"All I've been able to think about since they took you away handcuffed was how I had so many times to confront Darius over the years, and I never did. And if my silence was the thing that almost got you, or my daughter, or Christina killed… and how you told me you loved me even after he almost killed you. I'm so ashamed of what he's done. I'm so sorry about how this will affect all of you, and the house."

My voice broke.

"I'm so sorry for not telling you I loved you when you gave me the chance—"

"Aimee." He wrapped the meaning of entire worlds in the way he said my name.

The distance between us vanished, dissipating like vapor. He was suddenly very near me, his calloused palm on my cheek, a striking contrast to how gently his thumb traced my lips, easily parting them. His mouth immediately followed, soft against mine. Moments passed and he drew back, searching my face intently.

"Turns out I had some time to think about it this morning and I don't want to do slow anymore. Do you?"

His voice was warm, like embers kindled back to life.

The tears stung hot, blurring my vision, and I felt myself begin to smile. "No."

The next kiss was deeper, hungrier; everything we'd held back from each other unraveled at the realization that it might never have happened. "Jesus," I murmured breathlessly against his neck. "Thank you, Jesus."

"God," he said just as reverently, holding me close. "I've wanted this. Wanted you."

I looked up at him. "Thank you. Thank you for protecting my baby girl last night. Thank you for saving my cousin. I'm so sorry. So sorry for all of this."

"Stop apologizing." His tone was curt, humor rippling through it.

My breath shook as I let it out. "It was sketchy there for a few minutes last night, Mr. King."

"It certainly was." A smile played at the corners of his mouth as he brushed stray strands of hair from my face. "Was that your normal bedtime attire?"

My eyes narrowed. "Wouldn't you like to know?"

"You have no idea."

"Maren brought it back from Paris as a gift. She claimed it was breathable and would help me sleep well."

"Had the opposite effect on me. Took my breath away. Kept me up at the station all night."

"I'm so glad it was beneficial for one of us."

"Oh, it wasn't just me. Casey and the other officers send their regards."

"Jeremy King!"

I pushed him away, but his laughter drew me back.

"Shall we continue the rest of this long day, Mrs. Rojas?"

"Sure, don't you want the coffee?"

"I'll take it to go." He poured himself a cup.

The weathered wood sang mournfully under our feet as we walked across the deck. He paused at the top of the stairs and turned toward me. "Casey said there could be some additional formalities and paperwork I may have to fill out tomorrow, but I'll try not to be in your hair."

I slipped my hand into his, holding him back from starting down the stairs.

"Jeremy?"

He turned around.

"I love you. Please do whatever you need to as far as Darius is concerned."

A flame of amber ringed his irises, surrounded by a blue rivaled only by a cloudless summer sky. His mouth met mine once more, lingering.

"I love you too, Aimee Rojas."

He turned away and strode down the stairs, across the path and disappeared underneath his house, without once looking back.

"That was the worst night of my *life*."

Anna flopped forward on the pile of Jeremy's clean laundry I'd heaped on my bed. "I am never spending the night at the house next door again, and we are sleeping with the alarm system on tonight and every night."

I couldn't help but give her a little smile. "No one is going to spend the night over there again, love. Jeremy is going to stay out at SeaSplit tonight, and Christina's going to stay with us until her new bed gets delivered."

"When will Christina come back?"

"She's getting dinner with her daddy and Mike right now. He's helping them take a few last-minute things from their old house to SeaSplit. They'll bring her over when it's time to go to sleep."

Anna muttered, "She wouldn't let me look."

"What are you talking about, baby?"

"She wouldn't let me look when Jeremy was fighting the burglar. Jeremy sounded really angry and yelled for us to get down as soon as he turned on the lights. Christina told me to hide deep in the covers and she'd tell me when it was over." Anna's expression pinched at the memory. "I couldn't breathe and at first, I was mad at her because I could hear just as well as she could and would have totally known when it was over. But now I'm really glad because I don't ever want to know what that robber looked like."

My heart twisted. I'd never be able to get the image of Darius' face, bruised and half-dead out of my mind.

"I'm proud of you. You did exactly what Jeremy said to do. I'm sorry that you were so scared."

"It was mostly seeing the nasty blood all over Jeremy that scared me the most." She shuddered. "Ew. Can you imagine having a stranger's blood on you? A murderer's blood on you? He could have killed Jeremy, Mama. That man was a murderer."

"He could have been." The trembling socks I held in my hands were mismatched. I folded them anyway. "But you know what? Jeremy saved the man's life, even after he tried to kill him. Did you know that?"

"No, Mama." She sat on her heels, stunned. "Why did Jeremy save him?"

Because he knew it was Darius. I could have said. *Because it was the right thing to do. Because he's a good man.*

"Because that's what Jesus did for us, baby."

The truth manifested in her eyes. The rapid metamorphosis from disbelief to understanding was beautiful.

I picked up another pair of socks that did match. "The police took the robber to the hospital, and then they'll take him to prison. He's never going to hurt anyone again."

"And we are going to say our prayers, and turn our alarm on since Jeremy's not spending the night with us, right Mama?"

"That's right love." I sent Darius to the perimeter of my thoughts. "I'm so thankful Jeremy was there to keep you safe last night."

"I always knew he would keep me safe."

"You did?"

"Well, yeah. Jeremy loves us."

Maren's footsteps danced down the hall and into my room. "You know what else Anna Marie?" She stretched out like a cat next to her on my bed.

"She already knows," I told her.

Maren and Anna looked at each other, then at me. "Y'all kissed!"

Jeremy King
Praise Jesus.
It's summer break, and I don't
have to work for two months.

> *Take it slow today.*

I will.
Just need to stay out here until

Christina's furniture gets here.
Then I'm heading your way.

Jeremy's day may have started slowly, but mine didn't. After I saw Maren off in her Uber, my phone blew up.

Cecily Fontenot
Shug, I'm at the hospital now.
Darius is still in the ICU.
Surgery went well but he's being restrained
because the doctors are afraid the
withdrawals from the PCP and whatever
else he had in his system will make
him aggressive when he wakes up.
They may give him a morphine
drip to help him dose down as
long as he's in the hospital.
The police are here, ready to take
him when he's fit to be moved.
They have the warrant from
Morgan City as well as the report from
Galveston. The surgeon said the EMTs
wouldn't have been able to get him back
if Jeremy hadn't made the first tourniquet.
Tell J thank you.
Keep praying.

We are praying, and I will
let him know everything.
Please come home soon, Cici.
I'm sure there are time limits for
the ICU, and you need to rest.
Did you get any sleep at Kayla's place?

I did until Captain Casey called me.

> *Something is better than nothing.*
> *Come home soon.*

Jeremy King

> *Dr said you saved Darius' life, thank you.*
> *Pray for Cecily and Darius.*
> *Christina and Anna are doing well.*

Mary Cole
Chris and I are here if you need anything.
We can watch Christina or Anna
or both if you need to rest.

> *Hi Mary.*
> *Could you bring dinner over tonight?*
> *That would help a ton.*
> *Maren left this morning, and I*
> *haven't gotten to the grocery store.*

Yes, what time is good for you?

> *5? If that's OK? Love you.*

Love you too.
See you soon.

Jason Hamada
Hi Aimee, I just saw your text.
Thank you for letting me know
about everything.
Jeremy texted me too.
We're praying for all of you.

I won't be back from Seattle until
mid-June, but Lilly and the kids
will be back the week after next.
Please let us know how we can help.

David Tunc
Hi Aimee, I'm so sorry
we are playing phone tag.
Please give me a call as soon as you can.

I called him, but it went to voicemail. So much for that.

Gil Hoffart

Hoff, do you have a second?
I need to call you.
Nothing regarding C.

I'm free now.

Jeremy King
I'm at the store.
Need anything?

Just you.
Mary and Chris are bringing
dinner over tonight.
Why don't you and Christina join us?
I'm sure they'll bring enough
to feed a small nation.

I'll be there.

Cecily Fontenot
Jeremy is pressing charges.
Please tell him thank you.

I know it was hard for him
to make that decision.

Mary, Chris, and Jeremy are
coming over for dinner tonight,
please come home early.
You need to get some rest tonight.
And you can thank Jeremy yourself, he'll
be here and I know he'd like to see you.

OK Shug, I will.
I'll come as soon as the doctor
makes his evening rounds.

Drive safe, love you!

Love u 2 Shug.

Mary Cole

Turns out Cecily and
Jeremy will be here too.
Is that okay?

Of course, no problem.

Christina King
Hey Mrs. Rojas, can we watch
the first Lord of the Rings movie?
Anna says she's seen it
but it looks scary to me.

Silly girl!
I'm downstairs, you could come ask me.

Allison Nance

It is a little scary, but Anna has seen it before.
You can watch it if you want.
I'll be up soon to watch it with you.

LOL OK!

Jeremy King

Is Christina old enough to
watch Lord of the Rings?

After last weekend, yes.

Valid point.

Cecily Fontenot
Shug, I hate to ask you this,
but do you think you could
come up to the hospital to
hear what the doctor has to say?

Let me text Mary and Jeremy.

OK.

Mary Cole

Hey Mary.
I think Cecily really
needs me at the hospital.
Would it be too much to
ask if you could stay with Anna
until I get back this evening?

Jeremy King

Cecily asked if I could come to the hospital.

255

I'll take you.

I love you.

Mary Cole
Of course, sweetheart!
Do you need us to watch Christina too?

Yes, that would be wonderful.
Thank you so much!
How did you know to ask? ;)

Call it intuition.
Also, I can't see you driving
Jeremy's old beater into town.
LOL.

The hospital doors whispered open.

"Sorry about not keeping my schedule free," I said.

"Best laid plans." Jeremy sniffed. "All hospitals smell the same. Which floor is he on?"

"Fifth."

Cecily was waiting for us near the elevator bank.

"Oh, Shug!" She gathered me in her arms.

"Are we late? Did the doctor come already?"

"No, y'all are right on time. And you." Her gaze swung to Jeremy. "I know Aimee's probably apologized a hundred times already but please hear it from me, I'm so sorry. So very deeply sorry for what Darius has done."

"Cecily, please. There's no need—" he began.

She grasped his arms. "There's most certainly a need! I'm ashamed and yet so unbelievably grateful to you. The doctor is due to make his rounds soon, and I want y'all to hear what he has to say. Come on."

Cecily led us down the hall and hit an intercom.

"Name, please?" The intercom crackled.

"It's Mrs. Fontenot, Donnell."

The sterile tone of the speaker immediately warmed at the sound of Cecily's voice. "Come on in, Cici."

The lock on the door shot back.

I squeezed her hand. "Only you could make the hospital staff feel like family in under twenty-four hours."

Her eyes sparkled through the tears still in her eyes. "We'll check in first."

The guard hunched over the desk lifted his head. His chair groaned as he leaned back. "Do we have some guests today, Miss Cecily?"

"Yes, Clarkson, this is my niece and her boyfriend. I wanted them to be here to get the latest update from Darius' doctor."

Clarkson eyed us. "Three's a little tight, Miss Cecily. I can admit family," he nodded toward me, "but your boyfriend will have to wait out here with me. And I'll need your cell phones, too."

"Clarkson, Mr. King," she laid her hand on Jeremy's wrist, "was the man my son assaulted the night of his injury. Not only did Mr. King not kill him in self-defense, but he also turned right around and saved his life."

Clarkson's face remained motionless, except for his brows which shot up.

"You're gonna wear me down, Miss Cecily. I can tell." Clarkson chuckled and wrote something down in a large binder, then heaved it up to the counter. "I'm sorry, but Mr. King's gotta stay with me. We play by the rules here, which is four visitors a day, two visitors max at a time for ICU." His doe-eyed lashes blinked at Cecily. "Please sign here."

"Well, it never hurts to ask," Cecily chirped. "Thank you, Clarkson."

"Of course, Miss Cecily, and please remember to leave your phones here."

"I can take them." Jeremy held out a hand.

"Thanks, boyfriend." I planted a soft elbow in his ribs as I passed him our phones.

"Makes me sound too young."

Before I could turn, he wrapped his free hand around my neck, leaned in, and kissed me. The sterile air grew warm between us, hope rooting in the dim hallway. He let me go. "I'll be right here."

I caught up with Cecily and grasped her hand.

Muted beeps punctuated the silence in the intensive care unit.

An armed guard was stationed at the door of Darius' room.

"Evening, ladies." He checked his watch. "Normal intensive care visiting hours end in about forty-five minutes, and with the police hold we have on the patient, you're limited to twenty."

"He's not conscious yet. We're just here to see the doctor," Cecily said.

"I understand, ladies. Take care." He yanked the curtain aside, allowing us into the area where Darius laid.

He was bound in every way; handcuffed to the bed, right leg and both hands bandaged, eyes swollen shut. The bruising on the left side of his face had blossomed blue and yellow. His chest rose and fell mechanically with the rhythmic, precise timing of the ventilator.

I drew in my breath, readying myself to say something—anything—but the scraping of the curtain across ball bearings halted my voice.

"Mrs. Fontenot." A young doctor in turquoise scrubs with an iPad greeted Cecily then nodded to me.

"Hi. I'm Darius' cousin."

He shook the hand I offered him. "Nice to meet you." He turned back to Cecily. "We're in somewhat of a holding pattern. Currently there are three areas of concern, although I'm thinking that two of these areas will resolve fairly quickly." He flicked his fingers across the screen of his tablet. "The surgery to repair the femoral artery was very straightforward. We grafted a section of vein from your son's arm to the wound in his leg. I'm anticipating this should heal in four to six weeks. Minor lacerations on the patient's hand and face should heal normally with time, and honestly, I'm not extremely concerned with the concussive injury he sustained from falling. There's no hematoma, his spinal cord is uninjured, and the swelling is minimal."

"What's the most concerning part?" I asked.

"Darius has been unresponsive ever since he arrived just under forty-eight hours ago. It's difficult to determine why he hasn't emerged from his state of unconsciousness. We're still waiting for a final toxicology report to be generated, but the CAT scans and EEGs we've run so far haven't shown anything incongruent with injuries sustained from a fall. His cognitive functions are normal, and I'm expecting to take him off the ventilator within the next twenty-four hours. Depending on what the labs tell us, Darius may be in a comatose state for any number of causes ranging from the substances he used, to something psychosomatic." He glanced at Darius. "Or a combination of the two, depending on if he had a bad trip, or if the substance had time to alter his mind."

"His mind's been altered for the past fifteen years," Cecily deadpanned.

"He's in a coma?" My fingers twisted empty space on my finger where my wedding band had been.

"Yes. It may be transitory, or it could be prolonged. It's too early to determine at this point. However," the doctor passed a steady hand along his jaw, "the comatose state might work to his advantage. He's an addict?"

"You could say that," I murmured.

"It doesn't happen often and it's controversial, but occasionally, addicts seeking rehab ask to be induced into a comatose state.

It's a rare treatment we call a coma-induced detox. In some ways, it's a safer state for the patient to process the symptoms of withdrawal and easier for their care provider to monitor it. But it's not ideal and of course—as is the case with any withdrawal scenario—can still be dangerous."

"Dangerous?" I asked. "You mean he might not come out of the coma?"

The doctor's tone was clinical. "He could die. Undergoing an involuntary rapid detox could cause him to suffer a cardiac event due to the withdrawal. Or it could trigger a series of other conditions, including a stroke, or aneurysm, it's difficult to say."

Cecily's lips pursed. "So, all we can do is wait?"

Her final word resonated deeply inside me. For years she'd been waiting for Darius to come back, to end the addiction. We'd all been waiting for something.

"Yes. It's all a waiting game now."

"Can he hear us?" I asked.

The doctor's face softened. "Many coma patients who make a full recovery report dream-like scenarios where they can recall real conversations had by others who were with them."

Cecily stood near Darius' head as the doctor briefly examined the settings on the various machines that stabilized him. The doctor left after excusing himself, and Cecily reached her hand and gently stroked Darius's hair. Her gesture revivified a long-forgotten memory.

I had brushed my hand through his hair in just the same way when I was eight and he was three. Cecily's minivan roared down the highway on the road trip from Morgan City to Biloxi thirty summers ago. My mom and Cecily were laughing in the front and Darius slept with his head on my lap. His blonde hair was soft as a rabbit's foot. His lashes fluttered as I touched him, but he didn't wake…

The beep of the machinery pierced my thoughts, and I was surprised to find his hand was warm to the touch.

"Wake up soon, Dare." I spoke softly near his ear. "I love you so much."

"We should go, Shug." It looked like the last thing she wanted to do.

I took her hand.

The curtain rings screeched overhead once more as I drew it aside.

At the end of the hall near Clarkson's desk, Jeremy rose from his seat. His eyes flitted to me first, then Cecily. He dug his hand into his pocket and handed Cecily her phone, smiling at her gently.

From my vantage point, a seven-ounce device hitting her palm crumpled her in half. Jeremy's arms shot out, wrapping around her, supporting her as she sank onto him. He held her as she cried, telling her the same thing he'd told me, too many times over the last week.

"It's going to be okay, Cecily."

His eyes caught mine.

My mouth formed the words that my voice was too broken by emotion to speak.

"I love you." Tears ran down my face.

His lips moved silently over Cecily's bowed head. "Love you more."

Jeremy's truck was humming across the Galveston Causeway bridge when the phone buzzed in my hand.

"David?" I answered, relieved.

"Aimee, all praise to God! I'm so glad I finally got you on the phone."

"Me, too. You have no idea how much I've been meaning to call you, but with everything going on I've completely lost track of time."

"I understand entirely, which is also why I'm so sorry about what I have to tell you." His voice teetered. "I tried to reach you so many times. This is a matter which should be discussed if not in person, at least with the courtesy of a call… but I had no choice. I'm so sorry."

Deep in my gut, I knew what he was about to say.

"Someone else has booked your house. Starting next week."

Jeremy eased back against the cab door. The neon lights from Sonic soaked his smile purple as he watched hysteria drive tears slowly down my face.

"Lord." The laughter couldn't stop. "Of course, the end of this day would be capped by the news that I'll be homeless in five days."

"You're having an excellent attitude about it. Tot?" He tipped the carton toward me.

"No, thanks." I gasped for air, and the words jumbled together on the menu outside my window. "I'm pretty sure I'm soon-to-be-jobless, and now homeless."

"Nah, you're not homeless."

"I have nothing lined up," I said, wiping the tears from my face and calming down, breath by breath.

"Come stay at SeaSplit with me and Christina. All three of you."

I knew I was staring at him as if he was speaking a foreign language. "I remember we agreed to going faster, and trust me, there's nothing I'd love more than to see your handsome mug every morning. But don't you think moving in with you is pushing things a bit?"

"You wouldn't be 'moving in,' per se." He scratched the back of his head. "More like sheltering in place. Just at my place… that I'm still selling." He popped another tater tot in his mouth. "And we'll have to move your stuff over."

"That makes me feel so much better. Still, it gives the wrong impression, doesn't it?"

"To whom? The horses I don't own?"

"You know what I mean."

"I *do* know what you mean." He rattled the ice in his cup. "I had coffee with Jason at Red Light last week after everything blew up with your co-worker, but before everything blew up with your cousin. Asked Jason for his input about the possibility of you staying with Christina and I at some point."

I stared at him in disbelief. "You asked Jason—last week, before he left for Seattle—about us temporarily moving in together. And you're just now telling me about it?"

"Someone had to make plans."

His smile destroyed my last functioning brain cells.

"What did he say?"

"He said it was a generous offer."

"It is."

"He asked what my long-term intentions are."

"I, for one, would also love to know. What are they?"

"*Good and not evil.*"

"Glad to hear it. What else did he say?"

"To sleep with our children and to make sure there aren't any extra beds in the house."

"That advice," I said, "is bosh. You don't need a bed to have sex."

His eyebrows shot up. "Intriguing insight, Mrs. Rojas. One I definitely hope to explore with you in much greater detail soon. However, panning back to logistics involving more than just the two of us," he continued, "if we move you over on Thursday, I'd only be in the house with you for four nights, then I'll be in Miami for a week with that continuing education conference. You can house hunt while I'm gone."

"You've figured it all out, haven't you? Are you sure you didn't coordinate this with Darius?"

He shot me a look. "Not funny, Rojas."

"Too soon?"

He smiled, raising his green and purple wrists. "Yep."

"Hmm…" I took one of his hands and kissed the bruised knuckles. "Did Jason have anything else to say?"

"He did, as a matter of fact."

"Oh?"

"He said to love you well."

"A touch dramatic, coming from him."

"He also added a PS which was very to the point."

"Which was?"

I'd never seen a gleam quite like the one which illuminated his eyes as he said: "'Don't screw around, man. Lock it down.'"

It was impossible not to think of the events of the past weekend. Impossible not to think of Darius handcuffed to a bed in the ICU. But the grace and hope of our friends snuffed out the darkness running through my head.

Moving day arrived.

"Soon you'll have a place of your own, Cecily." I wrapped a blender she'd bought in packing paper.

Mary agreed, "Yes! I've got some places lined up for us to visit together after you get set up at Jeremy's."

"I'm thankful." A soft sparkle returned to Cecily's eyes. "God's will for us is life, so the best way to carry on is to go on living."

"Amen," Mary murmured.

"Ready to take a few things down to the truck?" I asked.

"Sure, if the boys are back."

"I think they are." I opened the door.

The day was cool, and I spied Jeremy and Chris leaning against Jeremy's truck, enjoying the breeze.

Jeremy straightened when he saw me. "Hello, beautiful."

"Hey," I smiled.

"Is there more upstairs?" He took the box from my arms.

"Just a few more of these. That's all."

"Give me the keys."

"Here. David said to leave them under the mat." I was happy to pass them off, letting him lock up this chapter in both our lives.

Behind me, Mary and Cecily cleared the cottage stairs. Chris grabbed the suitcases from their hands. "Jeremy sure got his money's worth out of that cleaning crew Casey referred to him. No one could imagine a crime scene in the place. Christina's bathroom was spotless."

Jeremy reappeared at the top of the stairs, the remaining two boxes in his arms.

"And that window installation you did was perfect!" Chris called out.

"The realtor didn't notice anything, which was my main concern," Jeremy said dryly.

"Did you pack the model ships, Jeremy?" Mary asked.

"No, I'm leaving them to help stage the place." Closing the tailgate, he glanced at the cottage. "I would be glad to sell them with the house if the buyer was so inclined. I'm ready to move on, and don't need to drag them across creation with us until we finally land somewhere permanent."

"That makes sense." Mary's gaze swept over the twin cottages, the path and boardwalk to the beach. "So many memories."

Jeremy gave her a soft smile. "Memories I'm content to let live in the past."

She looked at me, then back to Jeremy. "Of course!"

"Baby," Chris interjected, "we can gab all we want at Jeremy's show place."

"Chris." Jeremy secured the boxes with a tow strap in the bed of the truck. His ears reddened. "It's just another house."

Chris propped his elbow on the hood. "Be that as it may, I'm about half-starved. We've got some things to throw on the grill, so let's roll!"

I spied a bag of limes nestled between hardwood charcoal and five cases of Topo Chico.

"Are we making key lime pies as well?" I tucked a blue tarp over the groceries.

Chatter from the other side of the truck faded as Jeremy focused on me.

"I'm well acquainted with your predilections, Rojas. I thought we might spice up your Topo tonight, make us some unleaded spritzers." There was an unremarkable familiarity about the way he said it, something I longed for. The next four nights in his house would feel like four months.

"You're wonderful."

His lips tasted like salt and sugar.

The grit in his throat slowed his voice. "I should've made spritzers months ago."

"There's a season for everything, my love. See you at SeaSplit!" I called, catching up with Cecily and Mary at the Jeep, also packed to the brim with our things. We backed out of the driveway of the twin cottages for the last time, our small convoy making its way down the few miles to SeaSplit. I adored the excitement on Mary and Cecily's faces as we drove through the property.

Mary gasped when she saw the house. "It's even more beautiful than I imagined."

"Maybe I need to have Jeremy build me a house." Cecily piped up.

A small flash of pain blinked at the back of my head. "That's not a bad idea, Cecily."

Jeremy had intentionally kept me out of the house since the first time he'd taken me there. Anna and Christina planted themselves in the yard while Jeremy walked us through the house. He held my hand the entire time, watching my face as I noticed small things. Windowed closets, lit naturally by the sun. Reclaimed tile in the guest bathrooms. The way he'd built light and hope into every space. Seeing the house finished and partially filled with furniture was incredible, and I told him so.

"Also," my thoughts spun, "I have something to ask you. Not this week, but later. When you get back from your trip. We have time."

"Can't wait."

All of us girls—young and old—dressed for the beach and rushed to the ocean, leaving Jeremy and Chris to cook. Eventually, the smell of the grill drew us back to the house. The food healed us. We prayed, devoured the fajitas Jeremy and Chris had grilled to perfection, and alternately shrieked with laughter and groaned in response to Anna and Christina's lengthy recitation of dad jokes. Peace infused the house and soft, lengthening shadows lingered from the long summer day. I savored all of it, chatting in the glow of sunset with Mary and Cecily. Across the room, both Anna and Christina yawned.

"Girls," I called to them. "Why don't you get ready for bed? I think the adults are going to chat in the living room for a while."

Anna cast an anxious look at me.

I kissed her.

"Don't worry bug, we're all here together, and you're spending the night with me tonight, remember?"

"I am?" She smiled.

"Yep."

Content, she ran after Christina.

I plopped into the middle of the vast sofa and Cecily groaned, sinking into the leather roll armchair.

"Same," I murmured from under heavy eyelids.

Chris and Mary settled into the far end of the sofa.

In the kitchen, Jeremy made himself a glass of something decidedly leaded, unlike my spritzers.

"Chris? Ladies?"

"I'll have whatever you're having, son." Chris answered.

"Coming up."

"What's the latest from the doctors, Cici?" Mary queried.

Cecily's voice was hushed as she glanced down the hall, ensuring the girls were out of earshot. I couldn't catch their conversation.

Jeremy handed Chris a lowball glass and nestled himself into the corner of the sofa, near me.

"Tired?" he asked.

"Just a little headache."

He reached for me. "Come here, Rojas."

I glanced at the others, deep in their conversation about Darius. I settled into Jeremy's embrace, tossing the throw which resided on the couch across my legs. I leaned my head against his shoulder and the plush cushioning of the couch. It was the most comfortable I'd been in a very long time. The orb of ice in his glass clinked musically near my ear, and I caught the sharp aroma of his drink as he kissed the curve of my neck where it met my shoulder.

Chris' voice boomed good-naturedly from the opposite end of the couch. "Well, it looks like the cat's fully out of the bag now."

I shot him a smile before I closed my eyes, perfectly content to let Jeremy field this conversation. I'd already given him my keys and my heart. What more was there…?

Cecily's voice crowed, "Shoot, Chris, there was never much of a bag for that particular cat."

Mary spoke softly, "I'm just so happy…"

I heard Jeremy say, "So are we."

Their voices mingled, snippets of conversation lodging at random in my consciousness. "I never thought… a godsend… deadline for completion… she'll be happy out here… took long enough, you're not that young… cutting you off… haven't discussed it yet… dangerous because of the withdrawal… so many unknowns… he can't say…"

The words circled around my head like water down a drain. The pain in my head lessened as their whispers floated up into the ceiling, and I fell asleep.

I woke up with a start, reaching for the lamp on my nightstand, but my hand met empty space. I blinked, eyes adjusting to the lavender-tinged light that washed the house with a hazy glow. I was at SeaSplit, alone on the couch. The memory of Jeremy's arms around me flooded back. The steady rise and fall of his chest against my back had lulled me into a deep sleep. I reached for my phone on the coffee table.

5:02

I rubbed my eyes, trying to clear the sleep from my head. The last time I'd noticed it, the hour had been a little after 9, so…

Eight hours. I'd been asleep for eight hours. The scent of coffee mingling with fresh paint sharpened the air. Beyond the dining table, one of the doors to the deck stood ajar. Before seeking Jeremy out, I stole down the hallway and noiselessly opened the door to Christina's room. Anna faced me in the dim light, sleeping. I walked back down the hall, pausing in front of Cecily's room. Her light, whiffling snore barely penetrated the door. I smiled, very happy that she was enjoying a deep sleep. I crossed the great room and saw Jeremy leaning against the deck railing, watching the sun wake the day.

"Morning, love."

He turned. "Morning, beautiful."

"Did you get any sleep?"

"Not much." His smile was easy.

"I saw Anna in Christina's room."

"Keeping us honest." His arm came around me. "Christina's

upstairs. Mary and Cecily got them settled. No one wanted to wake you."

"When did you get up? I didn't realize you could be so stealthy."

"Maybe half an hour ago. You were out cold, it wasn't difficult." His hushed laughter was the best morning music.

"You didn't want to sneak away to your bed?"

"And leave you alone on the couch all night? Not a chance."

"We had one job to do. Three nights to steer clear of each other, and we couldn't even manage to spend one night apart in the same house. What would Jason Hamada say?"

"I'm pretty sure we know what Jason would say. Admittedly, it's not how I imagined our first night together would go. But it was lovely nonetheless."

I nudged him. "Jeremy King, you think about our first night together?"

"Don't you?"

"Well…" I blushed, turning my eyes toward the waves rolling unceasingly onto the sand. "You were a gentleman last night."

"Hardly. You'd be mortified if you knew even half of what I was thinking in the middle of the night."

"Mortified? That's a strong word. Why would I be mortified?"

He drew in his breath sharply and stood silently for a moment, studying the ocean.

"I was thinking about how many years and hours I've invested in this place. About how Christina and I could never live here. I've always been emotionally detached from SeaSplit. Building it has been more an act of worship than anything else. I put beautiful things in it because all beauty points to a Creator that cares. And I've always been prepared to let it go." His gaze followed a ribbon of rose-colored sky trailing through the clouds. "Until I spent the night here alone last week and saw how the light from the sunrise floods in through the windows upstairs."

In the sand below us, the grass rustled and swayed gently in the breeze.

"Right now, everything upstairs is still gray, but the sun is slowly bringing color back to the world." He faced me. "Last night, all I could think about was waking up there again and seeing the miracle of you lying next to me. I thought about how being with you would feel, first thing in the morning, amazed that everything up 'til then wasn't just a dream. I can't wait to see how the light will look, dawning on your skin.

"Last night, I was thinking that those are things I know I'd never get tired of seeing and feeling, no matter how many thousands of times I'd wake up next to you. The beauty you've brought to my life has taken me to a place I never thought I could stay." Intensity warmed his voice. "Beauty that's a constant reminder of a deeper love crying out, waiting to be answered."

I said shakily, "And that was only half?"

The light from the sunrise hit him square in the eyes, setting them aflame. He didn't kiss me, not at first. For a long time, he held me close, his touch devastatingly intimate. His patience, effective. He told me more, his voice softer than my hands on him, and the world fell away when his mouth closed on mine. By the end we were breathless; our hearts somehow irreversibly conjoined by a vow neither of us had uttered—but both knew existed.

At last he said, "Maybe that gives you an idea of the other half."

I nodded. "Jeremy?"

"Yes?"

"I love you." I'd never tire of saying it to him.

"I love you, Mrs. Rojas."

I caught sight of a single star, fading away into the glory of the daylight.

"Jeremy?"

"Yes?" The patient joy in his voice made me love him even more.

I laughed. "Why do you keep calling me Mrs. Rojas?"

In tandem with the rising sun, the roar of the surf grew louder.

"Well," he pressed his lips against my forehead. "It might cause a bit of an upset if I started calling you Mrs. King before we've said our 'I do's' don't you think?"

"Yes," I said. "I do."

"Cecily, Jeremy's going to make breakfast. He and Chris bought enough to stock a Michelin star restaurant yesterday. Amos must have been doing cartwheels. Would you like anything in particular?"

My voice echoed in her hollow room, even though it was partially furnished.

She sat at the foot of the bed, eerily still.

"Cecily?" I struggled to say her name a second time.

As soon as I saw her face, I knew.

"They called a few minutes ago, Shug."

Somehow, I crossed the room and fell at her feet, waiting for her to say words I never wanted to hear.

The afternoon was a blur, and reconciling the morning's joys and sorrows remained impossible.

Cecily stayed on the phone, coordinating funeral arrangements long-distance as I did a load of laundry and got Anna and I situated in SeaSplit's west wing.

The funeral would take place in Morgan City, but due to the legal proceedings with Valiant, I was bound to stay in the confines of state lines. Cecily would leave before dawn on Monday morning, taking the trek across I-10 to be with family in Louisiana.

Jeremy was already packed up, ready to leave for his week-long seminar. He would drive himself to the airport on Monday morning to catch his flight to Miami after dropping off the girls with Chris and Mary.

At Jeremy's suggestion, I invited Nat to spend Sunday night with us at SeaSplit so the two of us could ride to Houston for the deposition at 9. The Coles would pick me up and return the girls and myself to SeaSplit.

I sat on my bed, mindlessly rifling through my Valiant folio, still searching for a motive for Clint's actions. I spied my passport wedged in the back behind my presentation notes from the meeting I'd fled in Manhattan. I picked it up and thumbed through it, the colorful stamps from various countries comprising a flip book of the last ten years of my life.

I shifted my weight on the bed and glimpsed Anna and Christina working on a new shell garden by the boardwalk. Jeremy stood near them, watering the lawn. They shared a joke; Jeremy's grin lit his face and Anna and Christina's laughter barely penetrated the wall of glass where I sat. The moment lingered, seared in my mind.

I plucked my phone off the sheets and flipped it over.

3:16

"For God so loved the world…" I murmured.

Suddenly, everything clicked into place.

The phone flashed in my hand as I scrolled quickly and found his name.

The ringing was interminable.

His straw slurped. "'S'up, fellow perp?"

"Nat, could you do me another favor?"

Drenched in shade from the live oaks that framed it, the plaza was humid. We ran across it.

"I still can't believe you're wearing that." Nat panted, opening the heavy glass door for me as the Monday morning crowd jostled against us.

I hastily glanced down at the deep-cut double-breasted cobalt suit Maren had overnighted from Los Angeles.

"It's executive attire, Nat."

I threw my bag the color of kumquats into a tub and passed it onto the belt. A guard waved me through the metal detector.

Nat emptied his pockets.

"Are you sure you're ready for this, Aimee?"

"There aren't many options as far as timing goes, bud."

He caught up to me on the other side of security. The clicks from my heels echoed endlessly down the hallway. I put my hand on the brass doorknob, knowing the words I'd say inside the courtroom would be inscribed in time itself.

The concern in Nat's eyes made me pause.

"Hey," I squeezed his arm. "None of this would be possible without you, not any of it. You know that, don't you?"

He looked like a boy. "Really?"

"Really," I smiled. "Come on, let's go. We can't be late."

I took a deep breath and opened the door.

Valiant Oil and Gas, Incorporated

      Plaintiffs,

VS.

Clint Myers,

      Defendant.

      Videographed Oral Deposition of
Aimee L. Rojas, Director of Sales Activation Valiant Oil and Gas

Monday, May 22, 2023

Videotaped oral deposition of Aimee L. Rojas, produced as a witness at the insistence of the Plaintiffs, and duly sworn, was taken in the above-styled and austered cause on the 22 of May, 2023, from 9:45 a.m. to 10:12 a.m., before Donald Lambert, C&R, reported by machine shorthand at the offices of Lambert and Pless, 23000 San Felipe, Blvd, Houston, Texas, 77025, pursuant to the Texas Rules of Civil Procedures and the provisions stated on the record or attached hereto.

Q: Mrs. Rojas, how long have you known Clint Myers?

A: Since he joined Valiant in 2016.

Q: You were part of a committee that hired Mr. Myers?

A: Yes.

Q: You believed Mr. Myers would be an asset to Valiant?

A: Yes, and he proved himself to be so.

Q: What were his qualifications?

A: They were outstanding. Outside of his excellent track record at one of our major competitors, he held an MBA from an Ivy League School. His undergrad degree was a double major in engineering and marketing.

Q: Please describe his role at Valiant.

A: He was hired as an outside sales representative and successfully worked his way up to becoming Director of International Market

Activation.

Q: So, his proficiency at his job was undeniable?

A: Yes, he aided in netting almost two billion dollars' worth of contracts over the past seven years.

Q: You trusted him?

A: Yes.

Q: Did you have a personal relationship with Mr. Myers?

A: We were friends.

Q: Mrs. Rojas, prior to May fifth, were you aware of Clint Myers' relationship with a Miss Janelle Terill?

A: I knew they had seen each other in a romantic capacity.

Q: Do you know how long this romantic relationship lasted?

A: Clint never told me exactly when it began. To my knowledge it started in March sometime. He mentioned something the last time I saw him that made me assume it was over.

Q: The last time you saw Mr. Myers, you hosted customers from the Saipan-Velez project at an event in Galveston at the Grand Galvez on May fifth. Is that correct?

A: Yes.

Q: Was it a party?

A: Yes. It's not an uncommon industry practice to host a dinner or cocktails as a celebration upon the execution of a contract.

Q: Several of the customers at the party stated that you and Mr. Myers arrived at the hotel together and left the event together. Is that correct?

A: We did arrive together. We left our guests at the same time, but we did not leave the property together. I took an Uber home and Clint took his car.

Q: Mrs. Rojas, after your husband's death in 2020, did your friendship with Mr. Myers ever become romantic?

A: No.

Q: He was aware you didn't have feelings for him?

A: Yes, he was aware I had no romantic feelings for him.

Q: At any point was your relationship with Mr. Myers sexual?

A: No.

Q: Several customers from the event at Grand Galvez on May fifth testified that it appeared as though you were on physically intimate terms with Mr. Myers.

A: I'm sure it appeared that way. Clint made unwanted sexual advances toward me at the end of the event.

Q: You've clearly stated that Mr. Myers knew your relationship had boundaries. Why would he change the status quo, Mrs. Rojas?

A: I assume for the same reasons he embezzled money from Valiant, even though I'm certain he knew it was a felony.

Q: What benefit would he gain by making your relationship appear sexual in front of strangers, Mrs. Rojas?

A: In its crudest form, Mr. Lambert, sales is about desire and manipulation. The customers saw what Clint wanted them to see.

Q: The witnesses all stated that you didn't try to stop Mr. Myers' advances.

A: I was afraid.

Q: Afraid, Mrs. Rojas?

A: Yes. Clint said certain things to me which I considered threatening.

Q: Why didn't you confront him then and there, Mrs. Rojas?

A: Counsel, I'm going to assume you've never felt physically threatened by a man whom you once trusted. The situation on May fifth was complicated, but I'm sure Clint got what he wanted out of it.

Q: He wanted the opportunity to be physical with you?

A: No. He wanted to cement my utter disgust for him.

Q: Mr. Myers did not want to extend his relationship with you into the sexual arena?

A: You have quite a way with words, Mr. Lambert. Yes, I'm certain he wanted to terminate our friendship.

Q: Had he made any concerted efforts to end your relationship in other ways prior to May fifth?

A: Yes.

Q: Would you like to elaborate on these efforts, Mrs. Rojas?

A: In general, he was an ass. Regarding our work, he communicated with me in an unprofessional manner in our last few exchanges over the phone. Personally, he said certain things which eroded the trust I had in him. I'm sure you know I've been on medical leave for a majority of this year, Mr. Lambert. Clint took advantage of my trust and ultimately chose his own greed above any personal happiness he could have enjoyed from our friendship, or from our successful professional relationship. All of this took place at the expense of my physical and mental health.

Q: Investigators recently found an offshore account opened by Mr. Myers in August of 2020. This particular bank has a safe deposit box containing $2.6 million dollars in gold in today's valuation. Do you know Mr. Myers had two beneficiaries listed on this account, one of whom is Miss Anna Marie Rojas?

A: I have no appropriate remarks to make, Mr. Lambert.

Q: You're surprised?

A: Yes.
Q: Anna Marie Rojas is your daughter?

A: Yes.

Q: The other beneficiary is a Mrs. Jeremy King of Galveston County. Are you aware of such a person?

A: No.

Q: You do not know a Mrs. Jeremy King of Galveston County?

A: I do not.

Q: Why do you believe Mr. Myers chose to list your daughter as a beneficiary on this account?

A: I can't begin to speculate, Mr. Lambert, other than he truly cared for Anna. That's something I never questioned.

Q: Are you aware of any financial or material favors Clint Myers may have promised Janelle Terill in exchange for her assistance in his criminal activities?

A: No.

Q: You knew Mr. Myers well, Mrs. Rojas?

A: Yes.

Q: Can you speculate as to why Mr. Myers would neglect to list Ms. Terill as a beneficiary on this account, even though she allegedly aided him in the embezzlement of these funds?

A: He didn't care about her. She was useful to him, and he dismissed her after she'd served her purpose of giving him access to Valiant's accounting interface.

Q: And he cared more about a stranger—Mrs. Jeremy King of Galveston County—and your daughter?

A: It appears that way, Mr. Lambert.

Q: At any point, were you aware that funds were being transferred from Valiant's corporate accounts to this offshore account?

A: Of course I was unaware. That's why I requested an internal audit.

Q: Mr. Myers never propositioned you to join him in any efforts to embezzle from Valiant?

A: No.

Q: Mr. Nathaniel Si was the first to inform you about the breach in Valiant's invoicing system?

A: Yes.

Q: And Mr. Si informed you that only your login credentials had been used?

A: Yes, but with multiple IP addresses, two of which belonged to Clint and Janelle.

Q: Mrs. Rojas, have you received any communication from Mr. Myers since May fifth?

A: No.
Q: Do you anticipate Mr. Myers contacting you now or at any

time in the future?

A: I don't.

Q: Are you certain of this?

A: I'm confident, Mr. Lambert, but as you know, nothing's impossible.

Jeremy King
Just made it to the hotel.
How did the depo go?

> *About like we expected.*
> *Hoff said I was cool as a cucumber.*
> *The attorney was a jerk.*
> *Mary and Chris just dropped*
> *me and the girls off at SeaSplit.*
> *How is Miami?*

Hot.
Lonely.
Sure you don't need a
warrant for your arrest?

> *I can't even go to the funeral, love.*
> *And besides, even if I could,*
> *leaving the state would be a bad look.*

Nothing's a bad look on you, Mrs. Rojas.
I glanced up and looked through the windows. Christina and

Anna huddled near the boardwalk, diligently working on the shell garden, only a stone's throw from endless ocean.

Smiling, I picked up my phone and hit call.

"Hello?"

It was ridiculous that the sound of his voice could make my knees weak from a thousand miles away. But then again, it had been a very long day…

"You're really getting your mileage out of that, aren't you?"

Jeremy had lined the interior of the closet with cedar shelves and drawers. The scent transported me miles away from the sea as I hung up my shirts and folded my pants. The closet was larger than I remember from my first visit to SeaSplit. Glancing down the length of it, I caught my reflection in the mirror.

The glow of the sunset illuminated the closet, streaming through two thin rectangular windows set on either side of the mirror. There were so many empty shelves to be filled. I counted the pairs of shoes as I lifted them out of my suitcase. The wedges, my heels, several pairs of sneakers and the house shoes on my feet. I folded the few sweaters I owned and tucked them into the drawers which caught and closed silently as I slid them back into place. I smiled at the sweatpants and camisoles I'd survived in for months before shutting them in another drawer.

My cavernous suitcase was finally empty, and I carried it down two flights of stairs to the garage. Metal racks stood along one side of the wall, and I hefted my luggage up beside Anna's. That I didn't know when we'd be using it again was wildly freeing. I took stock of the garage before turning off the light. It was empty and still warm from the scorching summer afternoon. In the kitchen, evening light gilded the room in gold. The sapphire of the waves glimmered through the widows as miles of ocean beckoned to me; would always beckon to me.

My phone rang, pealing through the house. I scanned the kitchen counters and felt the pockets of my cut-offs, not finding it. The ringing continued as I wound my way back up the floating stairs on the window wall and briefly caught sight of the horses. As I cleared the landing, my phone stopped ringing. I crossed the bedroom and reentered the closet. I found it on the shelf by the mirror.

I tapped the screen and held it to my ear, walking slowly back toward the mirror.

"You've reached Jeremy King. I'm away from my phone, but please—"

I smiled and ended the call, turning the phone's ringer to silent and setting it back on the shelf to be forgotten.

I pinched the shoulder of the shirt I was wearing and brought it to my face. A vague aroma of jet fuel and sweat wrinkled my nose. I sniffed hard, peeling the shirt up and over my head.

Something in the depths of the house groaned, metallic.

I tossed the shirt into the laundry hamper and examined my half-naked reflection in the mirror.

My decollete flared under the black satin straps of the demi bra only just holding me in. I brushed my fingertips across my stomach. The lines Anna's dancing feet had made from the inside had both deepened and softened with age, a record of life written on my skin. My legs and arms were strong from my walks and workouts on the beach, and my skin borrowed a radiance from the sun. I blinked hard against the light streaming through the windows. Wayward sunbeams caught fire on my hand, scattering it across the walls as I twisted the band around my finger. Jeremy's t-shirts hung next to me, and I leaned into them, inhaling deeply.

Smoked bourbon. Brown sugar. Bergamot.

I flipped through them, the cotton pooling in my hands, thin and soft. I found one I'd seen him wear a number of times and pulled it off the hanger, slipping it over my head. It fit me loosely and was worn almost sheer as silk. The edge of the sleeves just brushed my elbows and the hem fell below my shorts. I tucked the front into my waistband and hugged myself, imagining this was as close as I'd ever get to disappearing completely into him.

"Aimee?"

My thoughts materialized as Jeremy's voice echoed through the house.

"I'm up here!" I called, my pulse quickening.

We both entered the bedroom at the same time.

"Hey, beautiful." He was hardly out of breath, even though he'd run up the stairs. The subtle note of shyness I heard in his voice made me blush.

"Sorry I missed your call. I've been up and down all day, organizing everything." I gave a quick glance around me and dug my hands into the back pockets of my shorts.

"It's okay. I just didn't know if you were here or not."

His eyes drank me in as he moved across the room and took me in his arms.

"I brought you something."

I smiled, hearing his shyness replaced by an overpowering confidence. "You did?"

The slow pressure of his hands mapping my hips spiked a thrill of euphoria up my spine.

"Yeah. It's outside on the driveway."

I pulled his head down to mine. "Should we go look at it now?"

"It can wait." His gaze darted through the wall of glass beside us, searching for something in the dunes, then returned to me. "The girls?"

"Mary and Chris have them for the next two days." My voice was barely audible, robbed of any strength by the passion welling up in my chest. "We're the only ones who know you left the conference early to come home."

The smile that had captured my heart flashed across his face. "Home?"

"Yeah." I etched the moment in my memory, knowing it would be the last word I would speak for a long time. "Home."

June

"Vietnam." Hoff swiveled in his chair behind a piece of furniture that could easily rival the Resolute Desk. The dizzying heat of downtown Houston burned up to the forty-second floor. He faced it, shielded by the glass enclosing his corner office.

"I'm not so sure," I smiled bitterly. "If he felt any remorse at all, he'd go somewhere else. He enjoys Pho Tai Chin too much."

"Remorse?" Hoff scoffed. "We'd be so lucky." He turned back toward me. "Latest from the FBI is he boarded a cruise ship out of Galveston bound for Cozumel, using a fake ID and birth certificate."

"You don't need a passport?"

"Apparently not for what's known as a closed loop cruise. Son of a bitch did his research, damn him."

"I'm not surprised. Clint was never one to leave loose ends. He'll put up a fight."

"I know," Hoff's brow furrowed. "But he can't hide forever. Clint Myers cost us seven million in revenue and even more in PR."

I flexed my high-heeled foot. "I'm sorry."

"It's not your fault, Aimee. He had us all hoodwinked. It was part of his job after all, to dazzle and charm. We never could have expected him to rob the company blind. He has no honor."

"No," I said softly. "I suppose from Cozumel he could get to Mexico City and go—"

"Anywhere," Hoff interrupted dejectedly. "The name he used on the forged license and birth certificate hasn't come up with any hits in Mexico. He may be traveling with more than one fake ID, though."

Clint spoke at least four languages fluently, and six others passably. I wondered momentarily if his Shangri-La extradited to the US. I decided it probably didn't.

"I know this has hurt you on many levels, Aimee." Hoff swiveled back toward me. "I appreciate you staying on this long."

"I appreciate you letting me stay on this long," I said in disbelief. "For all the help I've been this year."

"You came out of that fire Lambert put you through at the deposition like gold, Aimee. You single-handedly saved our asses from a public flogging at the expense of your personal life. For that, I'd have you stay on indefinitely. I'm truly sorry to see you go."

I adored this weathered brick of a businessman. "Thank you, Hoff. I'd be lying if I said I wasn't excited for the next chapter."
He fixed his eye on me, genuinely interested. "And what exactly is the next chapter?

"Real estate. Selling custom homes."

"Is that so? It's not oil, but it's definitely a steady industry." He gazed through the window at the city sprawling before him. "And in this town, you'll certainly have no shortage of business."

"No. And this go around, I have a trustworthy partner. He builds. I sell."

"I see." A spark entered his eyes. "Speaking of which, I'm reminded that congratulations are in order."

"Yes. Thank you so much."

"It truly is good to see you happy again." He returned the smile I'd given him. "You've done so much for Valiant over the years. We wouldn't be what we are today without you or Caleb, and I'm deeply indebted to you."

He drummed his fingers on his desk.

"You didn't tell Lambert everything, did you, Aimee?"

I stood up.

"Only the truth as it was at the time, Hoff. No more and no less."

"Of course." He rose and extended both of his hands over the desk, clasping mine strongly. "All the best, Mrs. King. Please keep in touch."

"It's gorgeous," I gushed. "It's a bias-cut column gown with a draped halter top. Backless and ruched along the hips, with a single strand of Swarovski crystals strung across the shoulders and beaded all over everywhere else. It hugs me in absolutely all the right places." I beamed at my mother.

My mother's eyes weren't aquamarine like Cecily's, but a deep sapphire. Her joy radiated through the screen. "I can't wait to see you in it, Aims."

"I can't wait to see you, Momma."

"What about me?" My dad chuckled off screen.

"I can't wait to see you either, Daddy!"

My mother flashed him a smile. "Your father thoroughly enjoyed chatting with Jeremy and getting to know him the other evening."

I rolled to my back on the bed. "Jeremy loved getting to chat with Daddy, too. I knew they'd hit it off."

"Because we're deep, brooding intellectuals?" My dad's voice boomed jovially in the background.

"Because you both love *Star Wars* and *Batman*," I laughed. "We're good for each other. All of us. Jeremy told me he really admired the compassion and openness you gave him, Daddy."

"Speaking of which, how did everything unfold at the King house?" My mother asked. "We've only heard snippets so far."

"Well, I can give you the full version now since Jeremy's down at the beach with the girls. The weekend we moved out here was the week before everything came to a head: the deposition with Valiant, Jeremy's conference. And we'd just been booted from David's house, and Cecily was thrown into making funeral arrangements with Kayla."

"I'm so sorry we weren't there." A shadow crossed my mother's face.

"It was an intense few days, especially with everything happening all at once. Jeremy and I were certain of where our relationship was headed, but timing was still an issue…" My voice trailed off. "Anyway, it was Friday afternoon and when I was unpacking, I just felt peace. Thinking about it now, I don't even think I'd call it a feeling, it was stronger than that. More of a knowing?"

"I understand." My mother's eyes shone.

"I called the county clerk's office. They said we had three days from Friday to Monday morning to fulfill the required waiting period for a marriage license. So, I walked outside and asked Jeremy if he wanted to go downtown and apply for one."

"Simple as that?" My mother smiled.

"Yep. He gave me a resounding yes. We told Cecily first."

"She'd seen it coming, I imagine?"

"From miles away," I grinned. "We threw the girls in the truck and told them what was what. They were thrilled. We arrived just in time to apply for the license and made an appointment for 8 on Monday morning with the justice of the peace, since Jason was still out of town."

"And then what? You twiddled your thumbs for another forty-eight hours?"

"Pretty much. As you know, we made a lot of calls. You were the first. Jeremy bought my ring the next day."

I was already twisting it around my finger. I glanced at it, a row of cushion cut diamonds countersunk and tension set between two bands of brushed white gold.

"He was very romantic about it. He said we'd both been through fire, but neither of us had ever been alone in it." The ring flamed in the light. "He said I deserved to wear some on my hand."

"I do love my new son," Momma said.

"Me too. Nat agreed to spend Sunday night at SeaSplit, so we could take two cars into town. The next morning, Jeremy dropped off the girls at the Cole's and we met at the courthouse on the island. The ceremony was simple." I had wiped the tears from Jeremy's eyes… "Then, Nat and I drove to Houston, and Jeremy left for the airport."

"Then a long four days until he returned?"

"Yes. Painfully long. I tried to occupy myself by giving the house a bit more of a lived-in look. Soften it up with some pillows. That kind of thing."

"I daresay he gave no notice to any of it the first evening he was back." My father bellowed.

"Daddy!" I shrieked with embarrassment. "And this from a theology professor." I rolled my eyes.

"The Spirit of the Lord directed the scribes of old to include the Song of Songs in the scriptures. There's no need to be prudish in the sanctity of matrimony," he chortled, obviously pleased with the rise he'd gotten out of me.

"Anyway, Jeremy did notice how I spruced up the place," I retorted. "And for your information, he stopped at the nursery just off the causeway on the way back from the airport. He bought me a gardenia bush as a wedding gift. Never mind that he forgot all about it and let it sit, dying on the carport downstairs for two days until we pried ourselves out of the house to pick up the girls."

Daddy laughed out loud. "What about your in-laws? What's old Jeremiah King like?"

"Ha! Not very old for one thing. The man only recently turned fifty-nine."

"A mere chick." My father grunted.

"Indeed," I smiled. "Jeremy had called his dad while he was in Miami to tell him everything, and after we picked the girls up from the Coles, we drove to Houston to meet Jeremiah and Lauren. Jeremiah's quite lovely, not at all how I imagined him. There's an air of eminence about him, and he's charismatic. But sometimes he seems lost. I'm wholeheartedly committed to praying for him."

"And your new mother-in-law?" My mother's sly smile made me roll my eyes in mock derision.

"I pray for her as well, Momma. We're the same age, and I can't even describe the look on her face when Jeremy introduced me as his wife. Jeremiah hadn't communicated any information to Lauren about me and Jeremy being married before we got there. It was awkward to say the least."

"I'm sure."

"Then there was double the fun when Christina announced that Anna was her sister. Do you know what Lauren did?"

"What?"

"She wept."

"No."

"Uncontrollably."

"From shock?"

"Probably. But I'd like to think it was also due to a healthy dose of shame."

"Aimee," she chided gently.

"I know Momma. I'm trying to forgive everything she's done to that family." I corrected myself, "My family. It will take time."

A door downstairs slammed as my three treasures stampeded inside.

"I can't wait for you to see the house and meet Jeremy and Christina. I've been given so much more than I'd ever hoped."

"God is good that way." My mother smiled gently. "I've adored all the pictures you've sent, my darling girl! Will the dress I sent you a photo of earlier be alright to wear to the wedding dinner?"

"Yes, it's perfect. We'll have everything catered here on the lawn at SeaSplit. I'm guessing there will be about forty people or so. The Kings, Hamadas, Coles, several other families from West End Bible and the school, and of course Maren." My eyes widened. "Speaking of which, Maren and sixth-grade biology Mike completely hit it off the day after everything happened with Darius at the cottage. I am still in shock."

"No!"

"It's purely an act of the Lord. He's exactly what she's always wanted, and from what I know of Mike, vice versa. He drove her to the airport that weekend when she had to leave for LA. I know they're talking to each other, and I'm sure he's picking her up from the airport again when she comes into town for our reception."

"I can't wait to see everyone." My mother's eyes sparkled. "I'm so happy that you invited Maria and Yordan also."

"Of course, Momma." Caleb's parents would always hold a special place in my heart. "Did you know Stephen is coming as well?"

"Is he?" My mother brightened at my brother-in-law's name. "He must go fishing with me!"

I laughed. "I'm fairly certain that's the primary reason he's coming. Although I know he wants to meet Jeremy too. I'm so thankful that the Rojas clan is excited to meet him. Are you and Cecily still planning your sister retreat?"

"Yes, we're going to Gruene. She's never been to the hill country."

"Good. I know I haven't contributed to her stress in the best ways. Your time with Cecily will be just what she needs."

"She's very excited about her house."

"Jeremy and I are, too, for many reasons. He's hoping to have it finished by the end of the year. Not only will Cecily have a home, Kingdom Coastal will have two builds under its belt."

"Kingdom Coastal." My mother grinned. "I don't believe your mind ever stopped spinning with ideas, even when you felt your worst, darling girl."

"Me neither. Another blessing of faith. Even when you can't see or feel the healing, it's still happening."

I glanced around our bedroom at this house—our house.

"Momma, I suppose I always thought of the possibility of being married again as some kind of do-over or second-best, but it's not like that at all. I never thought I'd get to experience joy like this a second time; being married to another wonderful man, being known and loved in that way again… it's so unexpected, all of it. But I guess that's what grace is, right?"

Her pride radiated through the screen. "Exactly."

July

The night was all-enveloping, and the voiceless roar of the sea rushed through the open door. My entire body pulsed. Sweat surfaced on my skin and tension coursed through me, rising faster than the tide.

Our noses grazed, his breath hovered over my lips. "Are you sure?"

Wayward beams of starlight penetrated the wall of glass, catching the gleam of fire on my hand as I touched his face.

"More than anything."

"Over easy?"

"Yes. I mean, wait, no. Scrambled. Hard."

Jeremy reached for a spatula. "We're still on for that meeting this afternoon in the East End, right babe?"

"Yep. At 1. Plenty of time for the consult with a little left over before we pick the girls up from school."

My phone rang.

"Perfect." Jeremy passed me my breakfast, hot off the skillet.

"Kingdom Coastal, this is Aimee." I tested a quick sip of matcha.

"*This call is from a person currently in a prison in Harris County…*"

I coughed, choking.

"Aimee?" Jeremy came to me.

"*… may be recorded by prison staff for your safety.*"

I cleared my throat and shook my head. "I'm alright, just a second."

"*… do not wish to accept this call, please hang up now. If you wish to accept the call, please remain on the line.*"

"What is it? You look like you've—"

I silenced him with my hand on his chest.

The line crackled.

My breath wavered. "Hello?"

"They…" His voice stumbled. "They said I had one phone call."

The morning was glorious, summer's scorching heat rendering color from every living thing. We drove through cotton fields, the bolls bowing their heads at eye level above the dense tangle of green foliage.

I slowly let out a deep breath. "I'm getting nervous, love."

"That's natural." On the armrest, his hand squeezed mine encouragingly. "Just remember: the authorities have had him the entire time, and God knows he's had a decent amount of time to process things. You've wanted closure for months, and you're going to be in a controlled environment."

He glanced over at me momentarily, taking his eyes off the road to drive his point home.

"He can't do anything to you, baby."

I gripped his hand as the truck slowed, nearing our turn-off. The state-imposed sign was barely visible in the cotton, small and ancient, as the road changed from asphalt to gravel.

A tiny jolt of pain raced across my head—front to back—and was gone.

"If only I could control my nerves. Residual anxiety is such a pain. Why does it have to rear its ugly head now?"

"Because today will make you relive everything. The night it happened, how you felt, everything he did."

The chain link fence towered, crowned with razor-wire furling over the top in rolls.

Jeremy threw the truck into park.

"We've prayed about this, and I know no matter how difficult talking to him will be, you're going to feel so much better when I see you again. It's going to help both of you."

"I know." I looked at my husband with the unshakeable assurance that he would support me through anything. "Sure you don't want to come with me?" I unbuckled my seat belt, leaving my phone and purse along with my fear in the seat as I opened the door and got out.

His wink made me grin.

"It would be best for all of us if I didn't."

The prison was different than I imagined. An armed corrections officer greeted me at the door. "You have an appointment, ma'am?"

Gray shirt and pants, gray boots.

"Yes, Aimee Rojas. I called last week."

"ID?" He moved to a kiosk with a computer.

"Yes sir." I pulled my driver's license from my back pocket. "Here."

"Just a moment."

The walls were white, sterile and devoid of any signs of creativity or habitation. Dim and muted, the hallway beyond the security checkpoint in front of me stretched out and ended in front of doors I imagined only a miracle could open. The officer placed a plastic tub on the counter.

"Your bag and phone, miss."

"I left them in the car. I only brought my license."

"Alright," he nodded. "License and shoes in the tub ma'am. This way."

He led me to the checkpoint and placed the tub on a conveyor belt. Before going through the metal detector, a female guard stopped me. "We'll do a visual inspection with the wand, and a pat down, miss."

I nodded, wordless.

"Arms out and legs slightly apart, ma'am."

She started with my arms, then deftly made her way down my sides and back. The wand clicked in the correction officer's hand as it hovered over my body, around my waist, up and down once more across my arms and legs.

"Come through." Another officer waved me on.

I took my sneakers and license out of the plastic tub.

"Conference room four," the first officer called to the latter.

"This way, ma'am."

To my surprise, the heavy doors slid open noiselessly, leading us into a brightly lit section of the hallway. Cells flanked either side, and I instantly knew why I'd been told wearing colorful clothing was required. Every inmate was dressed in a white tunic and pants. The corrections officer strode quietly beside me, not looking to either side of the hallway, but I couldn't help noticing the men's faces.

Solemn and silent as I passed by, they thirsted for any kind of color that would break the monotony of their cells and this hallway, any point of visual interest. In their bleak environment, my scarlet t-shirt looked like blood on snow. I wanted to believe the white of their uniforms signified a fresh start for at least some of the men… until the pit in my stomach reminded me that white would only be easier to bleach and give to another inmate.

We left the hallway and came to a large room. I followed the guard to the left, where another much smaller room awaited me. Riveted to the floor, two heavy metal chairs and a wide metal table were the only items in the room. Two cameras hung diametrically in corners, mounted to the ceiling. There was no glass, and there would be no division at all between us. I sat for what seemed like an age, waiting.

Finally, the door in the corner opened with a groan.

He was the thinnest I'd ever seen him, and his hair was cut in a way I knew he'd have never willingly chosen, buzzed short. His hands were shackled to a waist chain and his ankles were similarly bound. Nevertheless, he was still handsome.

As his eyes met mine, I gasped.

Despite the shackles, I was looking at the face of someone who was impossibly, undeniably free.

He lifted his wrists. "Guess we won't be shaking hands today."

He'd made a joke. *A joke.*

I covered my mouth, failing to stifle the sobs.

He studied me closely. He'd never once shied away from my tears, so I shouldn't have been surprised with the intensity he gazed at me. "I can't believe you're really here."

"Why?"

"Because of what I've done to you." He swallowed hard. "To your new family. Is Jeremy here?"

I nodded. "He's outside. He thought it would be better if I came alone." I attempted a smile. "He cares about you just as much as I do."

He lowered his eyes. "I can't believe that."

"Believe it." I unclenched my fists and put my hands on the table. "You look—"

"Terrible?"

"No." Every cell in my body wanted to burst with a sensation

I couldn't name. Then, I laughed. And kept laughing. "You look alive."

Hope chased the fear from his face, and he laughed with me.

The nerves in his voice jumped. "The guys in here, not all of them are bad. Of course, some of them are. But some have a hope I've never known, even though they'll be here for a long time to come… like me. They've helped me remember things I've forgotten. Things about Jesus."

He studied the chains on his limbs and suddenly shook himself from introspection. "What you must think of me…"

"I haven't stopped thinking about you. Not ever. I never stopped hoping you'd come back to us."

His eyes flicked up to me, living and aware, liberated from darkness. "You don't know what that means to me." His voice broke just like it had when he was twelve.

I reached across the table for him, shackles and all.

"Aimee *cher.*"

October

Dawn turned the night into an infinite spectrum of color. Morning persists, and with it, the promise of hope. My husband was gone from the bed, but I knew where I'd find him.

My feet whispered across bamboo flooring. I turned the handle and pushed open our portal to the sea. The fragrance of gardenia blossoms swept up to me on the day's waking exhale as I leaned against the railing. The breeze whipped my thin nightgown. I saw him, a shadow in the morning light. He was ankle deep in the surf, shoulders strong against the southern wind. The storm would come in time, but he was ready. He'd always been ready.

I waited for him, eyes on the heavens. Cirrus clouds brushed the sky, palms open to gather the waves below. Whitecaps rushed in the distance, relenting to the shore.

How long I stood there, I neither knew nor cared. I had learned to revel in the quiet space of not knowing. My husband turned. His joy shot towards me like an arrow, and he ran to me across the water, across the sand, across the grass and up our stairs.

He gathered me to him with his eyes first, then his arms and his mouth.

I savored the way he looked at me, the way he folded me into his embrace as we faced the gulf together, my shoulder blade against his heart.

"Sleep well?" His hands rubbed the growing swell of my stomach. The life inside me responded, fluttering at his question.

I gasped. "Did you feel that?"

"Yeah." Wonder knit his voice with emotion. "I keep thinking it's all a dream, but it's not. It's real."

"He's real."

"Nothing's impossible."

I turned and wrapped my arms around his waist. Jeremy's eyes glinted in the light, filled with a love that was all mine. "No," I murmured. "Nothing is impossible."

About the Author

Allison Nance has been writing and singing all kinds of words since before she can remember.

She holds a master's degree in Biblical Studies from Moody Theological Seminary, and her career in specialty dining and event management spans two continents and almost as many decades.

Allison currently resides in Houston, Texas with her family. If she's not writing, she's probably baking.

Acknowledgments

There are many people who are responsible for the life of this story, and to whom I owe my deepest gratitude:

For Shirley Leslie, who planted the seed for this book, and Steve Leslie, for sharing your insight into prison ministry. For my earliest beta readers, Laura Knott, Marianne Alfaro and Tera Balog, who don't know each other and yet have been my most steadfast cheerleaders from the very beginning. For Christina Cokenour and Mary Moore, dear friends who spoke life to me when I needed it most. For Ann Swindell. Your grace and gentle nudging was the catalyst I needed to run this race. For Griffin Covington, Vivian Nguyen and AJ Hill in sharing your technical, legal and medical expertise respectively. For Team Barnabus, especially Paula Peckham, Mary Hamilton, Paul Douglas Brown, Sara Meg Seese, Stephanie King and Lee Carver. Your hard criticism and soft hearts helped refine this story. For the Body at Renaissance Church and Solid Rock Church. Your love is laced throughout these pages. For Bob Gaines, and your enthusiasm for my writing. Thank you for believing in me. For Kerstin Stokes, your thoughtful eye and openness are a blessing. Thank you for shepherding this book so well. For Megan Whitfield and Holly Bollinger, and your gifts of artistry. For Sarah Crouch, best hype-woman on the planet. Additional thanks are owed to Kristen Terrette, Don Pape, Allison Byxbe, Laura Hartley, Michael Greenburg and Jackie Lea Sommers for your kind words and constant encouragement.

Most of all for Kayla, whose beauty, intelligence and compassion inspire me in countless ways. Someday I'll actually let you read the whole book. Promise. For Zac, lover of my body and soul at their best and worst. And for Abba. Thank you for teaching me how to sing your song in the dark, and for filling me with your hope.

Allison Nance

Explore the Hidden Shelf